MW01133578

HUGE X10

A MEGA MENAGE REVERSE HAREM ROMANCE

STEPHANIE BROTHER

© Stephanie Brother 2019

All rights reserved. This book or any portion thereof may not be produced or used in manner whatsoever without the express permission of the publisher except for the use of brief quotations in a book review.

This book is a work of fiction. Any resemblance to persons, living or dead, or places, events or locations is purely coincidental. The characters are all productions of the authors imagination.

Please not that this work is intended for adults over the age of 18 and all characters represented are 18 or over.

All rights reserved.

ISBN: 9781710514254

CONTENTS

HUGE X10

1

My name is Danna, and I want a harem.

There! I admitted it. To myself. In the mirror.

I sigh, roughly tugging my fingers through my dark wavy hair, trying to smooth out the effects of eight hours of my pillow and at least one panty wetting dream.

My cheeks pink.

That dream. Five tall, dark men in the restroom of the college bar. They wedged the door shut with the trashcan, lay coats on the floor so they could slide their tongues over my clit until I was wriggling and begging. Five cocks to show me what pleasure really is.

I shiver, remembering what it felt like to be owned so totally. I woke up with the wettest panties ever, wondering where the hell my imagination gets these images from. It's not like I've had an adventurous sex life. Two short term boyfriends don't exactly count as a sexual awakening.

I know where the ideas come from, though. My bestie, Laura, has a harem of her own. I know how crazy it sounds. Until last year I didn't realize it was a thing. Then Laura moved in with her new stepbrothers, and within record time, she was shacked up with ten of the most gorgeous men, enjoying a life of love and luxury.

I don't like being jealous of my friend. It's a creeping and unpleasant feeling that sits like lead in my stomach. It's not that I'm wishing bad things on her. I don't want her to break up with the McGregor brothers and go back to living the same dull, sex-starved life that I'm living. To be honest, I wish her all the happiness in the world. It's just that I'd love an exact copy of her life.

Maybe not exactly. Ten seems like a lot. I've seen those men in various stages of undress, at pool parties and while they're carrying out physical work around their mansion. I didn't want to drool over my friend's boyfriends, but when there's that much MAN around, it's tough not to.

I look away from my reflection, feeling ashamed. There are rules when it comes to bestie-relationships, and I feel like I've broken some of the more innocent ones.

Ugh.

It's time I should be leaving for college, but I have zero enthusiasm. Laura has taken some time out to have her first children. Little Hope and Hannah are just the sweetest little things. I don't blame her in the slightest, but I miss having her to hang out with. It's not the same without her.

I tug on some jeans and my favorite t-shirt which used to belong to one of my ex's and has now been modified with a slash neck and tied side. I smooth my hands over my thick thighs and full hips. Maybe, at my size, I should be wearing something a little more concealing, but I love my curves and don't want to hide for the sake of other peoples judgmental, body-shaming views.

It's warm out, so I dig for some sandals in my closet, and I'm good to go.

The house is so quiet.

Since mom passed, there just hasn't been the same feeling at home. Pop tries his best, but the life left our house overnight, and there's no bringing it back. In some ways, I feel that life has left me too. I used to be filled with sass and sparkle, but sadness has a way of smothering all of that. I miss my mom, and I miss myself too. Maybe that's why my dreams take me to fantasy places where I can be my confident self without the guilt of feeling like I'm enjoying myself too much.

My car is on its last legs, but I love it's slightly dented, or as I like to call it, preloved state. Laura and I made many journeys in this vehicle, singing badly to songs on the radio and gossiping like two old women. Those were good days. I wish there were more of them to come, but it's not likely. Laura has her own car now and a driver whenever she needs one. She is, for all intents and purposes, a married woman, and here I am, still languishing in singlesville, wishing for something different.

The journey to school is quiet too. Somehow, playing my music loud and singing alone just seems like a lame thing to do. As I'm parking up, my phone rings and my day brightens a little.

"Hey!" I say.

"Danna," Laura squeals. There's the sound of a fussing baby in the background, and my besties attention is gone already. "Sshhh…" she croons.

"Those babies giving you a hard time?" I ask.

"You have no idea. I thought ten men were demanding,

but two baby girls are so much more hard work," she laughs.

"Did the nanny start yet?"

"Yes," she gasps. "Thank goodness. You know I didn't like the idea, but I've got to say that having an extra pair of hands during the day time is brilliant. I can shower without having to dangle toys and sing nursery rhymes. It's restored my sanity."

"That's good." I pull into the car park, remembering the day that Laura's secret was exposed to the world. I thought that all that news coverage of her relationships would crush her, but she's got inner strength that neither of us knew she had, and everything worked out in the end.

"So, anyway, I'm not calling to tell you about my baby dramas. I've got some news."

"You're not pregnant again?"

"No," she snorts. "I mean if the boys had their way I'd probably be knocked up permanently, but I'm working on getting my body back and want to enjoy these babies before the next ones come along."

"Sounds like a plan, Stan," I say. "Get them to rubber up!"

"I am," she laughs. "There was much grumbling at first. I think they all got used to being free while we were trying to conceive."

"Damn," I say. "Those sheets must have been disgusting!"

"Danna!" Laura tries to sound shocked, but she's giggling her head off.

"So what's the news then?"

She takes a deep breath. "Well, you know after the television interview the boys did, the network got in touch to ask us if we'd take part in a reality show."

"Yeah. I remember Ford's reaction to that idea."

"Some were keener than others," she chuckles. "But I've been working on them."

"You want to go on TV?" I'm surprised. Laura was always a really private person, so letting cameras in to film her seems really out of character.

"It's not so much that I want to," she says. "It's more that I think it will be good for the family."

I know what she's getting at. There are still some grumblings about how the McGregor's have chosen to live. The traditionalist killjoys in the state are feigning shock while fucking their mistresses and shafting their employees. The usual bullshit. I'm surprised that Laura cares, though.

"You think it will be good for PR?" I ask.

"For sure. I mean, who could resist my gorgeous babies, or how amazing their daddies are?"

"Absolutely no one," I say. "It's genius."

"I hope so. And you'll be in it?" Laura asks, sliding in that bombshell as though she's asking me to pop round for milk and cookies.

"I don't know," I say. "You know I'm not into the idea of that kind of exposure. I like my anonymity. Plus, I think pop might disown me." There are a few seconds of silence as Laura digests what I've said. She's still sad that my parents were disapproving of her choices. Our friendship hasn't suffered, but their attitude did hurt her.

"Well, I just wanted to know in case it was something you might want to do."

Her voice sounds less sure that it did before and I suddenly realize that maybe she's asking me for my support here. "Do you want me to?" I ask.

"Not if you don't want to. You know I'd never make you do something that made you feel uncomfortable."

"But if I did?"

"Then I'd be ecstatic," she gushes. That one word tells me everything I need to know.

I may not want to do this, and pop may blow a blood vessel when he finds out, but this is my friend, and I'd do anything to make her life easier. Plus, it means that I get to hang out with the McGregors, which is always a whole heap of fun.

This day started off dull, but already it's looking up. I wonder if taking part in the show will involve me getting a new wardrobe because I don't think my old t-shirts and jeans are going to cut it!

"Okay," I say. "You let me know the time and the place, and I'll be there with bells on."

"REALLY?" Laura screams. "REALLY?"

"I may regret saying this but yes, really!"

"YOU. ARE. THE. BEST!" She whoops. The sound of screaming babies escalates at once, and I pull the phone from my ear. "I better go," she says. "These babies need feeding. I swear these McGregors are all obsessed with my boobs."

"TMI," I laugh.

"You haven't heard the half of it," she laughs. "Have a good day at college and remember your bedraggled, mom-friend who's currently leaking through her shirt and hasn't had time to clean her teeth yet. This nanny better get here soon!".

"I will, honey. I will."

When we hang up, I take a deep breath, missing my bestie already. Life changes fast, and I've been feeling left behind. Maybe taking part in this show will be good for us all. A chance for Laura and me to hang out and an opportunity for the world to see what a fantastic relationship Laura has with her boys.

I gather my things and walk to class.

Another day to get through but now there's a rainbow showing through the clouds.

2

It's the first day of filming, and I'm hanging out at the McGregor's with Laura. She's buzzing around like a restless bee while the boys are just relaxing all around us. I don't know if it's only these men, but stress seems to slide off them like water off a duck's back.

"Do the babies look alright," Laura asks me. They are sitting up in two bouncers looking picture perfect with matching fluffy pink rompers and cute little hairbands. I guess when TV stations market reality shows they are loose on the term 'reality.' There is no way that Laura is this pristine on a daily basis, and the boys are all preened to perfection. I glance around and then look at the floor because DAMN. It's just not normal to have to deal with looking at men this gorgeous all around you. One would be manageable, but ten!

"They look fine," I tell her. "Cute as buttons."

She exhales and perches on the edge of the sofa, gripping the cushions as though her life depends on them. "This was a bad idea," she says.

"Don't start that again," Ford grumbles from across the room. "It's too late to change your mind, and anyway, it's going to be fine."

There's a knock on the door, and one of the staff shows in the producer. "We're ready to start filming," he says.

The collective sound of ten men getting up and readying themselves to do something they're not really that keen to do is a loud rumble. Hope starts to fuss. "Oh, no," Laura says. "She's getting tired now. This is going to be a nightmare."

Cameron sweeps over and unclips his daughter from the bouncer. I say 'his daughter' loosely because they have no idea who the actual father is. They agreed not to find out too, so any of his brothers could be the real father. "Hey," he says as he hoists her onto his shoulder and bounces her up and down. "Come to papa."

Hope settles immediately, and Laura exhales again. She puts her hand on my knee and squeezes it. "Thanks for being here."

"It's fine," I say. "Who'd pass up all this excitement."

She gives me a withering look. "You in a heartbeat. I know you're only here because I asked you to be and you know that I need the support. It means a lot."

I smile. "You're crazy," I tell her even though she's hit the nail on the head. "After today I'm going to be famous!"

"Famous as the poor long-suffering friend of the woman with the most boyfriends in America."

I chuckle. "Maybe people will feel sorry for me. You

have ten amazing men, and I can't even find one."

Laura's eyes light up. "That's what we could do," she says. "We can find you a good guy."

"Only one," I say as though I'm joking.

Laura's eyes narrow, her perceptiveness, and the years we've known each other, causing her to evaluate what I've just said. "One wouldn't be enough, would it?"

"Well, I'm sure I could handle more," I joke, hoping she's going to laugh this all off. I don't know why I feel so awkward admitting that I want what she has. I guess because I don't want her to feel bad for living what is a dream life while I exist in studentsville.

"Yes you could," she says her eyes widening and a look of glee spreading across her face.

"You're scaring me with that look in your eyes," I say. "This show isn't about me, it's about you guys."

She grabs my hand and starts tugging me towards the door, following Casey who's carrying Hannah. "It's about all of us," she says.

The day passes quickly as the film crew captures every moment of the McGregor's existence. It's half staged and half natural, and I watch as Laura comes more alive with every moment that passes. It's as though this opportunity to show the world how happy they are, is fueling even more happiness. Her 'husbands' manage to keep going too, even though at least half of them objected to being involved. Aaron, in particular, was worried about how the filming could be twisted but he's made sure the contracts give them rights to see the footage before it's aired.

It's towards the end of the day that Laura plops

Hannah onto my knee. "Look how good you are with her," she says. "You'd be a great mom."

"One day," I say.

"Some lucky man has to snap you up first," she says. "Or lucky men!" She smiles with wickedness in her eyes. "I mean…I know this arrangement I have isn't something that happens every day, but it really should be!"

I find myself blushing, and she grins devilishly. "I think you've stumbled into a parallel universe, honey," I say. "This kind of thing doesn't happen to everyone."

"But would you want it?" she asks me. I see the camera moving closer out of the corner of my eye. I don't know what to say. My pop might hear about this, and he'd be mortified if I said yes, but to say no would make me a liar and would potentially make Laura look bad. This show is about her proving to the world that there is nothing wrong with her family life. Having her best friend throw shade on it would not be helpful.

"If I could meet even one guy who was as good as any of your husbands, I'd be a lucky woman," I say diplomatically.

"And if you met ten?" she probes, seemingly not getting the hint.

"Then I'd be even luckier," I say laughing. There. I didn't admit anything, but Laura looks like she might burst with excitement.

"They'd be the luckiest," she says. "Wouldn't they?" She nudges Barret who's sitting next to us reading the paper.

"They would be," he agrees. "Danna is hot."

Laura's head swings in his direction, and he bellows with laughter as she punches him on the shoulder. "Less hot talk about my friend, dude," she says.

"You'd never think it, but Laura here is a jealous little thing!"

She scowls. "I'm not jealous."

Blake pipes up from the end of the table. "She knows she has nothing to worry about. It's more that she's gotten used to being the center of attention."

"She's our sun," Donnie says dreamily from where he's currently sketching the babies who are sleeping next to him on the sofa.

"She looks like she wants to burn someone's ass," Antony laughs.

Listening to them all is like watching a game of elite ping pong, and I love it. I love the overwhelming feeling of warmth and safety that comes with being in such a big group of people. I'd give anything to be someone's sun. To have so many men orbiting around me.

My expression must give away my dreaming because Laura kicks me under the table. "Wake up, dreamer," she laughs. "We need to find you a harem."

I don't reply, but my face goes hot immediately.

"Yes, you do," Antony laughs. "Danna needs a harem for sure."

"There's not one man out there that'd be enough for Danna," Grant laughs. And just like that, my secret is out in front of the world.

3

I don't watch the first episode of the McGregor's Uncovered with them. Instead, I wait until pop has gone to meet his friends for a quiet beer and tune in from the comfort of my own living room. For the past week, I've been telling myself that the harem comments that Laura and the McGregors were making about me would be cut out or would be seen as a joke at worst, but as I watch myself on TV, I realize that my hopes were foolish. The blush on my cheeks and my discomfort are so visible. I might as well have worn a t-shirt advertising for men.

Ugh. I'm thinking about the douchebags at school who are probably watching this and the kind of reaction that I'm going to get at college tomorrow. Connor will have a field day, storing up his ridiculous attempts to make me feel like shit. We have the kind of hate-hate relationship that means I want to dig out his eyeballs with my thumbs whenever I have the unpleasant fortune of seeing him.

Laura's been trying to call me since the show aired this morning, but I've kept my phone on silent. I needed to see it first before I speak to her.

The screen of my phone lights up again with her name. This time I answer.

"Did you see it?" she squeals.

"Yeah, just now. It was good!"

She giggles. "I know. You should see the coverage we've been getting. It's been great. Our PR is over the moon."

"That's great," I say. "Exactly what you were hoping for."

"Yes," she says. "And there's more."

"What?"

"A woman saw the show and got in touch with the producers." Her voice is so excited it reminds me of how she was before we went on our school trip when we were eleven.

"What about?"

"About you," she says. "She has ten sons."

My heart skitters with a mix of hope and fear. "Ten sons," I say. "Her grocery bill must be astronomical."

"Her grocery bill isn't something you need to be thinking about right now," Laura says, sounding impatient. "She's looking for a woman for her sons."

"Oh yeah," I say, trying to sound nonchalant. I imagine the kind of men they might be, and there is no way they're anything like the McGregors. "Who are they? A bunch of weirdos?"

There are a few seconds of silence on the phone, and I

realize that what I've said could be negatively construed. "Not that you guys are weirdos!" I stutter. "You know what I mean."

Laura laughs. "I know what you mean, Danna. And I don't think they're weirdos. In fact, I've seen pictures, and they look about as far from weirdos as you can get...hang on a minute."

She pauses, and I can hear rustling as she fiddles with her phone. "Check these out." My phone starts to vibrate in my hand as the photos begin to arrive. The first one I open as my heart racing. A black and white snap of a gorgeous man with soulful, brooding eyes stares back at me. The next is of identical twins, the next of triplets...more and more photos arrive until I've scanned through counting ten of the most gorgeous men I've seen. They give the McGregor's a run for their money, and I never thought I'd be saying that.

"They're called the Jackson brothers," Laura says. "They own a ranch about three-hundred miles from here."

"And their mom is trying to hook them up," I laugh. "How lame is that?"

"About as lame as Roderick," she says. "And look how that worked out."

"Pretty damn well," I have to admit.

"She's asking if you'd consider going out to Broadsville to meet them all. She's asking if you'd really consider a harem of your own." Laura squeals with excitement, and I hear laughing the background.

"Who's that," I ask.

"Grant and Elliot are here," she says. "I can never get

any alone time in this place." She doesn't sound like she cares about that in the slightest. "But stop changing the subject. Will you go to Broadsville?"

"To meet a bunch of strangers?" I scoff.

"Everyone's a stranger until you've met them," Laura says, sounding exasperated. "These fuckers were strangers until I moved in here."

"Fuckers who all fucked you within a week," a deep voice pipes up in the background.

"That's just because I was sex starved," Laura says indignantly.

There's another ripple of laughter.

"This is what you want, isn't it?" she asks me. "I haven't gotten the wrong end of the stick."

"Do you remember how you felt when you overhead your husbands talking about what they wanted...you weren't exactly jumping at the chance, were you?"

"I know...but this is different," she says.

"How exactly?"

"Well, for one, you already have me, and I can tell you that harem living is amazing."

"Beginner's luck," I laugh.

"And for two, what have you got to lose?"

"My mind. My reputation. My sanity. My father," I list off my objections feeling more and more depressed as I do.

"Minor details," Laura laughs. "Just think about what you have to gain."

"Ten cocks," a deep voice says in the background, and there's another rumble of laughter.

"Ten cocks," Laura laughs. "Exactly!"

"One would be good," I say.

"But ten is so much better," she tells me.

Ten.

Ten men.

I remember when she told me about her father-in-law's plan. I remember thinking how amazing it would be to have all those men focused on pleasing you. I know when she was deliberating what to do, I told her to fuck them all. That Danna is still in here somewhere, buried under worries that never used to be a factor. I know that this is what I want, but sometimes it's hard to accept the way we feel inside. We try and force ourselves to live the way that others expect us and to make decisions that will make other people happy. I don't want to hurt pop, not when he's hurting so much already.

I never wanted to be this kind of person. I told Laura to go ahead and live the way her heart was telling her to live and damn the consequences. It's so much easier to tell other people to take leaps into the unknown than it is to convince yourself, and that realization makes me feel like a coward.

I've been dreaming about this. I've been thinking about it so much that I've made my panties wet and my heart ache. I want it so much that it's infiltrated my dreams. I have a chance to make my fantasies a reality, and I'm running from it. I'm finding excuses, and I hate myself for it.

I'm Danna Sandhurst, and I've got more balls than this. At least I used to before mom passed. Now I spend my time worrying too much that I'm going to do something to let her down. I want her to be looking down on me feeling proud, and she definitely wouldn't approve of this.

But if I don't go for it and I let this opportunity pass, I know what'll happen. It'll play on my mind, and I'll regret it. I don't need more regrets to kick myself over that's for sure. What I need is something to tear me out of this funk and drag the old Danna into the land of the living.

I want to get myself back.

"Fuck it!" I roar.

"That's my girl," Laura says. "I'm so excited."

"What if they're a bunch of weirdos?" I say.

"Then you run in the other direction, but if the pictures are anything to go by, I don't think you're ever going to want to leave!"

4

I can't believe that I'm actually going ahead with this.

After the phone call with Laura, she passed my telephone number to the woman who had contacted the show. Jackie Jackson – yes, that's really her name – called me almost immediately.

"Danna," she said. "It's Jackie. I'm so glad you agreed to speak with me."

"I nearly didn't," I say. "You can understand that this is a strange situation."

"Yes, of course," she says. Her voice is so warm and friendly that I'm immediately at ease. "When I saw the show I just had to call in. The arrangement that the McGregors have would suit my boys to the ground."

"Really?" I say. "I mean I know why the McGregors wanted it that way, but it seems like a pretty specific set of circumstances."

"I guess our circumstances are similar," she says. "We have a ranch. It's big and busy, and all the boys work here.

Without them, I'd never manage."

"And that's why you're looking for one woman for them."

"Exactly. I know what's gonna happen, Danna. I've seen it with my own brothers. They meet different women, and then they start to fight. Their loyalties don't lie with their family anymore. They take the side of their wife, and it all goes to shit…pardon my language."

I smile at her politeness. I get the feeling she's trying to show me that they're a good and respectable prospect, but her passion is showing through. "So, you have ten sons?"

"Yes," she says, sounding like a proud momma. "I wanted a big family. I have nine brothers myself, but when I married, I didn't fall pregnant, and after a few years we decided to adopt."

"So they're all adopted?"

"Yes. I have two sets of twins, a set of triplets and three other boys. There all good strong men with good hearts and good values."

I think back to the photos that Laura sent me. Ten big, strong, gorgeous men fill my head. Is it possible that this could be something I'm going to consider? Is it possible that they could fill my body and my heart too? "And they know what you're calling me about?"

There's a pause. "Not as such," she says slowly.

"What does that mean?"

"It means that they have no idea…well, it's something I've joked about over the years, especially when they've had relationships that have caused problems but not

20

something we've discussed seriously." My heart sinks. This is the reverse of Laura's situation. At least the McGregors all knew what their dad had planned for them, and most of them were willing to give it a shot. I run my hand over my face, considering the risks. It's one thing to be rejected by one man. When my last idiot boyfriend decided that 'he didn't love me anymore' my heart was bruised for months. It's not that I was love with him and heartbroken, it's more that I didn't like the feeling of being cast aside. I know that I'm not unique in that respect, but still. This seems a whole lot riskier now that I know this is just Jackie's idea.

"What happens if they don't want it?" I ask.

"Well…" Jackie pauses. "It won't work unless they are all on board. I don't want to divide my sons into two camps. That would defeat the object entirely."

"So it's all or nothing," I say.

"Exactly. So, when can you come and meet them?"

I take a seat on my bed, needing to regroup. Jackie's keen. Very keen, but am I? The silence stretches between us as I consider what to do next. I should tell her that this is a crazy idea and that there is just no way that it will work. I should say to her that I'm not up for coming to meet ten men who will probably balk at the idea of sharing one woman. At least in Laura's case, nine out of ten were ready to give it a go. She only had to convince Grant and herself! My struggle will be an uphill one. I know what I should do, but there's a little flame burning inside me that doesn't want to do the right thing. It's the part of me that told Laura to follow her dreams and damn the results. It's the part of me that's fueling my dreams and fantasies about an alternative life that I want to live.

I can't live a life that I'm not prepared to fight for. This is about me seizing an opportunity and giving it my best. It's what I've done all my life.

Then an idea pops into my head.

"I can come in a week," I say, my heart pounding with excitement as I start to follow its desires. "It's spring break, so I have time off from college."

"That sounds perfect," Jackie says enthusiastically.

"But there's one condition," I say.

"Anything!"

"I don't want you to tell them why I'm there," I say. "If I can get them to fall for me, then we're all good. If not, then I'll walk away."

"Are you sure?" Jackie asks. "Would it be better if they all knew exactly why you were here?"

I shake my head even though she can't see me, such is my reservation. "That would just make things awkward, and I don't want this to be forced. If it's going to work, it needs to be natural."

Jackie is silent for a while. "I just worry that it's a lot to hope to achieve in a week," she says.

She's right, but she has no idea how determined I can be nor how hard I will try and to be honest I'm just not comfortable with the alternative. "Can we just see how it goes?"

"Sure. I guess we'll have to."

Spring break with the Jackson brothers. My heart skips at the reality. "Can you just say that I'm the daughter of an old friend who wants to see what it's like to work on a ranch?"

Jackie laughs. "That's a good cover story. They'll be intrigued as to why I've never spoken of you before, though."

"We all have some secrets," I say, and she murmurs her agreement.

"I'll send you all my details," she says. "You can get a bus into town, and I'll come to collect you. Just forward me the details, so I know when you'll be arriving."

"Okay."

"I can't tell you how much this means to me," she says. I fought hard to make my family and want to do everything I can to keep it secure and united.

She sounds lovely. Precisely the kind of person I would be looking for in an ideal mother in law, but I suppose you can't really tell what someone is really like over the phone. Finding out if she's as lovely in reality is essential. Relationships struggle under the pressure of difficult mothers-in-law.

"This could be the best or the craziest thing I've ever done," I say, laughing nervously.

She laughs too. "Danna, whatever happens, I think we're going to have some fun together."

We chat some more, and by the time we say goodbye, all my nervousness has disappeared, and a sense of warmth has filled my chest.

I pull up the pictures of the Jackson brothers again and spend time looking at each of them, wondering what they're like.

Zack, York, Xsander and Xane, William, Walker and Wade, Tommy and Trent, and Samuel. I speak their names quietly, rolling my tongue around each one. The twins and triplets are all identical, so as well as having ten of them to get to know, I'm going to have to try and work out who is who within the groups. Now I know they're adopted, their differences really stand out. What must it have been like to grow up with so many siblings who aren't your blood family? Boys can be especially challenging when it comes to rivalries and competitiveness.

Being an only child has its challenges too, especially now. I would love a sibling to talk things through with. I guess that's why I value my closeness with Laura so much. She's like my sister from another mister.

I dial her number, wanting to share the details of the conversation with Jackie. Laura can't hold in her excitement.

"I can't believe it," she says. "Ten brothers. Just like mine!"

I'm laughing and smiling because her enthusiasm is so contagious. "I know. You couldn't make it up!"

"And they're all gorgeous!"

There's a shout of 'hey' in the background and Laura sniggers. "I said they were gorgeous, Casey. Not that I wanted to fuck them." The disapproving rumble continues, and she sighs. "I hope you're ready to deal with some ridiculous jealousy as well as the amazing sex."

"I think I could handle that," I say. "I think someone's going to have to take a feather duster to my nounie, it's had so little action recently."

"Well, I'm hoping it's gonna get a whole ton of action

when you head out to that ranch. I like a man who's good with his hands."

There's more grumbling in the background. "Will you knock it off, dudes," she scoffs. "We all know you're amazing with your hands. It's why I agreed to marry you all." A ripple of laughter replaces the grumbling, and it seems that all is right again in the McGregor household. I would never have believed that ten men could work so well together, but Laura's harem is different. They're all brothers, and they've grown up in a very structured environment with their father's wishes known and respected. By the sounds of it, the Jackson brothers are a less unified group altogether.

"I don't think I'm going to have it as easy as you," I tell Laura. "This is all their mom's idea, and she's only ever jokingly referred to it. They most likely going to be totally against the idea."

"So was Grant and he was the first to come around."

"The first to come in the sweet little pussy," Grant pipes up from the background.

"Eww," Laura says. "TMI."

"He's never gonna stop reminding us of that fact either," someone else says.

"You're just sour because you were last," Grant says.

"Fuck you, bro."

"I'm going to another room," Laura huffs. "You're all being very juvenile today."

When I hear a door close, I start to laugh. "You know you tell them off like naughty little boys."

"Let me tell you, Danna. My husbands are the sexiest, most alpha men I've come across but they can be so damn childish with each other. I've learned when to get up and leave the room so that they can bicker themselves to death and not annoy me in the process."

"I think it's worse for us because we're only children."

"Right," she says. "Exactly, but definitely don't let this put you off. It's a small blip in an otherwise amazing situation. I can't tell you how good it is…I mean, the sex." She whispers the last word as chastely as a virgin.

"You're a dirty bitch, you know that Laura, and I love you for it."

"Danna, you're gonna love it," she laughs. "You're going to be in your element."

"I really hope so. Because if this goes wrong, I'm going to have ten lots of egg on my face."

"Think positive," Laura tells me. "Be your sassy, hilarious self, and everything will be fine."

"Right," I say, but it's not that easy when you're missing someone and that weight of that loss tugs like an anchor on your heart day and night.

"So spring break harem style," she laughs. "Bet Connor would choke on his own tongue if he knew what you were about to get up to. That boy's been desperate to get into your panties for years."

"Now you're making me want to barf. He's the epitome of 'beautiful on the outside and ugly on the inside." A shiver runs through me because Connor is one man who really knows how to get under my skin. There was a time when I lusted after him to the point of almost madness but the more of his colors he showed, the more I went off him. They say love and hate are separated by a fine line. I think lust and hate might have the same insignificant division.

"Well, let's hope that none of those gorgeous Jackson men is anything like Connor."

"Here's hoping," I say.

5

I've told pop that I'm going to stay with Laura. He wasn't happy about that at all, but he wouldn't stop me. She's my best friend, and while he might not approve of the way that she's chosen to live her life, he also won't judge her for it. Judgment is something left to the higher power.

So here I am on a bus to a place I've never visited, to stay with a family of strangers to create a harem of my own.

It's surreal.

It's scary.

It's nerve-wracking.

It's more exciting that I even want to admit.

Jackie's going to be waiting at the station for me. She's told me to look out for a middle-aged red-head wearing a plaid shirt and brown work boots, so that's what I do. It's not a busy stop so when I step off the bus, hoisting my wheelie suitcase down the steps, I only have to glance around before I spot her and she's already seen me.

"Danna," she calls, raising her hand into a wave and smiling so broadly that I'm almost embarrassed. It's as though I'm the answer to her prayers, which, I guess in a way I am. She's fighting for her livelihood and her family right now and prepared to go to extraordinary lengths to do it.

"Hey," I say as she nears me and pulls me into a warm hug. I'm still holding the handle of my case, so it's awkward but sweet. "Jackie?" I don't know why I'm double checking because who else is going to be calling me by name and hugging the bejesus out of me.

"It's so good to meet you finally," she gushes, releasing me and then gazing up at me. She's shorter than I imagined and cuddly in a way that moms should be. Her bright eyes are smiling too.

"It's good to meet you too. Weird but good."

She laughs, reaching out to take the case from me. "It won't be weird for long. I promise. The truck is right over here."

Before I have a chance to gather my thoughts, she's off, tugging my luggage towards a large muddy vehicle which is parked with its wheels on the sidewalk. I hurry after her, gazing around at this new town. It's small and quaint, with a mom and pop store, a gas station, a diner, and a hard-wear store. Not exactly the bustling city that I'm used to. There's also a bar which looks like something out of an old school western and is called Joe's Place. I wouldn't be surprised to see a man exiting wearing spurs and a cowboy hat. It's funny how different two placed can be when they're only separated by a few hundred miles.

"I told the boys you were coming yesterday. Their

reactions were interesting," she says.

"How so?"

Jackie tosses my case in the trunk and yanks open the passenger door for me. "Well, mostly they were intrigued, but I have one very suspicious son who was looking at me funny and another son who likes his own company and isn't fond of guests. He didn't look too pleased about having a stranger around."

I like the fact that Jackie's so honest and want to ask her which of her sons she's talking about, but without pulling out my phone again to match faces to names, it seems a little pointless. I don't know how Laura managed to get a handle on the McGregors in such a short space of time because I'm feeling lost even imagining getting to know the Jacksons.

The truck smells of a farm but in a nostalgic rather than gross way. It's muddy in the foot-well, but the seats are clean, so I don't feel wary about sitting down. When Jackie slides in next to me and starts the ignition, the dulcet tones of Dolly Parton fill the cab.

"Don't you just love this song," she says happily, glancing over her shoulder and pulling off.

Jolene is one of my favorites, a song that my momma used to play sometimes. I agree, but I don't elaborate because I have a lump in my throat the size of a boulder.

"You're so pretty," Jackie says. "Prettier in person too. I just know my boys are going to love you."

My cheeks pink but I'm pleased. I guess that it doesn't really matter what she thinks of me. Boys don't listen to their moms much when it comes to picking girlfriends. We don't choose who we're attracted to either. So much of that comes down to gut feeling and instinctive preference. As I think this, the overwhelming reality of what I'm about to embark on washes over me again. I mean, what are the chances that ten men, who are not all blood related, are all going to fall madly in love with me. Pretty damn slim. I mean, I know I wasn't hit with the ugly shovel, but I'm no supermodel either. You either like big bums and thick thighs, or you don't. Dark wavy hair isn't everyone's preference. Big boobs might have more male fans than small, so that's a plus, but pale skin and freckles are definitely less broadly appealing than even, tan skin.

Ugh. I hate thinking about myself in a fragmented way. This is what our society does to us. Instagram model perfection is shoved down our throats, and the rest of us are just left to feel shit about our ordinariness.

I take a deep breath and give myself an internal pep talk. I know my own value, and I refuse to let anything about this next week undermine that. I don't need male approval to validate myself, and I certainly am not going to let a lack of it destroy my self-esteem.

"Well, I guess this whole thing hinges on whether they do find me attractive or not," I say. "It seems like a big thing to hope for all ten of them to be attracted to me enough to make this work, but I guess we need to be positive."

"Exactly," Jackie smiles. "Positive thinking is exactly what I'm looking for in a daughter-in-law!!"

I chuckle. "This seems very old fashioned, doesn't it?"

"You mean the 'introduction' aspect?"

"Yeah. Families would do this…find partners for their children. They still do in some countries."

"And I bet they have a lower rate of divorce than we do here. I mean, there is no one out there who knows my boys as I do. I reckon I know them better than they know themselves, especially what's good for them."

Jackie starts to indicate and turns off the winding road through a gate marked Jackson Ranch. We're here, and my heart starts racing instantaneously. It takes another five minutes to reach the house, and we drive through the most beautiful agricultural land I've ever seen; rolling hills of luscious grass, neat fences to keep the livestock in check, and sprawling fields just waiting to crop. When we pull up to the substantial wooden ranch house, I'm blown away. I mean, I was assuming it would be pretty big to house all the Jackson boys, but this place would give the McGregors a run for their money on size. It's huge. Obviously way more rustic than the McGregor mansion but with so much more traditional charm.

"They say home is where the heart is," Jackie says softly, "and they are right. I hope I never have to leave this place. We have got a family burial space over the hill there. I've told my boys that's where I want to rest next to my husband."

"I can understand why," I say.

She opens the car door. "Let's get you inside so that we can have a cup of coffee before the hoards arrive back for lunch. You can get settled in your room too."

I jump down from the truck with my purse, and Jackie slams her door, opens the trunk and drags my suitcase around. I follow her to the side of the house where we enter through a side door and into the kitchen. It's homely and rustic with oak cabinets and tiled counters. A vast table splits the middle of the room, and there are two colossal cord sofas on one side. It's quiet now, but I can imagine how noisy it must get when it's filled with the Jackson men. Noisy and packed.

"Here," Jackie says. "You take a seat, and I'll put the kettle on." There's a whining sound from the corner of the room and a shaggy dog with the droopiest eyes I've ever seen climbs slowly to its feet and starts to cross towards me. "You've been spotted." Jackie laughs and watches as the dog heads over to me and sniffs my legs. "That's Zack's dog, Ruffles. He used to go everywhere with him, but he's too old to go out much now. He keeps me company here, but he still pines for Zack."

I reach down to pet the dogs head, which it seems to like. I can see from the way it moves that it must be in some pain and I get down onto my knees so that I can rub its belly. Ruffles wags his tail slowly and makes a happy sound. "He likes you," Jackie laughs. "Zack might be a tougher nut to crack, but if Ruffles gives you the seal of approval, it'll certainly help some.

So Zack must be one of the brothers who's warier of my arrival. That's good to know. I wonder if Jackie will drop any more hints over coffee because it would certainly help me to know who's going to be approaching me with trepidation or negativity.

I stand, and Ruffles follows me to where I take a seat at the table. There are chairs at the ends and benches down the side I perch at the end of a bench and ruffles slumps at my feet.

Jackie asks how I take my coffee and quickly pours it black as I like it. She puts some cookies on a plate too and then comes to sit with me. I'm just taking a sip of the intense, bitter liquid when there's the sound of loud male voices nearing the door.

"We need to get York to look at that mare," someone says.

"He looked at her this morning," another voice says.

"And she's not getting any better."

"William, you've got to give the treatment a chance to work."

The door in the corner of the room flies open, and three men stomp in dressed almost identically in worn jeans, plaid shirts, and woolen socks. They've obviously left their work boots by the door which makes me smile internally. On the outside, I must look absolutely petrified. The chatter stops at the catch sight of me.

"Boys," Jackie says. "Come and meet Danna."

They move like a synchronized unit, and as they get closer, I realize they're identical triplets. Wow. I've never seen people look so alike. "Danna, this is William, Walker, and Wade."

I stand and hold out my hand, feeling ridiculously formal. They're so much taller than me that even though they're standing across the table, I feel swamped by man. With blond hair and light brown eyes, they're striking to look at, but it's their broad shoulders and swagger that has the butterflies fluttering. William shakes my hand firmly, his expression serious. Walker cocks his head to one side as he regards me with interest. Wade wraps my hand in both of his, smiling broadly. "Welcome," he says. "It's about time mom had some female company."

"You sure you know what you're letting yourself in for?" Walker asks.

I shake my head. "I'm an only child, so I'm used to a

quiet house."

"There's nothing quiet about this place," Walker says. "Even when everyone's asleep someone is snoring."

"Way to welcome our guest." Jackie shakes her head. "You know, Danna, I really tried to teach these boys manners, but this ranch just seems to dirty them all up again."

I laugh, already feeling like a fish out of water. What's it going to be like in here with ten Jackson brothers and just one of me? The prospect suddenly feels even more daunting, and I can now understand why Laura was feeling so conflicted and overwhelmed by the McGregor brothers. When I met them, it was all a big joke for me; ten sexy men all in such close proximity to my best friend. Now, the impact of why I'm here and what I thought I wanted is really hitting home. Trying to find one potential life partner is a challenge, but ten is something else.

I'm out of my depth massively, but as I look at these men, I try to feel okay about it.

I need to remember my frivolous and reckless attitude towards the McGregor brothers and apply that here. It's either that or get eaten alive.

"They seem polite enough."

"I hope they will be." Jackie looks pointedly at her sons, and they roll their eyes.

"Mom, we're grown men you know. And most women aren't looking for a gentleman. They're looking for men who are rough around the edges and good with their hands." Wade winks and Jackie swats him with her hand.

"You need to watch this one," she smiles. "He's always

been a huge bundle of cheek!"

"Wade thinks he funny," William says.

"Because I am," Wade says.

"Some of the time," Walker adds, being diplomatic. I wonder if that's his role with his brothers. It's going to be fun finding out.

"What are you boys doing home so early?"

"One of the mares is ailing. York came to look at her, but she's not improving," William says.

"We need to give it time," Walker tells his brother.

"I want York to come and check her out again. Is he in his office?"

"I don't know sweetie," Jackie says. "We've just come back from the bus station, and I haven't seen anyone else except you."

"You're going to go and find York, and he's going to tell you the same thing that I'm telling you," Walker says. "Your fussing too much. I know you've got a special bond with this horse, but York's done all he can."

"York was distracted this morning," William says. "His mind wasn't on the job one hundred percent."

"He's got a lot on his mind," Jackie says but doesn't elaborate. I try to recall what York looks like from the pictures Laura sent me, but the Jackson brothers are just a big blur of gorgeous man in my mind. I'm hoping it won't take me too long to be able to decipher them all.

"I'm hungry, mom," Wade says. "You got any of that fruit loaf I love."

Jackie beams broadly, as Wade comes to put his arm around her. "He's always loved my fruit loaf," she says. "Takes after his poppa."

There's a stillness in the room at the mention of the late Mr. Jackson. It's the same stillness that comes about when either me or pop mentions mom. I guess it's because memories come flooding back to fill the present and for a moment, everyone has to stop what they're doing and think.

"I'll get you some," Jackie finally says. "You boys want some too?"

William and Walker nod and Jackie sets about preparing a plate of slices of her homemade bread with lashings of butter. It looks delicious. When she's done, Wade brings over the plate and offers me the first slice. "You have to try this Danna. I swear it's got some kind of magic in it."

I reach out and snag a piece, happy to see that he's the kind of man who's gracious in sharing even the things that he loves the most. "You gotta tell me what you think," he smiles watching as I bring the bread to my lips. It smells of cinnamon and orange, and the first bit practically melts in my mouth. I chew and shake my head at how amazing it is.

"So good, huh?" he asks, and I nod. It's only then that he takes a piece for himself.

"Stop hogging the good stuff," Walker says, and William reaches over to take a couple of slices for himself.

"We gotta go," William says.

"You go and see if York is there. We'll hang out here," Walker says with a smile. His eyes are playful, and he drops himself onto the bench opposite me. I look to Jackie, and she winks at me encouragingly. Wade takes his brothers lead and sits too. While William stomps off with a frown on his face, Jackie pours two more cups of coffee and settles down next to me. I can almost feel the excitement rolling off her in waves.

"So, how come you're here for a visit?" Wade asks me.

"Well...I..."

"Danna needs a little break from the stress of college," Jackie pipes up, "so I thought it would be good for her to come and stay."

Both boys look to me as though they're expecting me to elaborate. "My course is really hard," I say. "And I've had some personal stuff going on."

There are a few seconds of silence before Wade steps in. "Well, we're glad you're here, and I hope you find the ranch restful."

"She'd be the only one," Walker laughs. "The work never ends in this place."

"Danna's a guest. I'm not expecting her to muck in." Jackie pats my hand.

"It's okay," I say. "I think I'd like to get hands-on if that'd be okay with the boys."

Wade's grin is broad, his straight, white teeth flashing his approval. "We'd love another pair of hands," he says. "As long as you don't mind getting them dirty."

Everyone's eyes seem to focus on my hands all of a sudden. I'm not a manicure kind of girl, so I'm glad my nails are mid-length and filed into neat rounds. They look practical and feminine rather than high maintenance. "I don't mind getting them dirty," I say. "As long as I get to clean up after."

Walkers eyes seem to flash darkly at me, and I'm suddenly feeling as though the W triplets might be on board with a little more than just friendly time. If they are, then that could be three out of ten. Thirty percent. Thinking of it that way makes this crazy plan seem just a little more achievable than I'd feared.

"Maybe the boys can take you out this afternoon then," Jackie says happily. "Did you bring work boots?" I shake my head, feeling very much like a soft city girl in my pristine white converse. These shoes wouldn't last five minutes in this place. "What size are you?"

"A seven," I say.

"Well, that's good," she says. "I'm a seven too. You can borrow some of mine."

I'm wearing jeans and a sweatshirt which I guess is suitable for whatever the Jackson boys might have me do. I sip my coffee as conversation switches into more ranch business. It seems the boys have an impressive stud horse that another ranch is looking to use to fertilize their mares. I had no idea that animal sex required so much advanced and detailed planning.

This all seems like a million miles away from my normal life.

I watch how the boys interact with their mom and find it natural and sweet. I know that they're adopted, but it doesn't seem to have had an impact on them all forming a close bond.

"So, Danna," Wade says. "You ready to get mucky?"

"I don't think any woman is ever ready to get mucky!" Jackie laughs. "We just put up with it sometimes. It's you boys who love the dirt."

"I think I'm ready," I say, "but I guess I have no idea what I'm actually letting myself in for."

"We'll look after you. Don't you worry."

We're just rising from the table when William is back, and this time, he's not alone. A tall man, maybe six foot three with spiky blond hair and the most piercing blue eyes I've ever seen follows William into the kitchen. He's carrying a large bag.

"You know we told William to give it more time," Walker says.

York shrugs his shoulders. "Don't know why you bothered wasting your breath. You know what he's like."

"A dog with a bone," Wade laughs.

"Exactly," York says.

Jackie gets to her feet. "York, this is Danna. She's going to be coming out with you boys."

York nods. "Welcome."

It's a short and not so friendly introduction. I get the feeling that York might be on the 'tough nut to crack' list, but that's okay. I get a good feeling about him. Any man who studies so hard just to be able to help animals has got to have a good heart in there somewhere.

"Right. Let me get you those boots." Jackie's off into a room at the side of the kitchen which I'm assuming is a mud room. I can see hooks laden with coats and other outdoor attire. It's at least as big as my bedroom at home. I guess on a working ranch, it's important to have these practical areas.

I stand awkwardly, with a half-smile plastered on my face. Walker and Wade clear the plates and cups from the table, and I get another happy surge because there is no way I could take on ten men who didn't know how to look after themselves. Ten lazy ass men would not result in a happy harem. "Here you go," Jackie says, strolling back into the room clutching an old pair of work boots. "These will suit you just fine."

"There's more mud on those than she's gonna pick up over in Hope's Meadow."

"We've got names for different parts of the ranch," Walker explains. "Hope's Meadow is our corner."

"It sounds pretty," I say and catch York almost rolling his eyes.

"It is," Jackie says, "especially list time of year when the flowers are blooming."

"You picked a good time to visit," Wade says.

I perch back on the bench to pull on the shoes. They're so muddy, and I'm conscious of getting the floor dirty, but it seems to be all over the sides, not underneath. They're big and clumpy brown things but really comfortable when they're on.

"There we go," Wade smiles. "We'll make a rancher out of you yet."

6

The boys all start heading towards the door where they begin to pull on their own boots. I don't think I ever realized how much of a turn-on it would be for me to see all these practical, working men. Mud hasn't been on my radar since I was a kid.

"So, Danna. How long are you going to be staying with us?" William asks.

"A week," I say. "I'll need to get back to college after next weekend."

"Don't you get work to do over spring break?" York asks.

I nod. "Some. I've brought it with me but I'm pretty on top of my studies. I like to be organized."

"Organization is a good trait," William says. As I follow them over to a large truck I notice that the triplets seem to fall into an identical walking pattern, each using the same leg at the same time. York trails them again. I wonder what it would be like to have triplets for siblings and be the odd one out. It's probably made even more difficult but the fact that these men are all adopted. The W triplets have each other but York is truly by himself in the crowd.

York opens the rear door for me and I slide inside. It's a mess in this truck. A muddy floor covered in cardboard in a vain attempt to preserve the carpet. The seats have a hay and dog hair coating. I have to admit that I'm feeling a little grossed out. York slides in next to me and as I glance at his profile I can see a hint of a smile gracing his lips. Is he amused by my discomfort? Probably.

"Someone needs a valet," I say, deciding to own it.

"You saying my truck's dirty?" William says.

"In a polite way," I say. There's a rumble of laughter from the rest of the boys as they take their seats.

"No fucking point in cleaning up when it just gets dirty again."

"You think that way about your underwear too?" York asks.

Everyone chuckles again and William's face is not best pleased. He's definitely the more serious of the triplets and I'm not really feeling any warmth towards him yet. York, on the other hand, has a darkly dry sense of humor that I love. His leg jiggles up and down restlessly next to mine and I have an urge to place my hand on his thigh to still it.

"You better get used to the banter, Danna," Wade says. "With so many men in the house, the conversation tends to get rough."

"I'm sure I'll cope," I say.

"I have a feeling that Danna can give as good as any of us in this car," Walker says, turning to look at me from the front passenger seat. His eyes are intense but his smile is broad. "I reckon Danna is going to take us all in her stride."

"I hope I am," I say.

"Either that or you'll need to buy some earmuffs," Wade laughs.

William starts the engine and we're off. We initially drive back in the direction that Jackie and I had passed through earlier but then we take a different branch in the road. There is a security gate that William waves a card to pass through.

The fences are high and there are visible security cameras pointed at the road. "You need security out here?" I ask. It hadn't even crossed my mind that rural areas would need it.

"Yeah, for sure. The livestock we have here is worth a fortune. We've had neighbors lose ten horses in a night. It's cost a lot to install but it's reduced our insurance some and making it so visible will hopefully put any ranch burglars off coming here."

"We've been lucky so far," William says. "But I think we need more."

"William would sleep with the horses if he could."

"He used to," Wade says smiling. "Remember when pop came to check on us and William wasn't in his bed. He'd wandered all the way out here in his PJs because Dancer was sick."

"The whole house was awake that night."

"Dancer needed me," William says softly.

"Mom thought you'd been kidnapped."

York chuckles. "Like anyone would have come into a house full of people and just picked William."

There's another round of laughter. "Yeah, they would have picked your pretty ass for sure," William says.

York doesn't reply but instead gazes out of the window. I can see the affection present between these boys but even so, York definitely seems more reserved and on the outside of the group. It makes me want to take his hand in mine and I'm surprised at the tender feelings I'm having towards him so soon.

Do tender feelings really have a place here and now?

I don't think I'm going to get ten brothers with tender feelings. My mom always told me the way to a man's heart is through his stomach but in reality, it's through his dick. They might try to deny it but good sex is top of any man's list for relationship goals. Fuck him, feed him, support him and comfort him in that order and you're on to a winner. At least, that's what it says in the magazines and who am I to argue!

I need to up my game because polite conversation is going to make me a house guest when what I want to be is a bed buddy. Just as I'm about to turn to York and put my hand on his knee suggestively, the truck comes to a halt. We're parked outside a huge barn type building which is surrounded by a huge fenced enclosure. There are horses everywhere and they are beautiful.

William is out of the truck first, slamming his door and striding over to where another man is securing a gate. I open my door but can't hear what's being said. "He's asking for an update," York says. "My brother is very passionate about his animals. Losing one is like losing family for him."

"It shows a good heart," I say and York nods. His blue eyes are cold all of a sudden, his full lips narrowed into a serious line. "Good hearts get broken easily, Danna. That's the problem." He turns his back and starts towards the stables, leaving me feeling chastened and hollow. I know what he means. It's only when we love that we make ourselves truly vulnerable, but without love, there is nothing that can touch our hearts. A heart without love is a cold and impenetrable thing.

A body without sex, too.

Wade grins over at me, always the lighthearted one. "Come on, Danna. Come meet our pride and joy."

I follow them towards the paddock to get my first look at the horses. All I can say is wow. They seem to be divided into two separate areas and I can see the difference between the two. "These are the Quarter Horses, our working breed," Walker says. "And these are our Thoroughbreds."

They're all beautiful, with glossy coats and thick manes, but the Thoroughbreds are something else. There's a majesty about them.

I watch York and William follow the other man into the stables. "So one of the horses is sick?"

"Yeah," Wade says. He's leaning over the fence, his forearms resting on the wood. All he's missing is a cowboy hat for him to fit into this picture perfectly. "William has a soft spot for her."

"William has a soft spot for them all," Walker says. "Pop always said he wasn't built to be a rancher. Too much compassion."

"Don't you need compassion? You're working with animals, day in and day out."

"To a certain extent," Wade says. "Maybe compassion is the wrong word. Compassion can involve you having to shoot your pride and joy in the head because they're suffering. William is too sentimental."

"It's funny but I would never have assumed that on first meeting him," I say. "He's the serious one."

They both laugh. "You categorizing us already?"

"Yeah. Aren't you making assumptions about me?" I say.

They both look amused and Wade, who is standing to my right, shakes his head. "I think you might be trouble, Little Miss Danna. Trouble with a capital T."

"I think you might be right," I laugh. "Do you like trouble?"

"Fuck yeah," Walker says. "The more trouble the better."

I'm not sure if I'm imagining them getting a little closer to me but they sure feel like they have. I'm like the meat between a chunky bread sandwich. I look up at them both, taking in their twinkling eyes and broad smiles. Wade's eyes are warm and Walker's eyes have that burning intensity I saw in the kitchen. "What about William?" I ask. "Is he good with trouble too?"

"Well, we don't do much without each other so I guess he's gonna need to come along for the ride," Walker laughs.

"Ride?" I say, shrugging my shoulders as though I have

no idea what he's insinuating. "Am I gonna get to ride one of these beauties?"

Walker leans in, his lips brushing against my ear in a way that sends shivers up my spine and heat between my legs. "No one ever called my cock a beauty before," he says, hot breath gusting over my skin. "But you can ride it any time you like."

Oh. My. Goodness.

I can't believe we're at the point of talking sex already but I'm going to go with it. Either these boys have been starved of fun between the sheets or I'm oozing pheromones. Damn.

Wade laughs, leaning against the fence he reaches to tuck a loose curl behind my ear. "Excuse my brother, Miss Danna. He's got a way with words that isn't to everyone's taste."

I lean in close to him, my lips brushing his ear in the same way his brother's brushed mine. "It's okay," I say softly. "I told you I don't mind getting my hands dirty."

I swear I feel him shiver and I get a rush from the power. This is me. This is the Danna I've been missing these past few months.

"Baby," he says. "It' won't be your hands you have to worry about."

I smile at them both. "Can I ride a horse too?" I say. Walker shakes his head as though he can't quite believe I'm real.

"Sure," he says.

There are voices coming from behind us and York and

William emerge from the stable.

"She's improving," York says. "The treatments working."

William looks a little embarrassed but relieved. "Seems I was worrying prematurely. Gary's got it all under control."

"Well, that's good news," Wade says. "Danna here wants to go for a ride."

"We've got to work," William says. "We're only half done and if we don't get our asses in gear, we won't make it back for dinner."

Walker rolls his eyes. "All work and no play makes William the boring brother."

"York can take her," Wade says. "We'll be done in a couple of hours and we can all ride back together."

7

York looks like he'd rather eat his own arm, but unless he's planning on taking William's truck, or snagging one of the horses, he's got no other way of getting back to the house.

"You ever ridden before?" he asks me. He slides his hands into his pockets and widens his stance, watching me with interest.

"Yes," I say, indignantly. "I had a pony party when I was ten."

Wade and Walker snort with laughter.

York looks less amused. "It can be dangerous to get on a horse if you don't know what you're doing. I'm not sure mom would be happy for you to take that risk."

"I'm over eighteen, York. I'm legally able to make my own decisions." I smile sweetly and am amused when there's a snigger from Wade and Walker.

"Okay," York says. "Let's get you on a horse."

I'm about ten minutes into the preparation for horse riding when I start to wonder if I'm actually making a terrible mistake. The horse seems so tall now I'm close to it. I guess at five foot five, I'm not exactly the tallest woman in the world. The horse whinnies at me, turning its head to nuzzle its long brown nose in my direction. Her mane is so coarse, and I reach out to stroke her a little, just to show York I'm not scared.

I am scared.

Terrified actually.

And annoyed with myself. It's just a horse. Kids do this when they're five and love it. I take a steadying breath.

"She's sensing your fear," York says. His tone is gentle and without judgment, so I'm not defensive.

"It's stupid," I say, touching her again. "New things always feel so daunting."

"That's natures protection mechanism," he tells me. "As children, we run headlong into danger. Our parents have to teach us when to approach with caution for our own survival, and we carry those warnings around for life."

"My mom always encouraged me," I say. "She wanted me to be brave and strong."

York smiles. "There's a difference between being brave and strong and reckless and foolish. I'm glad you're approaching riding with some trepidation. As much as it's fun and a necessary part of running a ranch, it can also be hazardous. Horses are unpredictable in the same way as all other animals. We can train them, but in the end, their own deeper instincts can take over when you're least expecting it."

"You're not filling me with confidence," I laugh.

"You'll be fine," he says. "And I'll stay close until you get used to it."

The idea of York staying close makes my heart skitter. I'm close enough to smell the scent of his skin; a fresh, alpine smell. His forearms are tense as he tightens the saddle, his huge hands working hard and I wonder if they're as rough as I'm imagining them to be.

"Okay, we're good to go." He moves to take the horse by the reins. "Put your right foot in the stirrup, grip hold here, and pull yourself up."

I inhale a steadying breath and lay my hand on the horse's side. She's so warm, lungs inflating rhythmically and feet shuffling just a little as though standing still is making her antsy. I reach out as York has suggested, take a big step into the stirrup and tug myself as hard as I can, swinging my other leg over the horse. York watches, keeping a tight grip on Daisy as she adjusts her footing again. "You did good. Put your other foot into the stirrup and take hold of the reins."

I do as he says, taking another steadying breath as I realize just how high up I am. Falling off Daisy would not be a pleasant experience. "I'm going to lead you around a bit so you can get used to her." York tugs the reins, and Daisy responds, moving into a gentle swaying walk that shifts me in the saddle. "Try and move with her," York says. "Shift your hips."

I do as he asks, trying to remember what people look like on riding horses on TV as reference. It's strange at first, but I finally start to get into a rhythm and York nods. "That's it." He lets go of the reins. "Keep going. You can use the reins to steer."

This sounds much more technical than I was anticipating. "I don't know," I say. "Are you sure I'm ready?"

"I thought you had a pony party when you were a kid. You must be ready."

I glance back at him, taking in the smugness in his grin and the challenge in his eyes. Those eyes. I could swear he has thicker eyelashes than mine, even when I've layered on the mascara. I focus ahead, taking on the responsibility of getting Daisy to trot in the right direction and of keeping myself firmly in the saddle. The last thing I want is to give York the satisfaction of failing.

"That's it," he says again. I'm trying to move my body to respond as Daisy picks up pace, but I don't think I'm quite getting it. The ground seems to whizz beneath us, even though the horse isn't going anywhere near as fast as it could. He's definitely showing more confidence in me that I am in myself. "Pull on her reins now so that you can slow down."

They're almost slippery in my hands, such is my nervousness. Daisy responds, though, coming to a standstill as we near York again. He seems to have her well trained.

"So, it seems the pony party has served you well." He smiles up at me, taking hold of Daisy and walking us back towards the stables. "Hold on, and I'm going to get Chipper."

The horse he comes back with is dark brown and glossy and quite a bit taller than mine. Daisy must be the training-wheels-version of the Jackson's stables. "Come on then," he says. I follow him around the paddock a few times, and then he unhooks the gate. Am I seriously going to roam around this ranch on a horse after only practicing for a few minutes? It looks like I am. The horses naturally move until they are side by side.

"We won't go too far," he says. "I don't want you to get too saddle sore."

I grimace. "I definitely want to be able to sit down later," I say.

York chuckles darkly. I wonder if his mind is in the gutter like mine is, imagining my pussy getting sore from fucking him. If his cock is in proportion to the rest of him, I think I'd be pulling back on the reins with him too. I wonder if I'll get the chance to find out.

We follow a trail, worn into the terrain by previous horse riders, I assume. The breeze is gentle against my cheeks, and the scent of the open country fills my nose. I didn't realize how much I needed to get out of the city until this moment. I've been burying my head in my college work and avoiding overthinking about real life for too long. Even so, the walls have felt closer than they should. I've found myself in this place looking for a harem, but as I soak up the sights around me, I think that maybe fate has brought me here for another reason.

"You know," York says, interrupting the tranquility with his gruff voice. "It's funny that Mom has never mentioned you before. I mean, she grew up in this town, and people rarely leave. I thought I knew all of her friends."

"Everyone has secrets," I say. "Not even secrets in this case. More like parts of their lives that they might not talk about."

"Yeah, but that's just it. Mom's not secretive," he says, eyeing me. "She's like an open book."

"Well, you know about me now."

York nods, but I get the feeling he's not buying my story. He's definitely suspicious, and I need to find a way to change the subject before I get Jackie into trouble. "So you're a vet?"

York nods. "When I was growing up, we relied really heavily on the vet in town. The bills could be astronomical, and sometimes, we wouldn't be able to get anyone up here to treat our livestock in time. It seemed to make sense for the family business if at least one of us went to college and trained."

"Your mom must be really proud of you."

"She is." He seems to grip his reins a little tighter, and his jaw looks clenched. "My father was a vet. My birth father."

It takes me a few seconds to piece together what he's saying. I don't know why, but I assumed that all the brothers we adopted as babies, but I sense that York is affected by talking about his father in a way that would indicate some pain there. "Wow. That's great that you've followed in his footsteps," I say, hoping that's the right thing to say.

"He won't ever know so I guess it doesn't really matter." York's back is straight, his expression tight. Death is a difficult thing to deal with, even when a lot of time has passed. Wounds can be deep and hard to heal, and it's too soon for me to be probing him for information.

"My mom passed away six months ago," I say. "I like to think she's looking down on me."

He glances at me momentarily. "You think she's watching you now."

"I think if she is, then she'd be laughing. I fell off the pony at my party and never wanted to get on a horse again after that."

He laughs in a full-bellied way that has me smiling. "Well, you kept that part quiet, Danna."

I shrug. "I don't like to show weakness."

He's quiet for a while after that. I wonder if that's how he feels too? I listen to the call of the birds and the whisper of the wind through the grass. This is a beautiful piece of country here, a place that could fill a person with contentment. Am I that person? I'm not really sure. The city gets into your blood, the hectic pace of life almost like an addiction. Slowing down can be a shock, like coming to a standing stop from a long jump.

"We are all weak," he says eventually. "Even the strongest of us have moments when we are on our knees. There shouldn't be anything wrong with that. We're humans, not gods. Our fallibility is what makes us human. But I know how you feel because I feel that way too."

"People have expectations for men and women. Men are supposed to be capable, and women are supposed to be soft and feminine. I never liked how I was expected to behave. At school, a lot of my friends were boys, and I wanted to have that freedom just to be myself."

"You think boys have less pressure," he says. "I think we have more."

"Maybe," I say. "I know that I get judged for the way I am because I don't conform to the stereotype. I'm not drawing on giant eyebrows or having fake lashes stuck to my eyes every two weeks. I don't have an Instagram account that I'm self-promoting on every five seconds. I don't really give a shit about what it takes to be a popular girl these days."

"Good for you," he says. "If anything, I don't think people are gonna judge you for that. At least no one that you should care about the opinion of. We need more people in this world who are prepared to stand apart from the flock."

I nod. "There was a time, before social media, that people could just have their own identity. We didn't sit around comparing ourselves to thousands of other people, maybe just to the people in our own school or own town. Now…"

"Now we're just tiny fish in a pond of seven billion people," he says.

"Exactly."

"Well, Danna. This is a small pond. Ranch life can still be like it was in the past. We only need to connect for business reasons, and there is no one here who is worried about eyelashes or eyebrows!"

I laugh. "You make it sound very appealing."

He glances at me again, this time with shyness about him. "Well, you're only here for a few days, but I hope that you get as much as you can from your trip.

I hope so too.

As we near the brow of the hill, my knees begin to hurt. "I think we might need to turn back," I say, no longer feeling as though I need to pretend a thing to this man.

"Sure," he says. "You can see the boundaries of our property from here."

I gaze around at the vastness of the place that York calls home and wonder at the difference with my own. Pop and our little house feel very far away. "This must have been a spectacular place to grow up."

"It was," he says, "but it wasn't meant to be my home."

"How old were you when you came here?" I ask.

"Six," he says. "After my parent's accident."

"I'm so sorry," I say. I can't imagine what it must have been like for him to lose his parents at such a young age and have to adapt to a whole new household and new family. No wonder York is so reserved.

"It was a long time ago," he says.

"But it never leaves us," I say.

He shakes his head. "Let's get you back to the stables."

8

Thankfully, the W triplets are done with work when we get back to the paddock, so we all pile into the car and head home.

I don't want to admit it, but my ass is actually really sore, and my knees are killing me. I could hardly straighten my legs when I dismounted. Who knew that riding involved so many muscles?

"Did you enjoy that?" Wade asks, smiling from the passenger seat.

"It was fun," I say.

"She did good," York says. "For a novice."

"Some people just have a natural way with animals," William says.

"The rest of our brothers should be coming back soon," Walker says as we pull up to the house.

"More names to remember!" I roll my eyes, and they laugh. "You'll get there. We all look pretty different, so it's easy to tell us apart."

"Except there are two sets of identical twins as well as you guys."

"Yeah, but you're not having trouble working out who we are, are you?" Wade asks.

I frown, realizing that I'm not. They have such different characters that their faces seem to be changed even though they're identical. It's the expressions, I think, and something in their eyes that gives them away. Oh, and their different shirts. Come tomorrow, when they've changed into different clothes, maybe I won't find it so easy to tell who's who.

"Who do I still have to meet?"

"Well, there's Zack, Xsander, Xane, Tommy, Trent, and Samuel."

"I love how your mom chose your names that way."

"She did for some of us," York says. "But some of it was luck. York was my name at birth."

As I open the door and slide off the seat, feet crunching on the gravel drive, another vehicle pulls up. There are two men in this one, and they look at me with interest. They slide out of their truck. "Where'd you pick up a girl?" one of them says. They're definitely identical twins with dark, tightly curled hair and piercing gray eyes. Their t-shirts are form-fitting in the best possible way, revealing broad chests and biceps that almost make my eyes pop out of their sockets. At least six foot four, I feel like a midget next to them.

"This is Danna, the one momma told us about."

They both smile. "We're not used to seeing women on this ranch except our mother. I'm Xsander." He holds out his hand to shake mine, and he does it with a firmness that has me clenching in the best place. "Welcome to the madhouse."

"Why you are trying to scare her off already," Xane says. He's leaner than his brother, but still as firm on the handshaking.

"If she can't stand the heat, no point hanging around the kitchen," Xsander says shrugging.

"I don't think Danna will have any problem with the heat," Wade says laughing. The other men glance at him and then at me with quizzical expressions, but I just smile. Let them guess what Wade's insinuating.

"Are we just gonna stand out here shooting the breeze?" William says.

"Guess not," Xane laughs as we all follow William into the house. I shuck Jackie's work boots off in the mud room while the boys do the same. Xsander and Xane are back to talking business, but I can't really get a grasp on what they're saying. Something about crop rotation and a new harvesting machine. Jackie sticks her head around the corner. "You're back!" She sounds surprised.

"Just about in one piece," I say.

"Well, that's good enough," she laughs. "Come on in and grab some hot coffee before you wash up."

When I've placed her boots on the rack, I follow the boys into the warm and welcoming kitchen. There's coffee in steaming mugs on the table and a plate of what looks like homemade bread, sliced into thick wedges topped with butter. The boys are munching hungrily. I guess feeding ten big, strong working men must be a fulltime job for Jackie. There's a gorgeous smell of roasting coming from the huge range cooker. Jackie's busy peeling potatoes at the counter.

"Can I help?" I ask her putting down my coffee and rolling up my sleeves.

"Sure," she says, smiling. She hands me her peeler and reaches into a draw for another one. "It'll be nice to have some company."

I start to tackle the mountain of earthy potatoes, wondering if they're grown here on the ranch. The boys are laughing and joking behind me, but I don't turn to see them. Slowly, they all head off to wash up, I assume.

Jackie hums along to the radio that's playing a country station. "Did you have fun?" she asks me.

"Sure. It was good. First time on a horse in over fifteen years."

"Good," she says. "I take it my boys looked after you well?"

"Yes. Very well."

"And any positive signs?" she asks, turning to me with a glint in her eye.

"I think so. I got a good feeling from Walker and Wade. And maybe from York too."

"And William?"

I shake my head. "He's been so worried about his horse that I don't think he noticed I was there."

She laughs, waving her peeler as she talks. "William has

always been the most reserved of my triplets. Give him time. It usually takes him twice as long to see what's going on as his brothers, but his heart's in the right place."

"Yeah. I think I can see that about him."

"And York? He's got to be one of the tougher nuts to crack."

"I think so," I say. "We talked while we were riding. We have some shared stuff."

"Shared stuff is the basis of all relationships," Jackie says knowingly.

I shrug. "I guess. This just seems like a mountain to climb."

"Ten mountains," she laughs but stops when I give her an overwhelmed look. "Just take it one day at a time, and don't hold back. You have nothing to lose here, only a whole lot to gain."

I toss another peeled potato into the bowl. "Okay. With that attitude, I think I could conquer Everest."

We talk some more until the pile of potatoes is reduced to peelings and shiny white rounds. "I'm going to stick these in the oven," Jackie says. "Do you think you could find your room with instructions?"

"Sure," I say. "Just tell me which way to go."

Jackie doesn't stop chopping for a second. "Go out the door in the corner, and up the stairs that you see in front. When you reach the next floor, head to your left until you see a room with 'meadow' written on it. That one's yours."

"Who are my neighbors?" I ask.

"Walker and Wade are next to you, and William and Zack are opposite. The rest are down the hall. You have your own bathroom, so don't worry about needing to walk around in a towel."

"Shame," I laugh and Jackie giggles too.

"Yes, that could have been one way to get my boys thinking along the right tracks. I'll ring a bell for dinner at around 7 pm."

I grab my suitcase and purse from the corner of the room and follow Jackie's directions until I come to a large wooden door with a white china nametag displaying Meadow in pretty cursive. The handle is cold wrought iron beneath my hand, but once inside I am filled with warmth. It's so cute with its sizeable canopied bed and rustic dresser and nightstand. There's a green velvet bedroom chair in the corner by the window; perfect for sitting with a book or enjoying the view. I dump my purse on the bed and pull the curtains back, taking in the rolling hills from a new angle. I'm just about the carry on my exploration when I see movement out of the corner of my eye. Ruffles is ambling along a path and behind him, a lone man; slim with dark, brooding features, he cuts a lonely figure against the landscape. As if he senses he is being watched, he turns and stares up at my window. I don't know how much he can see from where he is but I jump to the side, not wanting to be caught peeking. I use the curtain to conceal me and look again. He's still there, looking up at my window, paused like a wind-up soldier at the end of its motion.

Which brother is he? Zack? Tommy or Trent? Or maybe Samuel?

Then I remember Jackie saying that Ruffles is Zack's dog.

So this is Zack.

A tough nut to crack, Jackie said.

He looks lost out there by himself. Then again, I could just be romanticizing him like Heathcliff. I duck away again, my heart beating fast. Even from such a distance, I can feel Zack's intensity. A shiver runs down my spine. What would it like to be under a man like that? Would he grip my wrists in his hands and hold me down while he fucked me? Would he turn me over and slide it in from behind while he whispered dirty things in my ear? I don't know, but I really want to find out.

9

I'm showered and ready in no time, dressed in jeans and a yellow top with spaghetti straps and lace detail. It's pretty but not showy, a good combination, I think. I'm just finishing my mascara when there's a knock at the door.

With no spy hole, I have no idea who is out there, so I turn the lock and open the door just a crack. It's Wade. Then Walker appears from behind him.

"Can we come in and hang out?" Wade says, his eyes sparkling in the low light of the hallway. I get the feeling that hanging out might not be his sole intention. For a second, I'm paralyzed as the reasons I should say no run through my head, but then Jackie's advice comes back to me, and I open the door wider. I've ten mountains to climb in seven days. I need to get hiking. Most importantly, I remind myself that this is my dream, and I should be willing to go after it.

"So," Wade says slowly. "Just how much trouble are you really, Miss Danna?"

"How much trouble do you like?" I put my hand on

my hip, watching as Walker closes the door behind him.

"Oh, we like a whole heap of trouble," Walker says. "Can you handle a whole heap?"

Now that sounds like a challenge, and I'm really not one to flake out when the going gets tough. "I think I can handle what you got," I say, cocking my head and looking pointedly at Walker's crotch. I know my eyes aren't deceiving me when I see his cock hardening beneath his jeans.

"What about me?" Wade asks, taking a step closer and running his fingers down the bare skin of my arm. "Think you can handle my trouble too?"

I lean in close to his ear, breathing in the fresh scent of his skin. "I can't say for sure, but I guess there's only one way to find out."

I don't know what they were really expecting when they came knocking on my door, but maybe it wasn't for me to strip my top off before they've even kissed me. I unbutton my jeans too, sliding them over my thighs until they're a puddle on the floor.

Walker and Wade watch it all, not moving from where they're standing, just enjoying the view. They look hungry, and I don't blame them. I'm a lot of woman to take in when you maybe weren't expecting it. In this yellow polka dot lingerie, I look like a delicious lemon drizzle cake. At least, that's how I imagine myself. Positive mental attitude is the key to positive body image, and a positive body image is the key to amazing sex.

"Wow," they both whisper. Wade is the first to step forward, running his fingers up my arm and across my collar bone, dipping down the middle of my cleavage and over the roundness of my belly.

Walker moves behind me, his hands taking hold of the sides of my thighs and squeezing gently. I feel small between these two huge men but voluptuous too, like an overripe fruit just ready to burst with sweet juice.

My dream flickers through my memory; how it felt to have more than one man touching me, fucking me. My panties are wet, my pussy hot with anticipation.

Walker's hand stroke upwards, grasping the cheeks of my ass as his brother slides one bra strap from my shoulder. Walker's lips are the first to find my skin, skimming the back of my neck as he pulls my hair to one side. It's like liquid lightening up my spine. I make an involuntary sound, and Wade leans in to kiss it from my lips. "Sssh," he says. "There are eight other men in this house who'll be heading in this direction if they hear you making noises like that."

I want to tell him that it is the whole reason I'm here, but I don't. One step at a time. Or two, I think, as Walker kisses my neck again. Wade leans in to kiss me; soft lips teasing mine and the gentle slide of his tongue into my mouth is electric. My hands slide up his sides, the play of his muscles tantalizing beneath my fingers. This is everything I hoped it would be. Excitement mixed with the delicious sense of taboo that has me trembling with anticipation.

"You smell so fucking good," Walker says, his fingers finding the fastening to my bra and unhooking it.

Wow. This is moving fast, and fast is good. Fast will mean we can do this before Jackie rings the bell for dinner. There would be nothing worse than getting interrupted. Walker's hands tease my nipples, gently tugging each one and squeezing my breasts with a perfect tempo.

Oh. My. Goodness.

Wade slides his hand down the front of my panties, a wide middle finger slipping over my clit and down into where I'm aching and wet. "Shit," he grunts. "You're so damn slippery."

"I know," I whisper. "You're making me that way."

And they are. Every touch has me sizzling until I almost don't know what to do with myself.

I can feel the press of Walker's cock against my ass. It's big and hard, exactly as I would have expected for a man of his size. I'm standing here practically naked, and Wade and Walker are still fully dressed. It's time to rectify that.

It takes me seconds to pull on Wade's t-shirt enough for him to get the hint. "You want this off?" he asks me, his soft brown eyes like liquid chocolate.

"Oh yeah," I say. "Show me what you got under there."

"Yes, ma'am!" Wade strips his shirt off in the best way, tugging it over his head with one arm and damn, I actually swoon. Smooth tan skin and a physique honed by hours of manual work, Wade is cover-model fit. Tight pecs, abs that I could file my nails on, and arms that I know could carry me with no problem, make Wade one hot prospect. There's a rustle behind me, so I turn, finding Walker doing the same thing. Two unbelievable chests for me to run my hands over. Four arms to hold me. I don't know where to focus first, so I touch them both, fingers trailing over hot skin until I see them shiver. When my fingers meet their waistbands, they get the hint.

What is it about a man unbuckling a belt that is so damn sexy? The clink of a buckle and the rush of leather speed my heart. "Get them off," I say.

I don't think I've ever seen a man move so fast. "You're very bossy," Walker says.

"But you like it, don't you Walker?"

He grins wickedly. "I like it, but you need to know that we're running this show."

I put my hands on my hips. "Oh, you are, are you?"

My sass is like a red rag to a bull. In a flash, Walker has me in his arms and tossed on the bed. I would love to say that I land gracefully, but I'm sure I look like a sack of potatoes bouncing on the mattress. Whatever I look like, it's good enough for Walker and Wade, though. They stalk the bed like hungry predators, and I find myself shuffling backward until my head is on the pillow.

"I want that pussy," Wade says. He puts the finger that he slid between my legs to his lips and sucks. "You taste so sweet."

I swear that I almost combust. I don't know if I'm alone in sometimes feeling a little paranoid about oral sex. Having someone's face so up close and personal can be a bit daunting, but Wade has certainly brushed away any of my worries. He kneels on the bed, hooking his fingers in my panties and yanking them down, tossing them aside where they land over a lamp on the nightstand. I burst out laughing at the ridiculous sight, but Wade is more concerned with my now spread open pussy.

As Walker rounds the bed and climbs beside me, stroking and suckling my breasts, his brother takes time to part my folds, scanning gentle over my clit and down to my opening, spreading my wetness to lubricate his way. It's pure torture the way he doesn't quite touch anything for long enough to bring me relief. All the while he's starting between my legs. "You're so pink and pretty," he says, bringing his finger to his mouth again. "Can I lick your pussy, baby?"

I nod because who's going to say no to a man who looks like Chris Pratt's younger brother and can talk dirty too. I'm practically dripping before his tongue is anywhere near me. He nuzzles his nose against my skin, breathing in my scent. I shiver with the first lick against my clit and how amazing it feels when Walker sucks on my nipple using just the same rhythm. I stroke Walker's hair and grab at his muscular back as I try to find any way to hold on for dear life. Wade spreads my legs wider, his mouth sucking on my clit so ravenously that I have to arch my back.

The orgasm that is building is something fearsome, as though all my fantasies are there bubbling beneath the surface, pushing my pleasure even higher.

I know it's only day one at the Jackson's ranch and that some might consider my actions premature, but I don't care. These men are sexy as hell, fun, and respectful. What more could a girl want? And anyway, I'm not here to interview to be a nun. I need to know if we're compatible both in and out of the bedroom and I don't have much time to find out when there are ten of them.

My hips are thrusting in Wade's face, and his hand flies across my belly to hold me down. I'm squirming in Walker's arms, moaning as quietly as I can with so much sensation nudging me closer and closer to the stratosphere. I want to come so badly. I want to let out all the sexual tension that I've been brewing ever since Laura met the McGregor's and I realized exactly what turned me on. And now I'm really experiencing my first taste of group sex, and it's everything that I ever hoped it would be.

"I'm going to…"

I don't get a chance to finish because Walker silences me with a kiss as I come harder than I ever have before. Wade's tongue stops moving but presses down hard at the top of my clit, prolonging the orgasm that feels as though it is ripping me in two. My hands grasp the covers into balled fists as my legs go totally rigid. If Walker's mouth hadn't been over mine, I think I would have brought the house down.

Wade strokes my leg, and Walker strokes my hip, and I slowly return from seventh heaven to my room in the Jackson's home. I gaze around dreamily, brain fogged from pleasure in a state of confusion. Two gorgeous men smile back at me, chests heaving as though they've been running rather than focusing on pleasuring me into oblivion.

Two men.

I never thought this would happen to me in reality. Sometimes fantasies are just that; remote ideas with no chance of ever coming true.

Walker and Wade made my dream come true, and they look pretty damned pleased about it.

I don't know what to say to them. I want to tell them that they are amazing. I want to gush with gratitude for their mouths and their hands and their wicked, naughty streaks that had them deflowering me in their momma's house after only a few hours of knowing me.

I want to thank them for bringing back a small piece of me that's felt lost for a while. The wicked, naughty part that was happy to jump at whatever opportunity came my way.

I don't say any of that, though.

Instead, I kiss them both, one after the other, marveling at the different feeling of their almost identical lips, and then just as I'm about to get my hands on more of their sexy bodies, the bell rings downstairs and the spell is broken.

10

Walker and Wade look at me apologetically.

"When momma calls for dinner we all gotta run," Walker says.

"They won't start until we're all there to say grace," Wade adds. "We had better get you dressed."

"Better get yourself dressed too," I laugh. "I don't think boxers are appropriate attire for an evening meal, especially with new female company."

We all chuckle and start to grab our clothes. There's nothing awkward about the atmosphere, and I'm glad about that. I felt comfortable with these men from the beginning, and that's only increased as a result of what we've all just done. "So, shall we postpone until after dinner?" I say. "I'm a big fan of dessert."

"Fuck yeah," Walker says. "Although I wouldn't mind getting me some of your dessert too." He looks pointedly at my pussy and my clit tingles.

I tug my jeans back on while they thread their belts. I

don't know if it's a twin/triplet thing, but they seem to do so much in synchronization that it's mesmerizing. Then I remember that William is missing and it strikes me as strange that they didn't bring him along.

"How come you came without William," I ask them.

Walker and Wade glance at each other. "Well, we had the conversation with you when William wasn't around. We didn't just want to assume."

Walker puts his hands in his pockets. "And William can sometimes be a little less forward about this kind of thing."

"You mean he's slower to jump into bed with random visiting girls?"

Walker shakes his head. "I mean that he's less keen with sharing."

My eyebrows rise with surprise. For some reason, I was expecting the triplets to all share a similar attitude to sex and relationships and to be equally close with each other. I get the feeling that there might be a tighter bond between these two brothers than there is with William.

"Would you be up for him coming along later?" Wade asks. He's tentative with the question, I guess because he's worried about offending me or overstepping somehow. To be honest, I'm not really sure about that. We have a dynamic here between the three of us, and I really want to see how that plays out before adding a fourth and more.

Baby steps.

"Can we keep it to just us?" I say.

Walker nods and Wade moves to put his arm around my shoulder and tug me against his warm solid chest.

"Sure, Danna. Whatever you want."

There's an abrupt rapping on my door. "Dinner's ready Danna," a deep voice says. I think it's York. "Coming!" I call and Walker and Wade snigger.

"Yeah, you did," Wade says looking very pleased with himself and I swat him on the shoulder for being so smug. I'm finally dressed, and I smooth my curls a little to remove the 'bed-head.'

"I'll better look out the door to make sure no one's coming," I say.

"They'll probably all be downstairs by now," Wade says. "We're always famished by dinner time."

"Okay." I take a deep breath and open the door, sticking my head out to look left and right. The coast is clear, so I wave to Walker and Wade, opening the door widely and stepping into the hall. I'm grinning, and I know my cheeks are rosy from my recent mind-bending orgasm. Walker and Wade are just passing through the door one after the other when someone emerges from another room.

He's tall and blond with serious blue eyes and a swagger about him that tells me he's cockier than his W brothers. We all freeze, caught in the act. I mean, he wouldn't know for sure what we've just gotten up to, but I can see from the way his eyes find his brothers and a slow smile spreads across his wide mouth that whoever this is, he is making some dangerous assumptions.

"Samuel," Wade says. "Have you met Danna yet."

"No, but it looks like you have," Samuel laughs. "I hope my brothers have been treating you well, Danna."

I'm definitely blushing, and Samuel's expression just gets even more amused. "They came to get me for dinner," I say.

"Is that what they're calling it these days?"

I roll my eyes because I'm not admitting anything to anyone right now. If Samuel meets my expectations, then I might just give him a try, but right now, I'm going to leave him guessing.

"Come on," Walker says. "Mom will be getting antsy."

The boys start moving towards the stairs, and I follow, marveling at how well trained Jackie has her sons. I mean, I can't imagine what it would have been like to raise ten boys, and ten adopted sons would likely have been more challenging. I've worked out from what York said that he would have arrived in a grieving state. I wonder how many of the boys came here as babies and know no different and how many came as children who remember their past.

The delicious smell of dinner gets stronger as we near the kitchen, and my stomach growls in response. When we enter the door, I'm overwhelmed by the sight of everyone in this family in one room. There are seven men at the table and three looking back at me. "Where would you like to sit, Danna?" Wade asks.

I shrug. "Anywhere is fine," I say.

"How about here then," Wade says. It's next to one of the brother's I haven't met yet which feels awkward, but I guess it'll throw me in at the deep end.

"Sure," I say and step over the bench as gracefully as I can.

"Hi," the man to my left says. "I'm Tommy."

Wade steps in and slaps his brother on the shoulder. "Trent. You don't need to be confusing the poor girl right now. Isn't it enough that there are ten of us to remember without you pulling the switching-with-my-identical-twin routine.

"I'm Tommy," a man on the other side of the table says. "The five-year-old next to you is Trent."

I smile, and Trent bursts out laughing. "Sorry," he says. "I can never resist it."

"And how does Tommy feel when you pull that one on his girlfriends?" I ask, raising an eyebrow.

Trent's smile falls. "Sore topic," he says. Tommy's face isn't smiling anymore, either.

"You hit a raw nerve there," Wade says laughing. He finds everything so amusing, even when his brothers are obviously squirming.

"Sorry," I say, not really feeling sorry at all. Practical jokes are pretty low forms of humor, in my opinion.

"Danna, there you are," Jackie says, breezing in from yet another door, holding a huge steaming pot. "Boys, I hope you've all been looking after our house guest."

"Some more than others," Samuel says with a wry smile as he takes a seat next to Trent.

A few of his brothers give him quizzical looks, but he doesn't give any more away, and I'm grateful for that. I'm not sure how speculating about what Wade and Walker were doing in my bedroom would go down over dinner. I should think that Jackie might be happy I'm making progress, but I don't want to put the others off before I've had a chance to show them exactly who I am.

"Well, whoever's been treating our guest well gets good behavior points from momma." Jackie places the pot on the table on a large slate slab. She then grabs a large basket of bread rolls from the counter and then a huge pot of rice from the stove. It's a feast fit for twenty, but if the boys previous eating exploits were anything to go by, I'm sure they will make light work of this.

"We're not eight anymore, mom." The man I think is Zack stands and begins serving onto a plate. I'm thinking that he's going to sit down and tuck in himself, but he passes the plate across the table to Trent. "For Danna," he says softly.

I nod my thanks and Zack continues to serve up food for everyone, fixing his own plate last. Jackie's still placing more on the table; jugs of water and juice and smaller steaming bowls of vegetables that everyone serves onto their plates themselves. There's a rumble of activity, but everyone is quiet as Jackie takes a seat.

"For what we are about to eat, may the Lord make us truly thankful," she says. "Now tuck in boys."

It seems the Jackson brothers don't need to be told twice. I don't know what I was expecting, but the speed with which they consume their food is something to behold. For the first five minutes at the table, the only person to talk is Jackie. "So, Danna, is it good?" Her eyes are bright and hopeful, and I don't need to lie. This stew is the best I've ever eaten; meaty and rich, filled with vegetables to balance the flavor.

"It's so good," I say, using my bread to dip up the gravy.

"I like a girl who likes her food," she says, smiling.

"So do I," says Walker, giving me a wink.

I don't miss the look between brothers at that comment and the glances at me. I smile to myself. "My mom used to make something similar," I say.

"Home cooking is a dying art," Jackie says. "I wish I had someone to pass my recipes on to."

"Should have adopted at least one girl then, shouldn't you," Samuel says. There a little sharpness to his tone, and I turn to Jackie to see her response.

"Why would I want a girl when I have all of you trouble makers?" she says with so much affection in her voice and I wonder at the ability of moms to let comments pass without causing confrontation. It's going to take time for me to unpick the complexities of this family, for sure.

"What about when we all get married, mom? You're gonna have plenty of girls to pass on your wisdom to." It's one of the X twins who's talking.

Jackie just smiles politely. "I've heard that daughters-in-law are not usually up for receiving cooking advice from their mother-in-law, Xane, but it's a cute thought."

"Who has time for dating?" Xsander says. "Look at us all. Ten strapping men all at home with their momma." He laughs, but it doesn't sound genuine. "All work and no play makes the Jacksons a bunch of losers."

"Speak for yourself," Walker says with a twinkle in his eye. Wade shoots him a warning look which doesn't go unnoticed.

"There's nothing wrong with spending time with your momma, and you're all free to go out whenever you want, you know that," Jackie says.

"I'm sick of that bar in town," Samuel says. "Same

bunch of men eyeing up the same limited group of women. The pickings around here aren't exactly plentiful."

Jackie smiles at me, pointedly. "Well, you just never know who might fall into your lap, Sammie."

"It's usually Nadine Stonefield," he says. "And I feel like I need a sponge bath after that."

The table rumbles with laughter. "Nadine Stonefield is old enough to be your momma," Jackie says. "What's that woman doing hanging around in bars with men half her age? It's embarrassing!"

"She's looking for pickings herself, I'd guess," Tommy says.

"Just don't stand too close when she's reaching out to grab," Trent laughs.

"Oh my goodness," Jackie gasps, putting her hand to her mouth. "The thought of that woman putting her hands of my sons makes me sick."

"Maybe you need to come out with us as a chaperone," York says dryly.

"Maybe I do." The boys all groan at the idea.

"At some point, mom, you're going to need to accept that we're grown," Zack says gently. "I'm sure Samuel can handle Nadine just fine."

Jackie looks put out, and it's then that I realize that she was serious about chaperoning them. Now, I'm all for close mother-child bonds, but that seems a little excessive to me. Although, thinking about it, I'm here at Jackie's behest. It didn't seem like a big deal until now. There are clearly some of them who are less than happy with her overprotective and potentially interfering ways. It's funny how easy it is to overstep the line between a caring mom and momzilla.

"Never underestimate women, Zack. You know what happened to your Uncle Jack."

There's a murmur around the table. "Uncle Jack's wife took his kids and his business in the divorce. He never recovered," William explains.

"I knew that woman was a bad apple from the moment I laid eyes on her. I told him too, but Jack wouldn't listen. Men never do," Jackie says. She tears off some of her bread and stabs it into the gravy on her plate.

"We know, mom," Xane says. "We're not going to make the same mistakes."

"Damn right you're not," Jackie says. "Not if I have anything to with it." She smiles at me. "Sorry, Danna. I didn't mean to bring up the family's dirty laundry. I just need these boys to understand why I'm so protective."

"We know, mom," Samuel says with a roll of his eyes. "It's like a once-a-week mantra around here. Don't do what Jack did."

"Well, I'm sorry that I care so much about you," Jackie says. This time Samuel's comment seems to have hit a raw enough nerve for her to lose her cool.

"You know he doesn't mean anything by it," Zack says. His dark eyes flick from his mom to me, catching with mine and holding my gaze. They're darker than a pond in the moonlight, and for a second I feel like I'm slipping forward, mesmerized.

When he looks away, my chest feels hollow, and I don't

understand why. I've read about this kind of thing in romance novels but never experienced anything like it myself. Looking into Zack's eyes made me feel raw and open. Lonely too. I can't explain it, but I'm unsettled enough to have lost my appetite.

I stare down at my plate, wondering what the hell I'm doing sitting here with these strangers. I suddenly realize that I don't know how many days have passed since Mom died and feel terribly guilty. When did I stop counting and why? I've let life get on top of me when I should have been focused on home.

I feel a hand on my knee and turn to find Wade's worried face looking back. "You okay?" he whispers as the conversation continues around us. I nod, but I think he can tell that I'm not. He reaches across the table and pours me some water. I take the glass and take a few sips and a deep and steadying breath.

"Maybe Danna can come with us to Joe's," Xsander says.

"Yeah. That'd be one way to keep Nadine away," Samuel says. He winks at me, and I swallow against the lump in my throat. I need to get it together and stay on my game.

"I'll keep you safe, boys. Don't worry about anything," I say with a broad grin that feels as fake as the Cheshire Cat's.

"See, Mom," Samuel says. "Nothing to worry about."

Jackie looks to me and smiles. "You look after my boy's Danna, and you'll be welcome here always," she says.

I nod. "Of course, and thank you."

There's another murmur around the table. That's the problem with living with so many men; even a tiny exchange of comments sounds like a storm is brewing. Deep voices just sound so loud, even in a whisper.

"Shouldn't you be encouraging us to look after Danna," York says. "You know what those ranch-hands in town are like. They'll be all over her like flies on horse shit."

"Potty mouth," Jackie says disapprovingly.

"York's right," William says. "I don't think it's a good idea to take Danna anywhere near Joe's."

"You know I'm a big city girl?" I say, raising my eyebrows. "I've been to seedier bars than Joe's and survived to tell the tale."

The boys all make an ooo sound. "Well, that settles it," Samuel says. "Danna can keep an eye on us, and we can keep twenty eyes on her. Sounds like a good deal to me."

"But not tonight," I say. "I'm feeling like a need an early night."

"All the riding get to you?" York asks in a voice laced with amusement.

Samuel snorts and chokes a little on the water he's drinking. I give him a withering look. "Yes, York. The horse riding was a little more physically challenging than I thought it would be."

"Wait till we get you on a bucking bronco," Tommy says. "That'll leave you saddle sore."

"I think I might leave the bronco bucking to you strapping boys," I say.

"Yeah. You can be our buckle bunny," Trent laughs.

I don't know what that is, but it doesn't sound all that complimentary. "Don't be disrespectful," Jackie scoffs.

"Don't you think Danna would look great in some cowboy boots?"

"I'm sure she'd look lovely," Jackie says, "But that isn't what you were meaning, son, and you know it."

Trent grins as though he likes being told off for being cheeky. His dimples hint at the naughty little boy he probably was a couple of decades ago. "I'm going to do my best to get the full ranch experience," I say.

Wade nudges me under the table, and I grin. I guess he's thinking about the ranch experience that he's going to give me if we ever finish this meal. As if everyone around the table has been eating at the exact same speed, all of a sudden there is a loud clanking of cutlery on plates, and I look around to see that most of the boys have finished eating. My plate is still overflowing, and I'm really conscious that I don't want to upset Jackie. I scoop up a few mouthfuls of stew, leaving half my bread and most of my rice.

"I don't think Danna worked hard enough today," Tommy says. "Look at her plate."

All eyes are suddenly on me. Jackie tuts. "You don't draw attention to guests like that, Tommy. Haven't I taught you any manners?"

Trent laughs. "I think Tommy's hoping for Danna's leftovers."

"Tommy doesn't need to be looking for scraps from other people's plates. There's half a pot of stew there if anyone's still hungry."

I've never seen men move faster. Poor Zack can't keep up with the plates being shoved at him. I eat some more, glad that there's a distraction and when I'm done, I put my cutlery neatly and sit back to watch feeding time at the zoo. Maybe I'm being a little unkind. The Jackson brothers really do have excellent manners; they just really enjoy their momma's cooking.

I gaze around at them all and start to worry that I might actually be successful in winning over these men to harem life. How on earth would I live up to Jackie's standards and feed these hungry beasts? I know that Laura was overwhelmed by the idea of fulfilling ten men's sexual needs, but to be honest, it's their other appetites that are frightening me.

And what about kids? Laura already has two, and she's only just gotten started. Every child is another mouth to feed. At least Laura has the money to get the help she needs. The Jackson's certainly aren't poor, but they aren't rolling in servants like the McGregor's.

The next twenty minutes or so passes quickly with the boys asking me questions about college and what I'm hoping to do in the future. The only one who stays quiet is Zack, and he's the first to ask to be excused. He disappears up the stairs with Ruffles slowly trailing him. Jackie's eyes follow her son, her expression concerned.

The rest aren't far behind, heading off to watch TV in the den. I'm tempted to follow, but Walker and Wade have stayed in the kitchen. They're not forgetting about what was so rudely interrupted. But it's not only Walker and Wade who are waiting at the table. Samuel's there, and he has a look of glee in his eyes.

11

"I'll help you clean up," I say to Jackie as she starts to wash up the pans. All the boys were well trained enough to place their own dishes into the washer.

She waves me away. "You're our guest, Danna. You go and mingle." She gives me a wink, and I grin back.

"I'm actually tired," I tell her. "I think I'll get an early night. What time shall I come down for breakfast?"

"Well, that depends on whether you want to be up with the boys."

"Course," I say.

"Five am then." Her eyes sparkle.

"Sure," I say as though waking up the time I usually go to sleep after a Saturday night out is completely normal. This ranch life certainly has its drawbacks.

"I hope your room is comfortable, but you let me know if I can get you anything."

I say goodnight and start up the stairs, smiling as Walker, Wade and Samuel all kiss their mom's cheek and wish her goodnight too. If she suspects anything, she's keeping it under her hat.

I'm slow, and they quickly catch up by the time I'm outside the door to my room.

"So you're off to bed, are you?" Walker asks.

"She needs an early night," Wade says with a wink.

"I need an early night, too," Samuel says.

I smile, but I'm a little wary. Samuel is definitely a more difficult nut to crack than Walker or Wade. I like his cheekiness, but I'm not as comfortable in his presence yet. "Well, I was going to invite Walker and Wade in for a nightcap," I say. "Is that something you'd be interested in?"

Samuel nods, with wickedness in his eyes.

"Well, alrighty then," I say. "And then there were four."

I push the door open, but I don't turn on the overhead light. I'm looking for a softer effect, so I flick the switch for the lamp on the nightstand instead.

The door clicks shut, and I turn, finding three huge men in my small floral bedroom. I've seen what's under Walker and Wade's clothes, but Samuel is going to be something new. The atmosphere seems charged with the electricity that only comes when there is the expectation of sex in the air.

Wade is the first to approach me, and I'm glad. He's the one I feel the most comfortable with at this moment.

Walker isn't far behind. As Wade slides his hand into my hair, cupping the back of my neck, Walker takes his place behind me. The first press of Wade's lips to mine is all the more arousing because I know that Samuel is watching. I wish I could see the expression on his face. Is he turned on by this? I can only assume so.

Walker tugs the straps of my top down, the urgency in his action, revealing exactly how much he needs this. I can't blame him for that. They gave me my pleasure and had to sit through an entire family meal, thinking about what they could have been doing with me if the bell hadn't rung at that very moment.

Hands caress my breasts, my hips, and my back. My bra is removed, and the cold air stiffens my nipples even before their fingers find them. I feel crazy with the overwhelming sensation and the intensity of two men touching me, and one man observing.

"Take her jeans off," Samuel orders from somewhere in the room. He sounds distant, as though he's leaning against the far wall, but I don't open my eyes to check. Is this what he's going to do? Direct the action from a distance? Is he planning on joining in?

Wade's fingers find my belt and buttons and Walker's drag my jeans down until they're a pool at my feet.

"That's it," Samuel says. "Now get on the bed, Danna. On your back." His voice is husky, and I like that I can hear how turned on he's getting. I imagine him unbuttoning his own jeans and palming his big, hot cock, slowly stroking it until it's leaking arousal.

Walker steps aside, and Wade walks me back until my knees hit the soft mattress. My comforter is rumpled from earlier, and the boys waste no time in messing them up even more. This time it's Walker who drags the panties roughly down my legs and spreads my knees until I'm wide open for everyone in the room to see.

"Lick her," Samuel says. It's loud enough for anyone who's walking down the hallway to hear, but that doesn't seem to bother him.

Walker follows his brother's directions perfectly, swiping his tongue from my opening to my clit in one long lick. I shudder as Wade pinches my nipples, wanting to cry out but feeling a little shy.

I've never been the kind of girl to come easily. My previous boyfriends needed a lot of guidance to find the route to my pleasure, but not the Jacksons. It's as though they've read the book of me and know all the secret little things I like. The way they use their rough palms to caress my skin, their strong hands to grab me in a way that makes me feel as though they're in control. It's all perfect, and Walker's face between my legs is no different. My heart starts to speed to match his technique; fast, light licks have my hips bucking and straining for more contact. I know I'm going to come, but I need something more.

"Look at me, Danna," Samuel says.

And when I do, holy fuck.

He's sitting on a chair in the corner, his hand wrapped around his huge cock. His eyes burn into mine. "You gonna come, baby," he says. It's softer than I expected, and I grunt as the orgasm surges between my legs. It wraps around me like a snake and squeezes, my body rising and undulating with it. It's beautiful and terrifying; pure pleasure and total corruption.

I'm ruined.

Ruined for any man who comes after this. No one person could push my buttons the way these three have managed.

I have to make this work.

I have to find a way to make the Jackson brother's my harem.

Whatever it takes.

12

Walker and Wade stroke my body as I come around. My mind is sex fogged, my breathing so ragged, that it takes a while for me to process where I am and what I'm doing.

I gaze around, finding Wade smiling and Walker too. Samuel isn't smiling, though. His face is pained, his cock a straining angry looking thing that seems to be begging for attention. I wonder what his plans are. Is he going to make himself come or is he going to slide that big dick into my pussy, knowing that his brother just made it wet enough to take him?

I think I'd like him to do either. I've never seen a man masturbate before and it's one of the hottest, naughtiest things I've ever witnessed. His hand is slow. He's in no hurry, that's for sure.

Walker and Wade start to undress, and my eyes are drawn to Walker's gorgeous abs and thick, muscular thighs. My pussy clenches as he drops his briefs, and I get to see his magnificent cock for the first time. It's long and thick, maybe not quite as big as Samuel but way bigger than I've ever had before. I turn, and Wade is an almost identical copy to his brother. There are some differences. I think Walker must work out a little more because his shoulders are broader and his biceps thicker but they are both sexier than my eyes can take. I blink as they take hold of their cocks with their left hands and eye me like I'm a buffet filled with possibilities.

I suppose I am.

There's a moment where Walker and Wade turn to Samuel as though they're awaiting instructions.

"You know how to fuck," he says with that dark grin of his. "Show Danna how the Jackson brothers hit it."

Wade tosses his brother a condom which he fished from his pocket, and they wrap up two beautiful presents for me. Walker spreads my legs, raising himself over me and sliding his cock between my pussy lips. I'm so slippery wet that as soon as he notches into my entrance, he pushes deep in one thrust.

Fuck.

I arch my back to press my clit against him, and it feels so damn good. His eyes find mine, and he leans down to kiss me with soft lips and a tongue that slides against mine perfectly. I moan, because how could I not? This is everything I need right now.

Hot sex.

To feel desirable.

My fantasies fulfilled.

An escape from my everyday life.

A chance to just be me again.

Walker starts to move, his hips grinding against me. I slide my hands down the smooth skin of his back, marveling at the strength of him as he thrusts. His ass is working, pumping for my pleasure and his. I can't resist digging my fingers in and tugging him towards me harder.

He gets the hint, reaching one hand beneath my ass so he can get deeper. Oh my god. I gaze up at him, taking in his furrowed brow and his eyes closed in concentration. I turn to find Wade stroking himself. He climbs onto the bed next to me, kissing me with almost equal intensity as his brother, squeezing my breasts. When his mouth closes over my nipple, suckling hard I cry out. It's too much to feel this much pleasure.

"That's it," I hear Samuel say. I turn to him again, and this time, I can't turn away. His eyes capture mine, and when he smiles, I turn to liquid.

Walker rests back on his knees, hitching my legs over his shoulders, but I don't watch his cock entering me or his abs rippling as he fucks. I don't watch Walker as his hand slides over my belly, and his finger finds my clit. I don't see any of the things that are talking me so close to coming again that I'm almost scared. I don't even know if my body can do this again without breaking apart.

I can't take my eyes off Samuel as he strokes his cock in time to his brother's thrusts.

And when I finally come, stars swimming across my vision like a fractured blanket of ecstasy, I watch Samuel come too; his whole body seizing with the intensity.

I'm all wrung out. As floppy as a rag-doll, but I don't want them to stop. I just want more.

Samuel pulls a tissue from a box on the dresser and cleans his hand. He fastens his jeans, then without saying a word, he leaves the room.

So that's it. He didn't want to fuck me. He just wanted to watch. I don't know how I feel about that, but I don't get any time to think about it because Wade grabs my hands and forces them above my head and Walker leans forward until I'm almost bent in two.

"You feel so fucking good," he grunts in my ear, his voice tinged with a huskiness that tells me he's close to losing control.

Wade's fingers grip me tight, and I love feeling this overwhelmed. The powerlessness wipes all thoughts from my head, leaving me to slip deep into the moment. I know when Walker is about to fall into the oblivion he's been working towards when his body jerks. The release is amazing; his cock swelling inside me with pulses that make me want to fuck all over again.

It's usually at this point I begin to feel disappointed. I've never found a man who can fuck me as much as I need. But as Walker pulls out, his cheeks flushed with exertion, Wade is there to take his place.

"You still good?" he asks, and I nod, loving that he's making no assumptions here. "Hands and knees," he says with a pat to my thigh. I'm boneless, but I find just enough energy to do as he's ordered.

"Fuck," he says as I raise my ass in the air. I'm expecting him to enter me straight away. He's not going to have to work me up. My pussy is already so slippery that I can feel it on the inside of my legs and it just accommodated a cock which is pretty much identical to his. It seems that Wade has other ideas, though. He nudges my legs so that I have to spread them wider, then I feel the heat of his breath against my pussy. He licks a long, hot stripe over my clit and up to my entrance and I almost drop to the bed. Fuck that feels so good I don't even know what to do. He does it again, and I grunt, my elbows giving way so that I'm now resting on my forearms, my ass in the air. "I think she likes that," Walker says, reaching under my body to pinch my nipple. Wade licks again, and I gasp. "She definitely likes that." There's a smile in his voice that makes my heart skip.

"She's gonna like this too," Wade says. His cock presses against my entrance, and he's right. I am going to love it. If he doesn't give it to me right now, I'd beg for it.

When he thrusts, I grunt. He's thick and long and presses deep against a place that makes my knees tremble. His fingers press into my hips and ass, using the grip to bring our bodies together with perfect force. "That's it," he says. "That's it."

I like how his voice has a little tremor in it. I want him to feel as undone as I feel. Raw. Open. On edge. This is more than I could have hoped for. More than I could have imagined.

I hope Walker and Wade feel that way too.

I know for now this is about sex, but there is a connection between us even after this short space of time. A comfortableness that I don't find with people easily.

These men are good souls. Kind to their momma. Loyal to their family. Precisely the kind of men I need in my life. I just hope they feel that connection with me too.

I know I can't come again. I'm too past the sensitive stage, but the penetration feels good, and Wade has already given me more pleasure than I've had in years. It's time for him to take his.

"Fuck, Danna," he says. "I'm gonna…"

He doesn't even make it to the word come before he is. There's a fierceness in the way he grabs my flesh, holding us together so tightly I almost can't breathe. The weight of him, wrapped around me is perfect. The way Walker strokes my arm and tells me I'm beautiful, and the best thing to come into their lives in a long time is even better.

All I want to do is curl up onto my side between these two men and enjoy their strength and their warmth. I want the after-sex kiss and cuddle that makes all the passion and pleasure feel rounded off with comfort.

It's what I want but not what I get.

Instead, when Wade pulls out from inside me, there's a knock at the door.

13

We all freeze because we couldn't be in a more compromising position if we tried.

There's a pause, and we look at each other. "Should I ask who it is?" I whisper.

Wade nods.

"Hello," I call.

"It's William. Are my brothers in there?"

My cheeks flame because I wasn't expecting this to be common knowledge so soon. Has Samuel gone and immediately shared the news of our activity with all of his brothers? The thought fills me with shame.

"Hang on a minute," I say, scrambling from the bed and tugging on my clothes like a crazy person. Walker and Wade are doing the same.

"What shall I tell him?" I whisper.

"We can hide in your bathroom until you get rid of

him," Wade says. "If you want to keep this between us?"

I don't know what I want. I mean, I'm here for a purpose but is this too fast? Is this the right way for William to become involved? Will he feel left out? There are so many questions that my head is spinning.

"What do you want to do?" I ask. "He's your triplet. Are you comfortable hiding this from him?"

They both look grave. I guess I have my answer. "Get dressed before I open the door."

They nod, pulling on jeans and tees and fixing their hair. The room must stink of sex, but I'm not intending to let William in.

Opening the door is nerve-wracking. I have no idea what is going to be greeting me on the other side. Maybe it's not just William out there. Perhaps there are other Jackson brothers too.

When I finally pluck up the courage to turn the handle, I find William on the other side. His expression is grave, and he rubs his hand over his face in a gesture that screams stress.

"Abbey's taken a turn for the worse," he tells me. I have no idea who Abbey is.

"What happened?" Wade asks.

"I just had a bad feeling, and I went down there to check on her."

"Have you told York?"

"Yeah. He's getting his bag, and he's gonna meet us downstairs."

"We'll come now," Walker says. "I need to get some socks."

It's at that moment that William looks at us all, realizing that his brothers were actually in my bedroom, probably the last place he looked in the house. I'm sure, despite all the focus on fixing our clothes that we're not exactly looking pristine. In fact, Walker's hair is ruffled where I ran my fingers through it, and Wade actually has his t-shirt inside out.

Oh fuck. The hair we might have gotten away with but the shirt? Hell no.

"Sure," William says eventually. His eyes flick from his brothers to me, and I see a flash of hurt there. He knows, and he feels left out. I would never want to come between these brothers, but I have no idea how to fix this now.

Walker and Wade start towards the door, and I stand aside, feeling like the worst person in the world. I can't let them all walk away like this.

"Can I come?" I ask.

"I don't think that's a good idea," William says.

"Danna's here to experience ranch life. This is a part of it," Wade says carefully.

"You wanna come out and see a horse suffer, that's your business," William snaps.

I shake my head. "I don't want to see the horse suffer, or you suffer. I want to come for moral support if that's okay with you?"

William blinks as though he's trying to work out whether he can trust me or not. I understand that. We've only known each other a few hours, and he's definitely the most reserved of the triplets. I think he's potentially wavering because of what he's walked into.

"Okay," he says. "But you need to have some balls because we won't be able to deal with any emotional women's moments, okay?"

It's my turn to blink. What the fuck is an 'emotional woman moment'? And this is coming from the man who's been flapping all day about a horse. William definitely hasn't come across as tough guy.

"I'll bring my balls," I say, turning back into the room as if I'm going to look for them. Walker starts to chuckle. I obviously don't have any balls to bring so I grab my jacket instead. I'll need to find boots from downstairs too, but I'm assuming the boys will as well.

We wait for Wade to reappear with his socks and trudge downstairs.

I'm flustered as I try to pull my boots on. The boys are faster, and I don't want to be a burden. The air has a bite to it, the night so black that there are no shapes in the distance. In the city, there is always a yellow glow to the evening sky. Here the inkiness is overwhelming, and I'm grateful for the light from the house to illuminate the path to the car.

York is already standing at the truck, his bag in hand. He smiles as he sees me coming. "They dragging you out again too?"

"She begged to come," William says.

"I think begged might be a little exaggeration. I hold up my fingers to show an inch of space and York bursts out laughing.

"Let's just get in the car shall we," William barks.

York tugs open the rear door, and he allows me to slide in first. I'm in the middle this time, with Walker on one side and York pressed a little closer to me than he was when we first rode together.

Maybe it's the darkness that has filled me with anticipation, or perhaps it's the sex-buzz that's still surging around my body. I look around the car and want to giggle because less than ten minutes ago I was fucking two of these men.

I'm stills annoyed at missing my cuddle, but I'm hoping that I might still get one when we get back. I know all these boys need to get up early, but maybe Walker and Wade will be up for stretching their usual bedtime!

It's silent in the car, and I'm not about to interrupt the tense atmosphere with stupid questions or jokes. We follow the same rough track to the stables, and when we get there, I'll admit that my heart starts to beat faster. For all my bravado, I don't know if I'm going to be able to cope with seeing a horse so sick that it needs to be put down. This is part of everyday life for these men, but it's totally out of my comfort zone.

The smell of manure and hay is overwhelming, even in the coolness of the night. As we enter the stables, the horses whiny and shift positions, their shoes tapping on the hard ground. A man is standing at the entrance to the last stall.

"It's not good," he says, shaking his head. His cheeks are ruddy in the way that tells me he probably spends more time and money at Joe's bar than is good for him.

William's pace speeds and as he rounds the entrance to the stall. I see the moment his face falls and know immediately that it's not good news. He takes a step back. "Shit."

Walker and Wade slow as though they don't want to reach their brother and see what he's seeing. I hang back because this is harder than I was anticipating.

William turns to York.

"Be gentle with her," he says.

York pats him on the shoulder. "You know I will," he says. William nods and turns, striding past us all and out of the stables. His brothers watch him go but don't follow. I guess they know that he needs the space.

I don't go any closer as York disappears into the stall. I hear him unclipping his bag, and he makes soothing noises as he does what needs to be done. Walker and Wade stand either side of me, waiting.

My lungs feel tight from the tension, and I inhale deeply. My heart feels as though it left the stables with William. As the man with the ruddy cheeks kneels to assist York, I turn to Wade.

"I'm going to wait outside."

His eyes search my face. "You finding this hard?"

"I'm gonna check on William."

Wade's eyebrows rise just a fraction, but he nods, and I turn to walk outside. It takes a moment for my eyes to adjust, and then I see William's shape in the distance by the edge of the paddock. He's holding onto the fence staring into the blackness.

I take my time to reach him, making sure my feet

crunch enough for him to hear that someone is coming. He doesn't turn. I wonder if he thinks I'm one of his brothers. I stand next to him and rest my arms on the fence too.

"It must be so hard to raise an animal and see it die," I say.

William is silent and unmoving. I feel like I'm overstepping now. Maybe this was a big mistake.

"I'm not good with death," I tell him. "It makes me panic, but I forced myself to come tonight."

"Why?" he asks.

"Because I keep telling myself that it's just a part of life. An important part. If we didn't know we were going to die, we wouldn't have the urgency to enjoy life."

William nods, but he doesn't say anything, and I hate to leave silence to stretch too long.

"Do you always feel this way about the horsed dying, or was this one special to you?"

"She was special, but I always feel this way. My pop used to tell me that I needed to toughen up. I guess he was right."

I shake my head. "Empathy is something that makes us human, William. I'm sure your pop was a good man, but I disagree. Maybe, if we all hardened our hearts, we'd be hurt less, but we'd also feel less and feeling is a great part of life."

William glances at me, then quickly looks away. "Maybe he knew he was going to pass and was trying to get us ready," he says.

"Maybe. Or maybe he just didn't want to see you get so hurt. It's harder for us to watch the people we love hurting that it is to hurt ourselves."

William nods again and clears his throat. "You and my brothers..." He trails off as if he doesn't know what to say.

"Yes?"

He shakes his head. "They have a tendency to jump right in without thinking."

I chuckle softly. "Maybe we're alike in that."

"I wish I could be more like that," he says.

"You can be," I tell him. "All you have to do is take small steps forward when it feels scary."

William turns to me, gazing down into my eyes. He licks his lips, staring at my mouth. I can see exactly what he's thinking about and the war in his head. 'Should I kiss her? Should I not'.

I could make it easy for him. I could stand on my tip toes, place my hand on his shoulder and draw him to me, but that wouldn't be the right thing to do. If William wants what his brothers had, he needs to take that step.

He looks away, taking a deep breath. Then it's as though something snaps in him. He placed his hand around my back, pulling me towards him with a ferocity that I wasn't expecting. His lips find mine in a hungry kiss that's bruising and deep and perfect. He moans against me as though letting go is the sweetest relief. I stand on my tiptoes, reaching behind his neck to keep him with me. This is William taking a step into impetuousness, and I don't want to lose him halfway through. His hands grip my waist, then slide down to my ass, squeezing it and yanking me towards him. His cock is rock hard and pressed against my navel, sweet torture in the coolness of night.

"Fuck," he mutters against my lips, sliding his hands into my hair and taking hold of a chunk of it at the back of my neck. He pulls down, forcing my face up to his. William's breathing is ragged, his chest rising and falling fast.

"Did you fuck my brothers?" he asks. His eyes flash in the darkness, and I nod as much as I can with his hand holding my hair, the tug of my scalp sending heat to my pussy.

"Was it good?" he asks. I nod again, and he smiles.

"Do you want to fuck me?" he asks. I nod, my cheeks flushing with embarrassment that's laced with excitement.

His hand slides between my legs, pressing my clit through my jeans. I moan, and he smiles. "You don't leave me out again, Danna," he says. I nod, but he doesn't smile. Instead, he lets me go and walks back into the stables, leaving me alone in the dark.

14

For the next thirty minutes, I sit in the truck. William seems to have found the strength to face his demons, but I have not. There are some aspects of ranch life that I'm choosing not to witness too closely.

When the boys finally emerge from the stables, their faces are grave.

Nobody says a word the whole journey back, and by the time we're at the house, I have a lump in my throat the size of a boulder.

We trudge indoors, taking off our boots. Jackie's waiting for us.

"Did she go?" she asks.

William nods and Jackie shakes her head. "I'm sorry, son," she says, patting him on the arm. "How about we all have some brandy?"

The boys nod and Jackie pulls out a huge bottle that's already drunk half way. She gathers mismatching shot glasses from a cupboard in the corner and pours the amber liquor to the top. I don't know if this is some kind of tradition or if she thinks the warmth of the alcohol will chase away the chill of the night. Either way, I knock it back gratefully.

"Can you lock up?" Jackie asks William. He nods and begins to secure all the doors methodically.

"Are you okay?" Jackie asks me.

"I didn't go in," I say. "But it was hard knowing what was happening inside."

Jackie nods. "Death should be hard," she says.

"She's in a better place," York says. "A place without pain."

Jackie pats his arm too. "She was lucky to have you."

York shrugs and leans in to kiss his momma's cheek. "I'm gonna hit the sack," he says. "I'm beat."

"Me too," I say. This day has really taken it out of me, in good ways and in bad.

Walker and Wade glance over at me as though they're wondering what I'm expecting. The cuddle time that seemed so appealing before doesn't feel appropriate now. I smile a small smile and begin to make my way towards the stairs.

In the quiet of my room, I remove my clothes, wash, and dress for bed. I turn off the light and slide under the covers ready for sleep, but then I remember that I'd promised to message Laura to let her know I'm okay and fill her in on any gossip. She actually made me pinkie-promise like we were still in kindergarten. I'm about to pick up my phone when there's a knock at the door.

My heart skitters as I make my way to see who it is, but I'm not surprised to find it's William. He doesn't say anything, but puts his hand around the edge of the door, and backs me into the room. His eyes are intense, his body a shadow as he closes the door, and we are plunged into darkness.

He says nothing as he puts his hand between my legs, sliding it up the soft inside of my thigh, watching my face as I close my eyes with anticipation. He parts my folds, finding my clit and stroking it slowly and gently. Moving closer, he draws my face against his chest, curling himself over me until his lips are pressed to the top of my head. I moan as the stroking becomes faster, widening my stance, so he has the space he needs to work. His breathing is hot in my hair, his excitement growing obvious. I reach down, finding the hard outline of his cock behind his jeans.

William uses his hand to guide mine, squeezing against his erection with much more pressure than I would have used. He groans, pushing his fingers inside my pussy as though he's testing to see if I'm ready for what he has to give.

I am.

I don't think I've ever been more ready.

I'm expecting him to back me towards the bed so he can strip off his clothes, but he doesn't. Instead, he backs me towards the wall, turning me to face it. He slides the straps of my nightdress over my shoulders, leaving me in just my white cotton panties. His fingers find them at my hips, and he pushes them down my legs slowly, pressing kisses down my spine and onto my ass. His hands squeeze as his mouth worships, caressing the outside of my thighs, my calves, my ankles. I lean into the wall for stability resting on my forearms, my hands flat against the cool plaster.

Not knowing where he's going to kiss next fills each touch with so much extra sensation that I'm shivering and desperate within minutes.

"Fuck me, William," I whisper.

He bites the inside of my thigh. "So you want me now?" he says. "Not with my brothers."

His voice is level, but I can hear the hurt in what he says. "You know they came here without you. It wasn't my choice."

"Now I get to have you all to myself." He bites again, and I have to bite my lip to stop myself from crying out.

When he finally stands, and I hear the clang of his belt and the rasp of his zipper, I'm shivering. He rests the weight of his cock along the seam of my ass, leaning in to press kisses on my neck, using his hands to squeeze my breasts and tease my nipples.

In some way, his touch reminds me of his brothers, but in others, he's completely unique. I wonder if their styles are instinctual or if they've developed them by watching each other fuck before.

There's an edge to William that I didn't expect, and I'm not sure if it's driven by his hurt at being left out or if he's just darker in his approach to sex. Whatever it is, it's making my pussy wet.

He slides a finger down my spine until it reaches the dip of my back. "Arch your back," he says, pressing down. I do as he says, pushing my ass out and widening my stance. The first press of his cock against my entrance is a shock. It's so hot and hard, the crown parting my cunt and pushing deep in one thrust. His jeans are bunched around his thighs, a contrast to my nakedness. I press my forehead to the wall in between my flattened palms, closing my eyes to concentrate on the sensation.

He's deep; so deep that I grunt. I love the way his fingers dig into my flesh, the possessive tugs he gives my hips to sharpen each movement and bring us even closer together. I love how small I feel next to him as he wraps himself over me.

The smell of him is familiar, making me recall how his brothers felt as they fucked me too.

Three men with the same features but different hearts and minds.

I had no idea how intoxicating it would be to experience being intimate with these men.

I wish I could look into his eyes and see the passion burning there. I wish I could kiss his mouth as he fucked me, but somehow, this just feels right.

"Is this how you fucked my brothers?" he asks.

I shake my head, and he takes hold of my hair at my nape, tugging my head until my back is arched as far as is possible. "How did you fuck them, Danna?"

"On the bed," I gasp.

"Did they fuck you from behind like me?" he asks.

I shake my head. "Only Wade."

"Did you suck their cocks?"

I shake my head again. "Not this time," I say.

I hear a dark rumble of laughter. "Not this time," he repeats. "I like that."

His other hand slides over my belly, finding the hard button of my clit again. This time, it only takes him three taps to make me come. "Oh," I gasp, shuddering in his arms, my pussy clamping down on his cock. My knees go weak, and William holds me up, his cock still working.

"Maybe you can suck my cock now," he says, pulling out from inside me.

My pussy feels raw and empty, my orgasm now spamming against nothing. William backs me against the wall, kissing me deeply, his tongue sliding over mine until I'm breathless and boneless. His mouth moves to my nipple, suckling hard, then his hand on my shoulder shows me exactly what he wants me to do.

I drop to my knees, the carpet rough under my bare skin. His cock is dauntingly huge and glistening from my arousal. He smells of sex and man, and I take the tip of him into my mouth, earning me a hiss. "That's it," he says softly. "That's it."

I lick him, swiping my tongue around the smooth head and down over the length of him. My hand on his thigh picks up the tremor in his legs. I look up, and he's resting both hands on the wall behind me for stability.

He doesn't move his hips; not at first anyway. He lets me drive, and I love the feeling of being in control. Oral sex has a strange power exchange element. There's a fine line between acceptable and sexy, and degrading and abusive. There is nothing about this that makes me feel wrong, though. William hisses as I take him deep, using my hand to stimulate the whole of his cock. There is no way I'm getting it all into my mouth.

"Fuck," he mutters as my hand and mouth speed. He's getting close. I can tell from the way he tastes and the shudder that runs through his body. The closer he gets, the less restraint he has. One of his hands grabs my hair, his fist driving my mouth deeper over his cock. For a second, I feel as though I can't breathe, then I taste his release, and I swallow around him, relishing the feeling of control I have at this moment.

He groans loudly, and I'm momentarily embarrassed by the fact that I'm sure it would be audible from the corridor. I say a silent prayer that Jackie and the other boys are all in bed rather than wandering the hallways. I lick him clean, and he drops to his knees, tugging me towards his chest and holding me in an awkward hug that's more about propping each other up than about comfort. "Shit," he mutters. "That was…"

"Sexy as fuck," I finish for him.

He draws back and looks into my eyes, a slow, easy smile forming on this lips. "Exactly," he says.

He kisses me again, this time tasting his own pleasure on my lips.

"Life's short," he says. It's an incongruous statement, but I know where he's coming from. What happened tonight at the stables has left me feeling raw, and I guess it's affected him the same way.

I nod, stroking his face. "And sweet," I say.

He searches my face, his fingers twisting my brown curls absentmindedly.

"Can I stay?" he asks.

I have no idea if it's a good idea, but I think I'm past

worrying about making mistakes here. If he needs this, I'm happy to give it to him. It's been a long time since I fell asleep in someone's arms.

"Yes," I say.

He stands and helps me up, running his hands over my forearms as he looks at me in all my naked glory. "Where did you come from?" he asks, shaking his head.

I shrug. "Sometimes the universe knows exactly where a person should be and makes it happen."

"I'm glad the universe sent you here." William bends to pick up my negligée from the floor and hands it to me. He tugs off his shirt, jeans, and socks, then we make our way to the bed. I've just fucked this man, but there is something even more intimate about lying next to someone in the dark. He spoons me, tucking his arms around my middle. I feel him inhaling against my hair.

""They are not dead who live in the hearts they leave behind," William says softly. His words slip into my heart and make it ache. "It's a Native American saying. I read it around the time my pop passed on."

"It's beautiful," I say. I think about mom's smiling face and pink apple cheeks, and it's almost like she's in front of me.

We don't talk after that, and I listen as William slips into the world of dreams, his breathing soft and regular, his arm heavy over my ribs.

Day one has been something for sure. Not quite what I expected, but then the best parts of life never are. I fall asleep with the anticipation of the next six days and the unknowns they'll bring playing in my mind.

15

Fuck."

The bed moves behind me, and I force my right eyelid open to try and work out what the hell is going on. Where am I?

"Danna."

I turn to find the shape of man, sitting on the edge of my bed. I'm confused until I realize I'm not in my own bedroom.

I'm at the Jackson's Ranch.

"What?" I say as William struggles into his shirt and jeans.

There are loud footsteps on the stairs. "William, you lazy fucker. You're late for breakfast." I don't know who it is, but William is grumbling under his breath.

"Shit," he says. "You need to get up."

I look over at the window, finding it's still dark outside.

"It's the middle of the night."

"Not on a ranch," he says. He strides into my bathroom, and I hear the faucet and William splashing water on this face and washing out his mouth. I swing my legs over the edge of the bed, feeling like I've been run over and drowned in a bath of slime. God. If early mornings like this are required daily, I'm about ready to give up on my idea of a Jackson harem. That is until William walks back into the bedroom and I'm momentarily dazed at how gorgeous he is. He gives me a lopsided grin that's maybe a little shy. William is a barrel of contradictions; dominant and demanding in bed but serious and softhearted in life.

"I'm not a morning person," I say.

"Momma will have coffee in the pot. You think you can get yourself up?"

I nod. "Give me five."

He takes my hands and drags me to my feet, planting a kiss on my lips. "I'll give you anything you want, beautiful." Then he's off, opening the door with a quick glance left and right.

Wow. What a way to wake up.

I need to shower, but I manage to do it quickly, then throw on some casual clothes – gray leggings and a black sweater. I tie my hair into a knot on top of my hair and rub some moisturizer into my face. As much as I'd like to put a little make-up on, I get the feeling that it would only amuse the men downstairs. Who needs mascara when I could be shoveling shit?

I hope they don't make me shovel shit!

I'm the last one down for breakfast, and all eyes turn to me when I round the corner into the kitchen. I take my seat quickly and grab two pieces of toast and some eggs from the platters in the center of the table.

"There you are, Danna," Jackie says cheerily. "The boys were making bets on whether you were going to make it down before they left."

"Oh yeah," I say. "And who won."

"York."

"He was the only one who thought I'd get up in time?" I look around, feeling a little crestfallen. They obviously all think that I'm a spoilt city girl who's all talk. Ugh. Seems I have a whole lot to prove to these men.

"Nice that everyone has so much faith in me," I say, taking a big bite out of my buttered toast.

Jackie pours me a large mug of black coffee and offers me cream and sugar. I take both even though I don't usually drink my coffee that way. The clock on the wall is showing a time I've never been awake to see before. I'm going to need all the help I can get to stay awake.

"So who are you going out with today?" Jackie asks.

"Whoever will have me," I say looking around.

"Zack could do with a hand today," Jackie says.

Zack looks up at the mention of his name. "I'm good, mom," he says. "I'm sure the other need Danna's help more than I do."

"Nonsense," Jackie says. "You take Danna out and show her what it takes to keep this place functioning."

Zack still looks reluctant but nods his acceptance. I guess momma still carries some weight in this house.

I eat as quickly as I can, but the boys are way ahead of me, and most of them rise and leave before I'm done. Wade and Walker smile and wave as they follow William out. Part of me wishes that I was going with them. Zack seems a lot less friendly than his brothers, and the prospect of being out on the ranch surrounded by awkward silence doesn't exactly fill me with joy. He waits patiently while I fork the last of my egg into my mouth and wash it down with the dregs of my coffee.

"You good with wood?" he asks me.

I almost spit out the contents of my mouth until I realize he has no idea how rude that just sounded. Instead, I shake my head. "My pop likes to build things, but he never taught me anything. If I were a boy, he would have probably bought me my own toolbox."

Zack sighs. I guess taking me out with him would have been less annoying if I could actually help him with his work. "I make a good assistant," I say. "Just give me directions."

He nods, his dark hair flopping over his forehead. In a quick swipe, it's restored into place.

I take my plates to the sink as Jackie's tidying up, but I know better than to ask if she needs help. This is her domain.

"I'll see you later," I say to her.

"Sure, darling. You have a good day."

We pull on boots and jackets, Zack lending me one of his fleecy coats which is way too big but looks kind of cool in that girl-wearing-boyfriends-clothes kind of way. As we're leaving, Ruffles waddles into the mudroom. "Hey, boy." Zack grips Ruffles on either side of his neck and leans in to let the dog lick his face. There's a look of such contentment in both their expressions that my heart melts. Zack pats his pet. "Go on, boy," he says, pointing into the kitchen. "You know you can't come out with me now."

Ruffles hangs his head, and Zack sighs loudly. His eyes flick to mine. "He's got arthritis. He just can't get around as he used to and he misses being in the outdoors."

"It's a shame," I say, dropping to my haunches so that I can pet Ruffles too. He's such a sweet thing with kind eyes and skin that's drooping a little around his neck. His coat is warm and soft. He pants gently, and I can see what a strain it is for him to have made it to see his owner and say goodbye.

"I take him for a walk in the evening," Zack says. "Just around the house. He still needs to keep mobile but roaming the ranch all day is just too much for him."

I nod, but in my mind, I'm thinking about a solution. There must be a way that Zack could take his old friend out without it being detrimental to Ruffles health. I vow to think about it some more later when I can get on my phone and research.

"Bye, Ruffles," I say gently. He whines softly in objection, but I get the feeling he knows that it's futile.

"Has he been this bad for long?"

Zack nods. "Well over a year. It's been hard for him to accept that he's a homebody now. Even though mom's here a lot of the time, I think he gets lonely. He always used to love the wind in his coat. His favorite place was the front seat of my truck with his head hanging out the window." I can picture the image in my head, and it makes me smile.

"There's some fence to repair today," he says. "And I'll need to go to the store when it opens."

"Okay," I say. It'll be good to get into town for a bit and see some life outside of the ranch.

"We'll need to go to my pop's old workshop to pick up some wood."

Zack tugs open the door and holds it for me in a way that seems too gentlemanly for the gruff, working man he is. The morning air is fresh and damp. It feels cleaner than I'm used to, and I inhale deeply, relishing the crispness of the outdoors.

I follow Zack to a large red truck. It has an open area at the back which is draped with a waterproof cover. I guess that's where he keeps the lumber he needs.

We jump in the truck and drive around to the back of the house to a large outbuilding. "You can stay here," he says. "I'll only be a minute."

While Zack is gone, I quickly message Laura to let her know I'm okay. My phone starts ringing immediately.

"Why didn't you call me?" she says.

"It's been pretty crazy. I can't talk long. I'm with Zack. He's only going to be gone for a couple of minutes."

"Then you'd better fill me in quick, hadn't you?"

"I've made some progress!" I say with a smile in my voice that I know Laura will be able to hear.

"Oh yeah. How many?"

"Three and a half," I say.

She chuckled. "That's good going for one day. You beat me!"

"Well, I am on a mission," I say. "You had to be convinced."

"That's true. And what happened with the half? You get interrupted."

"No," I say. "He just wanted to watch."

Laura makes an approving noise. "That's sexy as fuck."

"Language," a voice says in the background.

"Yeah, Ford. Because you're always so moderate with your cursing."

There's a manly chuckle in the background. "I think my potty mouth has rubbed off on you too much."

Laura grumbles under her breath. "What's good for the goose is good for the gander," she says. "Now stop interrupting my conversation with Danna." She takes a breath. "So, how was it?"

"Good," I tell her. "Better than I could have hoped for, but I'm not sure if any of this will translate into anything permanent. I just have to go fast and will hopefully gather them on route."

"I don't think there's anything to be hopeful about. They're gonna be trailing you for good," Laura laughs.

"Maybe some of them," I say. "But there are definitely gonna be some who are harder to convince. Even Jackie, their mom, agreed. Like the guy I'm out with now – Zack – he's much more about keeping himself to himself.

"Grant was like that, but in the end, he saw the light," Laura reassures me.

"He saw more than the light," Ford says. "Unless the light is your new name for your titties and your…"

"Ford!" Laura shouts. "TMI!"

He chuckles again. "You're currently asking your best friend how many guys she fucked yesterday. I really don't think that TMI is a thing right now."

"The man has a point," I say.

"You go, Danna. Grab those guys and show them what they've been missing," Ford says.

Just as I'm about to fill Laura in on the details, Zack emerges from the shed carrying a large toolbox."

"I've gotta go," I say. "I'll call you later."

"Make sure you do this time," she squeals. "I'm dying here."

I'm laughing as I end the call and drop the phone back into my purse.

Zack places the toolbox on the back seat and then slides in next to me. "You calling home?" he asks.

"Just speaking to my best friend."

"Filling her in on how countrified we are out here?"

"No," I say. "Just letting her know that I'm okay."

Zack nods, starting the engine. I stare out of the window, watching the sun beginning to rise and cast its long beams across the landscape. The silence stretches between us, but I decide that for once in my life, I'm not going to try and fill it. Zack's not a chatty person, and I feel as though I should respect that. To be honest, I don't feel uncomfortable being in his company like this. Zack is a big, strong, reserved man and being with him is like sitting under a tall tree on a sunny day. There's a solidness to him that reminds me of my pop.

Eventually, he clears his throat. "We're heading on over to the western perimeter. There's been some damage to our fencing over there."

I turn, taking in his profile; the strong, Romanesque nose and long lashes, the unruly hair and beard that needs a trim. He's sexy in an 'I don't care how I look' kind of way. Like a model on vacation. "What kind of damage?"

Zack doesn't answer straight away. His brow is furrowed as though I've asked a question her really doesn't want to answer.

"Malicious damage," he says.

"Who'd want to damage your property?"

He sighs, and I get the feeling he really doesn't want to have a conversation about this. "There's some rivalry around here. Other ranches."

"Really? That doesn't seem very neighborly."

"It isn't." He taps his finger on the steering wheel.

"So, what do you do about it? Are the police involved?"

Zack continues to look straight ahead as the truck bumps and lurches over the rough track. "No."

I frown, gripping onto the sides of the seat, my knuckles whitening with the effort. "Maybe they should be?"

"Sometimes silence is all that is needed to ease problems away," he says.

"What does your mom think?" I ask. I can't imagine that Jackie would be too happy.

He glances at me, his dark eyes flashing. My heart skitters. "Mom doesn't know, and you need to keep it that way." His voice is calm, but the warning is clear. I nod, and he turns back to the road.

When we reach the western perimeter, I can see exactly what he means. It's as though a demolition truck has driven into the fencing and kept on going. The wires between the wooden posts have been torn away, and at least fifteen posts have been ripped from the ground. It's going to take a lot of work to put his back together.

"So what does your mom think you need to do out here?" I ask. "Why did she say you needed help if she doesn't know anything about this?"

"I told her I'm upgrading the fencing. That's all." Zack stops the truck and is out to unload his tools before I've even removed my belt.

I leave my purse in the car and slide out of the seat until my feet hit the dusty ground. Around the back of the truck, Zack is unloading more wire on a large spool, a sizeable pointed spade that I'm assuming will dig out post holes and some bags of mix. "Mom wouldn't sleep well if she knew," he says.

"I can understand why. The damage is…well, it's pretty extreme."

Zack nods. He glances down at all of the items he needs to work. I reach out to take hold of the spade and tuck the wire spool under my arm. His expression darkens as though he doesn't like me carrying his tools. He's either a gentleman for not wanting me to move heavy things, a misogynist for thinking I couldn't possibly help him or a control freak. I get the feeling it could be a mix of those things.

"Where do you want to start," I ask.

He surveys the damage. "Over there," he says, picking up his tool case and heading to the nearest part of the damage.

Zack starts by cutting away the twisted and torn wire. When he has two posts clear, he begins to drag one to the posthole it had been situated in. I carry the spade and hand it to him when he's frowning into the hole. It's already filled up with rubble. He looks momentarily shocked that I'm actually being helpful. When he takes the shovel, I start to collect the discarded wire and leave it in a pile by the truck. We continue like this for over three hours while Zack sets the posts to rights, and I work around him to make everything happen faster. As the sun rises higher in the sky, we both begin to sweat, and Zack heads to the truck, returning with cold bottles of water. We drink thirstily until they are almost drained. Zack pours the last of his water into his palm and wipes his face, using his wet hand to smooth his unruly hair too.

Wow.

He really has no idea how damn sexy that is, or he wouldn't be doing it in front of me for sure.

His lips glisten, and I imagine tasting the freshness of his mouth. His eyes meet mine, and I blush because surely he can feel how attracted I am to him. Even the sweat that's soaking through his shirt in the middle of his chest and across his back is turning me on. I bet he smells delicious even when he's been working all day.

"You hungry?" he asks.

I nod, handing him my bottle that he's reached out to take.

"Let go into town now then. We can grab something to eat and get the supplies I need. Those two posts are too damaged to use again," he says. "And I'm all out of wire."

"Sure. Sounds good."

In the truck, Zack puts on some soft country music, and we both open our windows, allowing the warm breeze to cool our hot bodies. Zack's right leg jitters as he drives in a restless way that makes me want to put my hand out and still him. If I could take a peek into the minds of any of the Jackson brothers, it would be Zack. I'd love to know what's going on behind his restrained exterior.

If I were sitting next to any of the W triplets, I'd be flirting by now. I even managed to get York to open up a little too, but Zack is a whole other species. Or maybe he isn't. Perhaps, his reservation comes from shyness. Perhaps all I need to do is be myself.

That's what my momma always told me. 'Be yourself, and if people don't like it, then that's their business.'

So I decide, with much trepidation, that I'm not going to hold myself back. I'm going to do what I feel. I rest my hand on Zack's knee, and it immediately stills. His head jerks down to look at where I'm touching him and then quickly back to the road as though he can't believe what I'm doing and has no idea what to say as a result.

"You were fidgeting," I say, taking my hand away. "Is that a habit, or are you worrying about something?"

"Habit," he says.

I don't push anymore because I think I've unsettled him enough. We're pulling out of the ranch and back onto the road I traveled with Jackie. I know it's not far into town and I'm excited about taking a walk and getting back to some normality. I'm also looking forward to seeing Zack outside of the closed family environment.

As we enter the main street, Zack pulls over into almost the same spot his mom collected me from.

"Lunch first," he says.

We jump out, and I follow Zack to a small diner on the corner opposite Joe's bar. It's an old fashioned place with red leatherette seats and Formica tables. The waitress, who's currently resting huge burgers onto the table of another couple, looks up and grins as we walk in. "Hey, Zack," she says cheerily. Her eyes flick to me, and her smile falters. "You want the usual?"

"We'll see the menu," he says, sliding into a seat that I'll bet it his usual too. I get the feeling that Zack is a man of routine.

The waitress, who has Brandy on her nametag, presents the menus to us.

"The specials are on the board," she says, her eyes scanning me and then flicking to Zack. "The meatloaf is good."

"I'll take a Caesar salad," I say. "And sparkling water."

"Can I get meatloaf and a coke?" Zack asks.

"Sure." Brandy takes our menus and looks me over again. I smile, feeling like I should ask her what the hell she's looking at but I don't want to be rude. It's pretty apparent that she has a bit of a thing for Zack. I don't know who wouldn't to be honest. She's probably just wondering who I am and sizing up the competition, so to speak.

As she retreats, Zack begins to fiddle with the salt and pepper shakers.

"I think she likes you."

He glances towards the bar where Brandy is fixing our drinks. "We had a thing," he says. "A long time ago."

"Oh," I say. "She looks like she wishes you still had a thing."

"We had nothing in common," Zack says. "She needs someone more like my brother Samuel."

I remember how Samuel looked at me last night, as though he wanted to devour me. "Why do you think she's more suited to Samuel."

"He's more of a jock. Brandy was a cheerleader in high school. They're a match made in heaven."

"Just because we're something in high school, doesn't mean we're going to be like that for the rest of our lives."

"She likes to watch trashy reality shows and hang out at Joe's. It's not really my thing."

Brandy's coming back with the drinks, so I wait to respond. She places everything on the table neatly, staring at me again. "You from around here?" she asks.

"No, just visiting," I say.

She frowns, flicking her hair over her shoulder. "I really feel like I recognize you from somewhere. Have you stayed in town before?"

I shake my head.

"Strange," she says.

"Maybe I have that kind of face."

Brandy looks me over again. "I'll bring your orders out when they're ready," she says.

As she retreats, Zack watches her over his shoulder. "She's not a bad person," he says. "I just felt like I had nothing to say to her."

I smile. "You are a man of few words though, Zack."

Zack's cheeks pink and he slumps forward a little on the table, watching the movement of his hands and the shakers. "What's the point of talking when there's nothing important to say?"

"I don't know…I guess some people like to converse and other people don't."

"I like to converse," he says. "But most people don't seem to get me enough to bother."

"What's not to get?" I ask.

He sits back in his seat, placing his big, rough hands in his lap. His shoulders look so broad, filling his side of the booth, his biceps stretching his shirt almost to breaking point. "I'm a simple guy," he says. "I love my dog, my family, my home."

"In that order?" I smile.

"Ruffles depends on me," he says. "Having a dog is like having a child. He's my responsibility, so he comes first."

I love the way Zack thinks about life. It's way more mature than any of my previous boyfriends. Their only concern was about their social life and their appearance.

"Ruffles is adorable," I say, and a smile spreads across Zack's face as though I've just said the sweetest thing in the world. I haven't seen him smile that way before, and it fills my heart. They say the way to a man's heart is through his stomach, but for Zack, it's really through his four-legged best friend.

"He's getting old," he says.

I nod and shrug. "It'll happen to us all."

"I don't know what I'll do..." He trails off, obviously lost for words.

"You'll be sad, and you'll miss him," I say. "And it'll be hard, but life will go on."

"But it's never the same," he says. I'm expecting him to carry on, but instead, he slides out of the booth. "I'm going to wash my hands."

And that's it. Conversation over. One minute I think we're bonding and the next he just cuts me off. I get the feeling that Zack is carrying around some serious hurt. Prying isn't something that I'm very comfortable with, but I think I'll need to ask Jackie some more about her oldest son or I'm really doubting that I'll ever be able to make the kind of connection with him that I need to.

16

The salad is delicious, and Zack looks as though he enjoyed the meatloaf. Brandy stares at me some more but still doesn't work out how she knows me. I've never thought I have the kind of face that people mix up with others, but I guess I have a doppelganger somewhere in Broadsville.

We head over to the hardware store, and Zack picks up the posts and wire that he needs to finish the job.

We spend the whole of the rest of the day together exchanging only necessary sentences about what we're doing and where we're going.

Maybe I should feel more uncomfortable, but I don't. This is Zack. He's exactly what his mom called him; a tough nut to crack. But I find that I want to break that nut. I want to get under his skin and into his heart. I want to know what's beneath his protective exterior, but other than the conversation about Ruffles, I haven't found a way to penetrate him.

On the way back to the house, his leg is jittering again,

and I rest my hand gently on his knee.

As it did in the morning, he stills under my touch.

"Thanks," he says. "For today, I mean."

"That's okay," I say. "It was fun and good to see everything back the way it should be.

He snorts. "For as long as it stays that way."

"You need to tell the police what is going on here, Zack. I know you don't want to worry your mom, but you can't just leave these things to happen. Someone could get hurt."

He doesn't say anything in response, but I hope I've gotten through to him enough that he will think about what I've said.

Back at the house, I tug off the work boots, so glad to be without their heavyweight. I hang Zack's jacket up, sad to be without the faint scent of him surrounding me. Zack doesn't wait around for me to finish and is in the kitchen on his hands and knees with Ruffles in a flash. Both man and dog are the purest version of happiness I think I've ever seen.

Jackie breezes in and smiles broadly at her son. "Did you have a good day?" she asks me.

"Yes. Lot of busy hard work."

She pours me a mug of coffee. "I hope Zack didn't work you too hard."

"Danna's very capable," Zack says. "She was a big help."

"Well, that's great," Jackie says happily. "Looks like

132

you're fitting in perfectly around here." She gives me a wink and Zack glances up at us curiously.

"I need a good shower," I say. "I'm gonna take this up."

"Sure. I'll ring the bell for dinner," Jackie says. "Keep an ear open."

I pat Ruffles and tell Zack that I'll see him later. My thighs hurt as I ascend the stairs, but it's a good hurt. Pain that comes from hard work.

In my room, I lay on the bed and close my eyes. I'm so drowsy from all the fresh air that I know, if I stay here too long, I'll fall asleep. I take hold of my phone and call Laura.

"So what's your total now?" she asks in greeting.

"Still three and a half," I laugh.

"But you've had all day!"

"Yes, but Zack is a lot more reserved than his triplet brothers."

"Ah. Well, that explains it. Do you like him at least?"

I sigh. "Yeah. He's the gorgeous, silent, brooding type. What's not to like?"

Laura giggles. "Well, I guess you're gonna have to work a bit harder!"

She's not wrong. I actually can't imagine getting to the point of intimacy with Zack. What would it take to break down his walls? I wonder how far he allowed Brandy into his personal space. They seem so unsuited that it's almost laughable.

"I'm not sure how fruitful any work will be in that direction, but let's see. Maybe, if I can get the rest of the Jackson's on board, Zack will follow."

"Well, that worked for me. Grant was set against the idea, but he came around."

"Yes. After you had sex. I think getting Zack to do more than have a one-word conversation with me is going to be a miracle."

"Mmm…I suppose Grant might have been a bit of an easier situation. What about the rest?"

"Well, Samuel is a strange one too. He wanted to watch, but nothing else."

"Well, as you say, you're halfway there with him."

"York is cute. We flirted yesterday, so I'm hoping that all I need is a little more time with him."

"Okay…so that's five."

"The rest are still to be tackled."

"Wow…I'm loving your attitude," she laughs. "There was me feeling guilty and struggling with the idea of a harem, and you've crossed into a whole other world to try and assemble yours."

I turn onto my side, bringing my knees up. "Momma always told me you've got to work to get where you want to be. She told me I shouldn't wait for things to just fall into my lap because most often it just won't happen."

"Your momma was a wise woman," Laura says gently. "And you're doing the right thing."

"I hope so," I say. "There is a very real chance that all

of this is going to blow up in my face."

"Maybe," she says. "But at least you'll know that you tried to find the life that you want. It would be worse to always wonder what might have been."

"True," I say.

"So how was the sex?" She whispers the last bit, and I'm left wondering who might be in the room with her.

"Amazing," I say. "Perfect, and so different."

"So you went straight in for three at the same time. You're one brave girl," she laughs. "It took me a while to work myself up to two!"

"Two I say, with one watching."

"And the other one?"

"After, by himself."

"And how do you think you'll get on with more than two. I remember how encouraging you were of me. Does it feel different now you're in the driving seat?"

"Maybe a little. I don't know. I guess it'll just depend on how connected I feel with each of them. With Walker and Wade, it just felt right to have them together. They work well together."

"I know what you mean. My twins are the same. But how come the triplets didn't all want to be together? It surprises me that they'd do that."

"I know. It surprised me too. I think they were worried about being too much for me and also that William might not be as up for something so soon."

"Ah...well, I suppose they know him better than anyone else. So what's the plan for later?" Laura asks.

"You know I have no idea. Dinner with the Jacksons, then I need to find a way to get to know the other brothers. There's Xsander and Xane and Tommy and Trent."

"Don't tell me they're sets of twins," she laughs.

"Errr, yes. It seems like your father-in-law, and Mrs. Jackson used a very similar naming convention for their huge number of sons."

"Well, at least it helps you to remember who is who," she laughs.

"Exactly. I miss you guys," I tell her. I feel very far away from my life. "By the time I come back I'm going to be desperate to give your babies a cuddle."

"We miss you too, sweetie," she says.

"Yeah we do," a voice pipes up from the back.

"I AM NEVER ALONE," Laura says exasperatedly.

"Don't complain about that," I say. "Being alone is highly overrated."

We say our goodbyes, and I leave my friend to go back to being the center of a vast family universe. I hear voices on the stairs as the boys come home and then the sound of the pipes groaning as everyone starts to freshen up.

I spend a long time in the shower, washing away the dirt of the day, and trying to find my mojo again. Being with Zack has brought out my serious side, but what I need to be this evening is my flirty fun self. Two days have ticked past, and I have a whole lot to achieve. I wash between my legs and remember the way that Walker, Wade, and William made me feel. I had no idea it was possible to come so much in such a short timeframe. Their brothers have a lot to live up to.

As I'm getting dressed, I see Zack walking Ruffles, traveling the same path as he did yesterday. He looks as serious too, as though he's carrying the weight of the world on those broad shoulders.

I choose my favorite sweater dress to wear tonight. I rub plenty of lotion into my legs and slip on my sandals. My hair dries into perfect waves, and with a touch of make-up, I'm feeling really glamorous.

I'm ready before the bell rings, so I decide to go down early and offer to help.

Jackie is bustling around, but she sends me off to the den, refusing my offers of assistance. It's strange to wander around the house as a stranger with no escort. I can hear the TV and follow the sound. The door is open, but I still feel really awkward walking in, especially as I have no idea who might be inside.

I hang around in the doorway, finding Tommy, Trent, and York reclining on large sofas. Tommy is looking at his cellphone while the others are watching football highlights. It's York who senses me first.

"Hey, Danna," he says, straightening himself up. "You coming to hang out?"

"Yeah. Your mom just sent me packing."

York laughs. "Yeah. She's not a fan of having people under her feet when she's cooking."

I take a place next to him, sliding back into the comfortable, cord seat. Tommy and Trent watch and smile. "I would have thought that she'd be begging for help with all you hungry boys to feed."

"She's used to it," Tommy says. "I don't think she'd know what to do with herself if she wasn't looking after us all."

"Yeah," Trent says. "When we start getting married and making our own families, mom's gonna be popping round to deliver dinner to all of us."

"If she ever lets us leave," York says. He laughs, but I get the feeling that there is genuine underlying worry about changing anything around her. Maybe that's why none of the boys have girlfriends right now.

Jackie seems formidable in the eyes of her sons. A real power to be reckoned with. I remember how forceful Roderick McGregor was with his sons. He was also the instigator of the harem idea for his sons, and he made it very clear what he wanted. Jackie's not being open with her idea, but her sons are conscious of her likes and dislikes.

I wonder how they'll feel when they discover that my being here was completely Jackie's idea.

"So, how did you get on with Zack?" Trent asks.

"Yeah, good. We were really busy all day."

"He doesn't talk much, does he?" Tommy says.

I smile. "He talks enough."

The boys glance at each other with interest. I have no idea what they know about what happened last night with their brothers and me. I get the feeling that Samuel wouldn't keep anything a secret but that the triplets would be more discreet. Still, no one here is acting in a way that would lead me to believe that they're aware of anything.

"He's always been like that," Tommy says. "Moody and mute."

"He's just more reserved than the rest of us," York says. "He went through a lot before he came here. Mom told me that she's tried to bring him out of his shell over the years but that he's too set in his ways to change him."

"We can't all be the same," I say, pulling a pillow into my lap. "It's our differences that make us interesting."

Trent grins. "Girls are always interested in Zack. I don't know why but they always seem to be drawn to the moody guys."

"Girls like a challenge," I say. "They like to think that love can change people."

"You don't believe it can?"

I shake my head. "I don't think so. Not really. We are as we are. At least, that's what my momma told me. She said that when I was born, I had my own ways about me and nothing she could do changed who I was at the core. In the end, we can modify ourselves, but we always come back to who we are at the root."

Trent looks across at his brother. "So I need to stop bothering to try and make this guy a normal human being then, do I?"

Tommy doesn't look up from his phone but grabs the cushion next to him and tosses it at his twin.

We all laugh. "I think your momma was probably right," York says. "It's a good way to think, anyway. If you accept people for who they are, there won't be so much disappointment."

"Exactly," I say. "It's easier said than done, though. My momma used to nag my dad something chronic. When they got married, she knew he wasn't the most dynamic man in the world, but she still expected him to be."

"But they were happy?" York asks.

"Yeah, they were. I think my dad put up with a lot. Maybe if he had been more dynamic, they wouldn't have lasted as long as they did."

York nods. "Relationships are funny."

"What the fuck is he doing?" Trent shouts, slamming his hand down on the arm of the chair.

A player on screen obviously isn't performing the way he's supposed to be. I wish I understood football better. Maybe if I'd had a brother. "Language, dude." York chucks a pillow at Trent, and suddenly there's a full-blown pillow fight happening around me.

You'd never believe that these men are all in their twenties. I cower in the corner of the couch, praying that I'm not going to get caught in the crossfire.

Eventually, after a lot of arm punching and wrestling, the three brothers slump back into their seats.

"So, Danna…you got a boyfriend?" Tommy asks.

There's a rumble from his brothers. "Dude, you can't ask things like that?" York says. He looks at me apologetically."

I put my hand up to diffuse the situation. "It's okay. I don't mind answering. I don't right now."

"You want one?" Tommy grins at me, and his brothers reach for pillows again.

"What girl wouldn't want a man to show them a good time?" I say, grabbing the cushion from York before he can launch it and sets it on the sofa next to me.

"You'd be surprised," Trent mumbles.

"So you like a good time?" Tommy says, suggestively.

At least the conversation is moving in the right direction. "Who doesn't love a good time?" I say again. This line I'm treading is a fine one for sure.

"Ignore my brother," Trent says. "He's worked his way through most of the girls in town, and he's feeling lonesome."

"Ah. You a player, Tommy?" I ask.

"Not a player," he says. "Just a man who's very enthusiastic about women."

"That's one way of putting it."

"What's the male version of a nymphomaniac?" Trent asks. "Whatever it is, that's Tommy."

"The male version of a nymphomaniac is a man," I laugh.

Tommy gets up and sits next to me, grinning widely. His green eyes are dancing with amusement, and he rubs his hands over his beard as he considers me. I hold my head up high and maintain eye contact with him and his brother's whistle.

"I think you might just have met your match," Trent laughs.

"I think he has," York says. "Danna, you can come and sit over here if you want to get away from Tommy." He pats the seat on the other side of him, and I smile at his thoughtfulness and protectiveness.

"It's okay. Tommy, what you going to do? Grope me in front of your brothers on your momma's couch?"

"It wouldn't be the first time," Trent says.

"Or the last," Tommy jokes.

"And what about when momma calls dinner. You gonna walk in there with wood?"

York is sipping from a bottle of beer and manages to snort it through his nose.

"You gonna give me wood?" Tommy asks.

I look into pointedly into his lap. "I think I have already."

"Shit!" Trent laughs. "I really think you've met your perfect woman, bro."

Tommy covers his lap with a pillow. "I think I have too."

"So, are you boys going to head into town later?" I ask. "I walked past the infamous Joe's today. I wouldn't mind taking a look."

"We could," Trent says.

"Definitely," Tommy says. "Whatever the lady wants."

I laugh and pat his knee. "Be careful what you promise, baby. You could get yourself into all kinds of trouble."

Trent and York laugh some more and then the bell rings, and they are up in a flash.

"Thank fuck for that. I'm starving." Trent is first through the door, driven by a ravenous belly by the looks of it. York follows him, glancing back at where I'm still seated next to Tommy. He pauses for second as though he wants to wait for me but isn't really sure what my thoughts are about Tommy. Does he need to protect me, or am I into his brother?

Tommy leans forward. "You're really sexy, Danna. You know that?"

I smile sweetly. "Do you think your momma would like to hear you talking to me this way?"

He leans forward even more. "I think my momma likes you a lot and would prefer me to get with you than any of the other girls in town."

"Get with me?" I say, putting my hand on my chest to feign shock.

"I heard you last night," he says softly. "I heard you whimpering. Did you make yourself come or did one of my brothers get to you first?"

I don't answer because I'm not going to reveal anything that the others might not want to become public knowledge. His green eyes, framed with gorgeous long lashes hold mine hostage.

"You want to make me whimper?" I whisper.

"Oh yeah. More than you'll ever know. He rests a big

warm hand on the bare skin of my leg. God, he's sexy and naughty in the best possible way. His lips look so soft and warm, and all I can think about is tasting them.

"Later," I say, getting up and walking away before he has time to say anything else.

Tommy doesn't follow me immediately, and I smile to myself that he's waiting for his erection to go down. I'm wet between my legs, but no one can see that, thank goodness.

The kitchen is bustling, and everyone else has already taken their seats. York looks at me questioningly, and I smile, taking a seat opposite him, next to the two brothers I've had the least interaction with; Xsander and Xane.

"Hey," I say.

"We saved you space," they both say in unison.

"Well, that's very kind." I take bread from the bowl in front of me and reach for the butter.

"Our brothers have been keeping you busy," one of the says. I'm not sure who is who yet, but he's sitting to my left.

"They have," I laugh. "But there's enough of me to go around." I catch York's eye as I say it and I'm sure his cheeks have flushed a little bit. There is definitely an attraction there. With Zack, I'm not sure, but with York, I can feel it. I can also sense his trepidation. I guess, unlike some of his other brothers, he's thinking about the possible consequences of a thing with me. Like, would his mom be angry with him? Would it be awkward?

Walker, Wade, William, and Samuel didn't seem to have any worries in that direction, and Tommy certainly doesn't.

I kind of like that York does. That little bit of respectfulness and concern about appropriateness goes a long way with me.

"I'm not sure about that," the twin to my right says.

"I have no idea if that is a compliment or a criticism," I say.

Jackie bustles over with a large tray of chops and roast potatoes. "If there's not enough, I can feed her up," she laughs, giving me a wink. She gets a few quizzical looks from her sons that make me smile. If only they knew!

We all serve ourselves and dishes of salad and coleslaw are passed around too. The conversation moves to ranch business, and I glaze over, watching the brothers interacting with each other and enjoying the ways they laugh, joke, and poke fun with each other.

Towards the end of the meal, Tommy announces that he's taking me to Joe's and asks if any of his brothers want to come.

There's a rumble of agreement from most of the Jackson brothers, and I look down at my clearer plate, wanting to smile broadly but wanting to maintain my cool too. I glance over at Zack wondering if he'll come, but he's twisting his serviette rather than joining in with his brothers. My heart aches at the thought of him staying behind.

"Let me help you clear up," I say to Jackie.

"Nonsense." She grins and waves her hands as though she's ushering me out of the door. "You go and enjoy yourself. This is your week of vacation, not your week so skivvy around this house. You've already done a load of work to help Zack."

"Wow…mom's letting Danna off chores," Samuel laughs. "She really must be something special."

Jackie grimaces at her son. "For that, you can pick up extra chores."

It's Samuel's turn to grimace, but he doesn't backchat his mom.

"Let's go," Tommy says, pushing back his chair.

"I need to grab my purse."

"Let's meet back here in five," York says.

I nod and slide off the bench, heading up the stairs first. When I'm about to open my door, there are footsteps behind me. "How was William?" It's Samuel, and he's standing close. Damn. His blue eyes are the color of the Caribbean Sea, and when I look into them, I feel like I'm slipping under water.

"You just saw him," I say knowing full well what he's referring too. "Why are you asking me?"

"You know what I mean," Samuel says. "I would have liked to have seen that too."

I turn so I'm facing him full on, drawing myself up as tall as I can. He's still nearly a foot taller than me and broad enough to block out anything behind him.

"Watching isn't half as much fun as doing," I say, raising my eyebrows.

"I don't know about that," Samuel says.

I lean in closer so I can lower my voice. "You prefer the feel of this?" I say, taking hold of his right hand. "To the feel of this?" I take his hand and press it against my pussy. His blue eyes flash hot, his lips rising into a one-sided smirk. I want to grab his spiky blond hair and push him to his knees. I want to make him worship this thing that he seems to like to look at but not touch.

"I prefer to get off without complications," he says, leaning in close to my ear. "I get the feeling you're anything but complication free."

I shudder at the feeling of his breath against my cheek. "Nothing in life comes without complications," I tell him.

"Well, at least you're honest," he says.

I turn and brush my lips across his jaw. "When you're grown up to deal with more than just your hand, you let me know." Then I turn and open my door, closing it behind me.

Shit. My heart is hammering in my chest. That man has a kind of serious intensity going on. I feel like a mouse who just got its tail caught by a cat, but I'm pleased that I gave as good as I got. I can imagine him standing outside my door with that smirk on his face, and I'd like to wipe it right off some time, but now is not the right moment for Samuel.

I grab my purse and a jacket, fluff my hair and powder my nose, then I'm ready for whatever is going to come next.

At least I think I am.

17

The car journey to Joe's is eventful. There are two large trucks in convoy filled with Jackson men. Oh, and little-old-me!

I'm wedged in the back between Walker and Wade, not that I'm complaining in any kind of way. Their muscular thighs are spread, and now I know exactly what they're packing between those sexy legs, I can't help getting flustered and hot.

They've been asking me about my day; lots of idle chit-chats that won't give anything away. I wonder if they know about William. He's driving, and I can feel the static of attraction rolling off him in waves. York is in the front passenger seat, seemingly oblivious to the undercurrent that is running through the rest of us.

In the car in front, Xsander and Xane and Tommy and Trent are being driven by Samuel. He has a battered old truck that looks as though it's seen better days. When I say that, William tells me it used to be their dad's, and Samuel has been keeping it going in his memory. It shows a softer side to Samuel than I would have imagined existed from my interactions with him to date; a side that I look forward to uncovering at some point.

"So, you ready for your first taste of Broadsville nightlife?" York says.

"I have no idea what I'm letting myself in for," I say.

"You let us know what you think later on," William says.

Wade squeezes my knee with his big, rough hand. "We'll be there to take care of you."

Walker does the same on the other side. "If anyone gives you shit, you just let us know."

"I can handle myself," I say indignantly, all the while secretly loving the fact that I have these two huge men offering to keep me safe. If I was honest, I know that any one of the nine brothers who are escorting me tonight would step in. It's how they've been raised, and I love their momma for doing such a fantastic job.

We pull up outside the bar, taking two spaces on the opposite side of the main street. The air is fresh but not unpleasant, but I'm glad that they make their way inside quickly, rather than standing around shooting the breeze.

Joe's is precisely what I thought it would be. Old fashioned saloon décor, working men, and women dressed in clothes that are a little too small and tight to be decent. I feel like I stick out like a sore thumb in my sweater dress and flat sandals.

All eyes turn to us as we walk in the door. There are some manly calls of approval for the Jacksons; drinking buddies who are glad to see them. Then gazes turn to me. I guess they're probably not used to seeing strangers in these parts. I keep a smile on my face, not wanting to appear hostile. There's some definite hostility amongst the women, probably from the ones who want to get into the pants of these gorgeous Jackson men. I have sympathy, I do.

"So, here it is. Our one local place to hang out," Tommy says. He throws his arm around my shoulder and surveys the surroundings. "What are you drinking?"

"I'll take a beer," I say.

He looks at me surprised, then grins. "My kind of girl," he says with pride in his voice.

The W triplets are watching with interest as he strolls off to order. It's beers for everyone.

The music is loud with a country vibe, and there are at least ten men in the place wearing Stetsons. I feel like an extra in a movie.

"So, Danna. What do you think?" Xane asks me. I know it's him because he's quite a lot slimmer than his brother.

"It's cool," I say. "Rustic."

"Cool and rustic?" York shakes his head. "Never thought I'd heard those two descriptors applied to one place."

"You know what I mean," I say.

"I think you mean it's more countrified than you ever thought you'd experience, but you don't want to hurt our feelings."

I pat York's shoulder. "I know you're all big boys. I

think you could take me being honest. I actually mean that it seems fun."

"You should see it on a Saturday night," Xane says. "Carnage."

"More babies have been conceived in the lot behind this place than the beds of Broadsville," Xsander says.

"Well, I think I'd better avoid the lot then," I laugh.

The X twins are so tall that I'm craning to look at them and so broad that block out everything behind them. There's something about their features that makes me think they've got some African roots; the tight curls to their dark cropped hair and warm caramel skin tone. I wonder how much they know about their backgrounds. How much to adoption agencies share?

"There's a lot of things you need to avoid in here," Xane says. He glances around, his brow furrowed. There's an uneasy watchfulness about him that I hadn't noticed before. Around us is a sea of white faces and I'm wondering how easy it must have been for them to grow up in this kind of environment.

"I'll bear that in mind," I say.

"There you are," a woman's voice squeals from behind me. A dark-haired, middle-aged woman, wearing tight pink jeans and a white tube-top, launches herself at Samuel. "Nadine," Xane grins. "She really has a thing for him."

"Is that the woman Jackie was talking about?"

"Yeah. Mom and Nadine used to go to school together."

I grin as Samuel puts his hand on her upper arms and

tries to extract himself from her grasp. She's leaning into him as though she wants to plant a kiss on his lips and he's craning backward to avoid it. "Has he slept with her?" I ask.

Xane shakes his head. "Samuel can be a bit of a dog, but he doesn't slum it."

"Has Tommy?"

Xane and Xsander exchange looks. "Brothers don't tell," they say in unison.

"The bro-code," I laugh. "Okay. I get it."

Nadine is chatting to Samuel at a hundred miles an hour, and he's still holding her at arms-length. I see my chance to help him out and think it's probably a good move, so I shoulder my way between the X twins until I'm standing next to Samuel. "Hey," I say to him.

Nadine stops what she's saying immediately, staring at me with narrowed eyes.

"Samuel. Can I talk to you for a minute?" He glances at me and nods.

"I'll catch you later, Nadine," he says. "Okay?"

I've definitely made an enemy in Nadine, that's for sure. "Yeah, course." She simpers, taking hold of Samuel's hand a squeezing. "I'll be waiting."

I begin to walk towards the door, and he puts a hand behind my back, steering us through the crowd. When we're far enough away from Nadine that she won't overhear I turn. "You owe me big time."

He shakes his head, but he's smiling. "What do I owe

you, Danna?"

"Oh, I don't know. Eternal gratitude and sexual favors."

He cocks his head to one side, his eyes flashing with interest. "Eternal. That sounds like a serious amount of gratitude."

"And sex," I say. "Don't forget the sex."

He places his hand on my upper arm and leans in until he's close enough to my ear that I can feel his breath and smell his cologne. "How could I forget the sex?" he asks.

"I don't know," I say, "because I sure as hell can't."

"You liked me watching, didn't you," he says.

I shiver, remember the way his eyes caressed me, almost as intensely as physical touch. "Yes."

"But you wanted me to touch?" His runs his finger over the roundness of my shoulder and down my arm, setting the hairs standing.

"I did," I say. "But maybe this is good."

"In what way?"

"I think maybe you like delayed gratification. Maybe, if I make you wait, you'll want it even more than me."

His beautiful eyes sparkle, the dimples on his cheeks evident for the first time. "I think you're a very wise woman, Danna," he says.

"Maybe," I say as I take a step back and edge around him in the crowd. "We'll have to wait and see."

As I make it back to where his brothers are gathered by the bar, Tommy is holding two beers. "There you are," he says, handing me my drink. "I was beginning to think that you'd been kidnapped.

"She swooped in to rescue Samuel from Nadine," Xane laughs. "Danna is a regular superhero."

"I'm not sure Nadine will feel that way," Tommy laughs.

"She's like a fly on shit," Xsander says.

"What Samuel needs is a girlfriend," I say.

A look passes between the brothers that is impossible to miss. "What?" I ask.

Xane shrugs. "Samuel doesn't really date."

"What do you mean? He's celibate?" I say. It would explain a lot.

"No. He just…he sometimes hooks up with a girl in the next town…but it's nothing serious."

"He has a fuck buddy?" I ask.

There are shrugs all around. "He never said that's what she is," Xsander says. "We just know he goes over there sometimes."

"They could be playing Scrabble," I say, and there's a ripple of laughter. "You don't know Samuel very well," Tommy says. "The dudes dyslexic."

Just as he finishes saying that Samuel appears behind him.

"Who you talking about, Tommy?" he asks coldly.

Nobody says anything, and the silence is so uncomfortable that I actually shiver.

"Have you got a beer?" I ask Samuel desperate to ease the situation.

"It's here," York says, passing his brother a bottle.

"So do you guys just stand around talking ranch?" I say. "Or is there something else exciting that goes down in this place?"

"Mostly lots of ranch talk," Wade admits, laughing. "And if we get drunk enough, there might be some dancing."

"Some nights there's live music," Walker adds.

"And that's just Walker's drunken singing," William says.

There's some brotherly jostling, and I put my hands out to diffuse them again. Boy! Keeping these brothers in line is a full-time job.

"Hey guys," a woman's voice says from behind me. I turn to find Brandy from the diner, looking around hopefully. "Is Zack with you?"

"He stayed home," York says.

Brandy's face falls, her disappointment totally transparent. Her gaze finds me, and she narrows her eyes. I'm waiting for her to say something. It looks as though she wants to but can't quite find the words.

"Samuel, there you are!" Nadine's back and in Samuels face again.

"Hey, Nadine," Brandy says. "You recognize this girl? I

swear I know her from somewhere, but I just can't work out where from."

Nadine turns to me and narrows her eyes, just like Brandy did. I want to slap them both for staring at me like a piece of meat. How damn rude can some people be?

"You from around here?" Nadine asks.

I shake my head. "I asked her that already," Brandy says, as though everyone should be aware of exactly what we discussed earlier at the diner, even if they weren't there.

Nadine cocks her head to one side, studying me again. York steps forward, obviously sensing that I'm getting pissed off. "You know what girls," he says, "you're making our friend feel uncomfortable."

"Didn't anyone ever tell you it's rude to stare," Tommy says, taking my hand and pulling me back into the circle of brothers, behind York's broad back. Nadine cranes her neck to catch another glimpse of me.

"I've got it," she says. Her hands wave in the air as she tries to put the pieces together in her brain. "You're Danna from that reality show."

Brandy leans around to look at me. "That's it. Laura Plus Ten. I love that show."

The boys all turn to look at me with eyebrows raised. "You're on TV?" Xane asks.

My face reddens, and my stomach drops.

This is about the worst thing that could happen right now.

I shouldn't have come out tonight and risked getting

recognized, but I had no idea that Laura's reality show had such extensive viewership, and now I'm about to get exposed.

I can't very well lie, can I?

When I nod their eyebrows raise even further. "What kind of show?" Wade asks.

"It's about a woman who's married to ten men. You must have heard of them. The McGregors...the ones who own McGregor Corps."

"The developers?" Walker says.

"Yeah. They all fuck the same woman," Nadine says crudely.

"What do you do on the show?" Xane asks.

"I'm the best friend," I say softly, my cheeks on fire with embarrassment.

"She's the best friend," Brandy says. Her eyes narrow again as she looks at me, then scans the faces of the Jackson brothers who are standing protectively around me. "The one who's looking for ten men of her own."

There's a moment of silence in the group as all eyes fix on me. The music in the background seems to fade away as I stand exposed for all to see.

I have no idea what to do next. "Is that why you're here?" Nadine asks. "You looking at the Jacksons to be your Harem?" As she says the words, a smile forms on her face. She realizes she's onto something from the way my cheeks are flaming. My pale skin does nothing to hide my emotions, and it's infuriating.

"What?" William says. The others are waiting for me to answer and I just don't know what to say, especially in front of these jealous women who seem so gleeful about getting one over on me.

I can't just stand here like this. This isn't the way I wanted the boys to find out, and I'm certainly not about to start admitting or explaining anything now. I take a fortifying breath and then turn, muscling past Tommy and Trent towards the door. I'm outside in the cool air before anyone can catch me, but once I'm there, I have no idea what to do next.

I don't know where I am. There are no buses this late and certainly no cabs. I have my phone in my purse, but I don't know anyone for miles around, except Jackie.

I could call her, I think. I could tell her what's happened and ask her to come and collect me. Except, I don't get the chance because as I'm deliberating, a wall of Jackson men has formed around me.

18

Nobody says a word, and I have no idea how to deal with this situation.

I could be honest. I could tell them that their mom called me and arranged for me to stay with them. I could tell Wade, Walker, and William that what happened between us yesterday wasn't just about the hottest sex that I've ever had. I could tell them that I'm here for a week to try and get them all to fall in love with me and want me to be the center of their world.

I could, but I don't.

People are coming and going behind us, and I feel the eyes of Nadine and Brandy through the window. Are they expecting some kind of show? Are they hoping that we'll cause a scene?

That isn't my style.

"I think maybe we should go home," I say.

Tommy's in front of me, and he takes a step closer. "I don't think so," he says. "I think you need to explain exactly how you know our mom."

I shake my head because I'm not going to lie. This situation is bad enough, but if I keep digging, I'm never going to be able to get out of the hole.

"She called you, didn't she?" York says. His brothers all turn to him. Does he know something? "She watches that show. She told me. Mom called you and told you to come down here."

I stand like a mute.

"She called you because of what you said on the show, and you came…"

"You came to make us your harem?" William says, incredulously.

I look down at my feet, chastened to have been discovered and fearful of their anger and rejection.

"What is a harem?" Xane asks.

"You know…like the emperors and kings used to have in the old days. One man with lots of wives, except in this case reversed."

I don't look up to see Xane's eyes widen at the explanation. I wonder how many of the other brothers were confused as to what was being said.

"That's what you want?" Xane asks.

I glance up, meeting his ethereal eyes. My heart is a hammer in my chest, but I can't just ignore him, so I nod.

"Ten men?" he says. "How would that even work?"

"How do any relationships work?" I say. "I've seen it

work for my friend…I want it to work for me too."

"But why us?" Xsander asks.

"Because there are ten of us, dude," Tommy says. "It's got nothing to do with us as people. It's just simple math."

"Because mom wants to keep us together on the ranch," York adds. "Danna wouldn't be here if mom hadn't called her. She wouldn't be here if mom wasn't planning."

"Mom wants us to be with one woman?" Trent says. "Shit. I would never have seen that coming."

"You know mom worries about the future of the ranch. Now pop is gone, she wants to make sure we stick together to keep our business together."

"And she thinks this is the solution?" Samuel says incredulously. "What the fuck?"

"I think we should go back to the ranch," I say. ", and I don't want to bring anything bad on your family. Let's go back, and I can leave in the morning."

There's silence, then Wade steps forward. "You're right, we should go. But I don't want you to even think about leaving tomorrow." He slides his hand into mine. "You're our guest until you need to go back to college. I want you to stay."

Walker moves to stand next to his brother. "Me too."

William is there. "And me."

"Is there something you guys want to tell the rest of us?" Trent asks.

Samuel laughs. "Yeah. There's a whole lot of

something going on there."

The Jackson brothers all start talking at once, and York puts up his hands. "Home," he says. "Now. We've aired enough dirty laundry outside this dive for one night."

His brothers hear him and start to cross the road to where the trucks are parked.

"It's okay," Wade says softly. "We'll sort this all out."

"You think?" I say, not really able to imagine how that might be possible. I wish I could hear what each of the brothers is thinking right now.

We make the journey to the Jackson Ranch in silence. York turns to at one point and smiles a small, tight smile. Walker and Wade have their hands on my knees protectively, and I feel less vulnerable as a result.

The other truck arrives before us, and the boys are out of it like a shot. I then remember that Zack isn't with us and so he doesn't know anything about what's been said. What on earth is he going to think?

And Jackie. I should have sent her a message to warn her, but my brain is scrambled, and I'm just not thinking clearly. William is the first to throw open his door, followed by York. Walker and Wade ask me if I'm okay in unison. I shrug because who knows what's waiting for me inside. There could be ten receptive men and one happy momma or a colossal ruckus that's about to kick off.

Ugh.

I hate drama.

I hang back as the brothers make their way into the kitchen. I can hear the sound of raised voices, and I lurk in the doorway, not wanting to intrude into a family confrontation which feels as though it should be private.

"Just listen for a minute," I hear Jackie say. "Where is Danna?"

"She's outside," Wade says. "I don't think she wants to come in."

"Go get the girl," Jackie says. "You don't leave our guest out in the cold, dark night, for goodness sake."

Wade emerges again and takes my hand, practically dragging me inside as I drag my heels. He shuts the door behind me as though he's imagining that I'm thinking about making an escape. It's ridiculous because there's nowhere for me to run too. It's pitch black out there and over a mile to the road. This is certainly not the time to go rambling.

"There you are," Jackie says, coming to stand beside me. She gives me a hug, and I immediately feel better, then I look around at the boys over her shoulder, and my heart sinks. This is not about to go well.

"Mom," Samuel practically growls. "What the hell?"

Jackie turns and raises her finger as though she's about to reprimand a bunch of naughty eight-year-olds rather than the room of the strapping sons that are standing in front of her in reality.

"Don't you use language like that to me, young man," she says. "You think you're all so clever, bringing home girls with no capacity for ranch or family life. Wasting your time with girls in other towns, thinking I don't know what's going on. You think you know it all, but you don't. You have no idea what it takes to keep a family together, to raise children in a happy relationship. You have no idea how challenging it can be when there are people from outside the family involved. Do you think that if I left you to go out and chose your own wives that this ranch will still be here in one piece in ten years? If you do, you're crazy."

"Crazier than you thinking that we could all marry the same woman?" Samuel says. "You think that would work better than ten marriages we choose ourselves?"

"We have one of the highest divorce rates in the world, and we're a country where people are marrying for love. You know what happens to love in those cases? Look at your Uncle."

"Jack again!" Samuel says, rolling his eyes. "It doesn't have to be like that for everyone," York says. "You know that."

"But if it's like that for even one of you, this ranch will have to be sold. Divorce is costly, and anyone marrying in will have rights over our property and land."

"So we're supposed to believe that we could all love Danna?" Xane says. It's not mentioned in a mean way, more that he's intrigued.

"Danna is a lovely girl. She wants this. She's seen it work for her friend. She's willing to give it a try for that reason. I want you to give it a try for the reasons I've outlined. What do you have to lose?"

"What do you think people are going to say, mom?" Xsander asks. "Me and Xane have a hard enough time in this town without you turning us into sexual deviants."

"I'm not turning you into sexual deviants. I expect you to treat Danna with the respect she deserves and what ya'll do behind closed doors is your business, not the rest of the worlds."

There's a pause as everyone seems to digest what's been said. Then there's a noise of a door opening behind us. Zack emerges from the den.

"You guys are back early," he says, rubbing his face and yawning. "Did something happen?"

"You can say that again," Trent says.☐

19

I've never been so embarrassed as when Samuel explains that I'm staying with them because I want to fuck them all. Jackie is furious at that and waves her finger at him so rapidly that I'm worried it's going to fall off. I wait until everything's calmed down until I tell them that I'm going upstairs to pack my things.

"I don't want you to do that," Jackie says.

"Neither do we," the W triplets say.

"I just think it'll be for the best."

The other brothers glance around at each other. "Stay," Tommy says. His twin nods. Xsander and Xane raise their heads in agreement. York nods too. Samuel shifts his feet as though the whole situation is making him antsy. Zack is crouching down, tickling Ruffles under the chin.

I inhale deeply and pass my breath out through my nostrils in a whoosh, the way I was taught to do by my grief counselor. When I came here, I didn't imagine things turning out this way at all. I did wonder how they might take the idea of a harem when it eventually came out, but I hoped by that point I would have gotten to know them all well enough that they'd consider the idea. Can I expect that now?

"I'll leave you guys to discuss this," I say. "And you can tell me what you think in the morning."

Jackie pulls me into a fierce hug. "Sorry," she whispers in my ear. "Maybe I just should have told them from before."

As I leave the room, I feel many sets of eyes watching me go, and by the time I get halfway up the stairs, I have a massive lump in my throat.

I can hear raised voices from below, continuing to discuss the reason for my visit. I can still feel the coldness from Samuel's eyes, and I can't imagine how he'd ever come around to an idea that he's so vehemently against.

I close the door to my room behind me and slide down the door until I'm sitting on the soft, cream carpet with my face in my knees. As much as I knew this was a long shot, I'd been stupid enough to develop hopes that this could work. I already felt such a connection to so many of the brothers, even the ones I hadn't spent a lot of time with. Imagining that I might need to leave tomorrow with nothing to show for my trip is heartbreaking.

When we strive towards our dreams, failing seems so much more painful.

I reach for my phone in my purse and scan the home-screen. I'm expecting to see a message from Laura, but there isn't one. I consider calling her for advice, but I don't think I could speak to her without bursting into tears. I know if I do that, her momma-bear instincts will come rushing to the surface. She'll be jumping into her chauffeur-driven limo before I can object.

I've gotta admit that the idea of her coming to rescue me is really appealing, but it wouldn't be fair. She's got babies to look after, and ten men to keep happy. My heart sinks. There's no one else I can call to ask for advice. I wipe my eyes, tears threatening behind my closed lids. I take a shuddering breath in and swallow the lump from the throat. I really need to get a grip on myself.

I'm just about to get up off the floor and focus on getting myself ready for bed when there's a soft knock at the door. I'm expecting it to be Jackie, coming to check if I'm okay, but when I open the door, I find York.

"Hey," he says, looking awkward as he stuffs his hands into his pockets.

I wipe my eyes again as he studies me. I'm guessing that I look like I feel; upset and blotchy, sad and embarrassed.

"This is…it wasn't the best way for you to find out," I say holding the edge of the door for stability.

"Can I come in?" he asks.

I back up, allowing him into my room and watch as he closes the door behind himself.

"You must think I'm crazy," I say.

"I don't know what to think, but I wanted to talk to you rather than sit down there listing to my brothers go on and on."

"What do you want to know?" I take a seat on the bed and indicate to York that he can sit on the chair.

"I guess I want to understand why this is something you want."

Now there's a question.

"If I'm honest, I've loved reading ménage romances for a while; one woman and two men…it always just seemed so nice that she had two strong men to take care of her. Then I saw my friend get into this situation with the McGregor brothers. There are ten of them, and I could immediately see how amazing it is. They have so much fun together, and she has so much support. And from their family perspective, the future of the business is secured because they think as one unit. When your mom called me, I was wary because I knew this wasn't something that you all wanted. This was her idea of something that could make things better for you all, but then I thought I should go for it. I should try to find the thing that's going to make me happiest, even if it's a long shot."

"And you think you like us all enough to give it a try?" he asks.

I shrug. "I've been here for two days. I've spent time with some of you, but there is obviously a whole lot for us to find out about each other. I think if you guys were all willing to try that there's a possibility that I could…" I trail off because how do I phrase this next bit. What does a relationship need for it to work? Respect, compatibility, humor, love. These are the things that we would need to build together.

"You could?" York asks, leaning forward in his chair.

"I could develop feelings enough for you all to make it work."

He leans back again, his hands resting on his muscular, spread thighs. With his blonde, spikey hair and piercing blue eyes, he's a stunning picture to view.

And his body. Those strong arms developed through

genuine hard graft than vain gym attendance. Those hands that can heal, that chest that is broad enough to make me feel safe in exactly the way I need. York is a good man through and through.

"How does it work for your friend?" he asks. "You know…in practice."

For a minute I'm not sure what he's asking. They love each other, obviously, or else they wouldn't be on TV talking about their relationship. Then I realize that he's probably talking about the practicalities.

"They all live together in one suite."

"That must be a big suite to have so many bedrooms," York says.

My cheeks heat. "They have one bedroom."

York's eyes seem to flash brighter. "They all sleep together?"

"It works better that way. No jealousy or frustration. They all have access to Laura whenever they need her."

"And you'd be comfortable with that…with us?"

God. Do I really need to spell this out for him? I decide to take the bull by the horns as York digests the implications of my answer. "It's what I'm looking for."

"Have you shared a girl with anyone before?" I ask him. I'm surprised to see his cheeks pink and know pretty much that it's a no, even before he says it.

"I don't think that happens much around here…maybe in the city."

I shake my head. "Your brothers wouldn't agree." It's

time that he finds out what happened with Walker, Wade, and Samuel. I think it might help if he thought this was something his family was already indulging in.

"My brothers?"

"Walker, Wade, and Samuel," I say. I won't elaborate too much because as I add each name, York's eyes seem to widen. I don't mention William either because he was with me by himself.

"How do you know?" he asks. Oh hell. He hasn't quite realized that I mean they shared with me.

"Let's just say I had some personal experience last night."

York's eyebrows almost hit his hairline, and he shakes his head. "I should have made my move sooner."

I blush as his eyes scan my face and move down over my body. I don't know if he realizes how suggestive his gaze is or if the talk of sex has made him forget himself. All I know is that my nipples are aching to be sucked.

"There's no queue system," I say gently. "And as far as I'm concerned, there's no need for any bro-code about who's girl I am or who's marked their territory first. We're all grown-ups."

"You've got to understand, Danna, that this is a lot for us to take in. You're on board with it. You've had time to realize that this alternative lifestyle is what you want. We got on the train when it was traveling at full speed."

"I do understand, York."

"I'm not saying that…" He looks away, gazing at the black and white framed sketch on the wall. It's of two love-birds, their heads close, their eyes dreamy. "...that I'm not interested. Or that I'm bothered that you've..."

"Slept with your brothers?"

"Yeah."

"So what's stopping you?"

York inhales and exhales slowly. "My own concerns that this might end in tears."

"Whose tears?" If he's worried about me, I'd find it cute but infuriating too. I'm a grown woman who can make my own decisions, and I certainly don't need him to be fussing over my potential heartache.

"Who knows," he says. "What you're proposing has so many people involved that it's hard to see how it could possibly end well."

Now I could spend the next half an hour debating the pros and cons with York, and we'd get nowhere fast. I get the feeling that he's not the biggest 'take a risk' kind of guy in this house, but I can also tell that he's interested. If he wasn't, he wouldn't have excused himself from the debate downstairs to follow me up here.

I decide that it's time to take things into my own hands, so I get to my feet and make my way over to where he's sitting. York immediately sits up straighter, watching me with interest. When I'm in front of him, I bend, resting my hands on his knees. I watch the pupils in his eyes enlarge as I lean in. I think he's expecting me to kiss him, but I put my mouth close to his ear. "Are you worried about getting hurt, York. Is that what this is?" He shakes his head. "Are you worried about me getting hurt?" He shakes his head again. "Then what are you worried about?"

"My brothers; Samuel and Zack."

I pull back because I'm so surprised, then take two steps backward while I contemplate what he's said. Zack I can understand, but Samuel. "Why?" I ask.

"They have issues," he says. "With trust."

"And you think this situation would hurt them?"

"I worry that others will run before they can walk…some of them already have…and the others will be left too far behind."

I nod, and York stands, coming closer and placing his hand on my upper arm. "I like you, Danna," he says. "I felt an attraction to you when I first saw you and felt a connection after we spent time together yesterday. I don't know exactly how I feel about this crazy idea you've cooked up with my mom, but I think I'm willing to dip a toe in to see if it could work."

"Just I toe?" I ask, smiling.

York snorts with laughter. "Maybe more than a toe!"

We gaze at each other with a new understanding, and for the first time since Joe's, I feel a glimmer of hope. I have at least one Jackson brother on side for trying out my crazy idea. I have three who've already dipped more than a toe in the water.

The rest…well, who knows.

For now, I'm not planning on leaving.

And as York leans in to kiss my lips, I allow myself to enjoy the moment.

A perfect kiss to end a not so perfect day.

20

York is a true gentleman, and he knows how to kiss.

And if things weren't quite so precarious, I would have pushed things further and faster. As it stands, that's all we do; enjoy a very erotic and tender kiss that has me standing on tip-toes and leaning in, even as he's pulling away.

Then, York excuses himself to rejoin the discussion downstairs.

So, I'm here getting myself ready for bed, without the desperate feeling of despondency I had before he came to talk with me.

I put on my cute white satin pajama shorts set that's trimmed with lace, and I settle into bed.

I send Laura a message that says 'my secret is out...will tell you more tomorrow,' and then I turn off the bedside lamp.

Voices are still audible from downstairs, and it's so frustrating not being able to hear the discussion. After five minutes of straining to listen to the odd word, I decide that enough is enough. Sliding out of bed, I pad to the door and make my way to the stairs, taking a seat at the top. The entrance to the kitchen is open, and I can finally hear what's being said. Now, working out who is saying what might be a little trickier.

"I just don't get it, mom. Why didn't you speak to us before inviting the poor girl?"

"Because I knew there would be some of you who would reject the idea out of hand," Jackie says. "And I was right, wasn't I?"

"So what was the point if you knew that? You think that us seeing Danna and spending time with her was going to convert us to believe that this thing could work?"

"Yes, I did. Or at least, I hoped. And it's worked, I gather. For some of you at least."

"This is just some girl with a fucked up fantasy. She's probably had a fucked up childhood and thinks that this is going to solve all her problems. Or she's after our ranch. I mean, this just isn't normal."

"Why? Because it's something that you don't see every day?" Jackie says. "Or maybe it's just something you see in porn and not as a healthy relationship situation. If you watched the show, then you'd understand how amazing the McGregor family are and how well it's worked for them. They were my inspiration for thinking that this could be a possibility."

"You know I don't watch shit like that," another voice says.

"You boys need to watch your language. I understand that you're riled up, but it's no excuse for dropping the manners I taught you. You might be angry with me, but

I'm still your momma, and I expect to be treated respectfully, whatever the circumstances."

There's a rumble of 'sorry,' and my heart swells at how good these boys are to their mom. Some of them might have distorted images of what I am, but that's not surprising, given the circumstances.

"I just feel like you've brought Danna here under false pretenses."

"Danna knew exactly what the situation was, and she wants this enough to put herself on the line to try. All I'm asking is for you to do the same."

"You're asking us to become the laughing stocks of Broadsville."

"You think we'll ever be able to go into Joe's again?"

I think the last two were Tommy and Trent and I rest my head against the way as I wait for Jackie to respond.

"I think, boys, that if Joe's is the only thing that you have to worry about, then this is a done deal. Half the men in that place are desperate, and the other half are there to escape from their wives. You think their opinions matter?"

"I think that I don't want to be the subject of gossip, mom," Samuel says.

"You already are, Sammie," she says. "Everybody knows about the girl you go to visit, or at least, they know that's the story you tell. The rest speculate about whether you're using it as a cover story and are actually gay."

"What the fuck?" Samuel snarls. "My life is my business. Where do other people get off saying shit like that about me."

"Language," Jackie reminds him. "And you know it doesn't bother me either way, I'm just saying that none of you is whiter than white." There's another rumble as the boys take in what Jackie's saying. "Have you even thought about how much courage it must have taken Danna to come here and try this. Have you thought about how she must be feeling up there, waiting for you all to debate the pros and cons of starting a relationship with her?"

"She's wobbly," York says. "Even though she's saying she doesn't regret this I can tell she's wavering."

"And if you let her go, then you've not got the sense I tried to raise you with," Jackie says.

"It's better if she goes now," Samuel says. "She's not really serious about any of this. She might say she is, but when push comes to shove…when she realizes how tough it is to be a rancher's wife, she'll be running back to her easy city life."

"I don't agree," I softer voice says. I think it's Zack. "She got really stuck into helping me with the fences the other day. I expected her to sit around a watch, but she wanted to do it all."

Samuel scoffs. "That was one day, Zack. Not a lifetime."

"But it's not up to us to judge Danna, is it? On two days? She's here with an open mind and an open heart, and we're down here debating on whether she can hack it on a ranch. It's not like we need her out there shoveling shit, is it? We've got enough labor."

The room goes quiet as everyone takes in what Zack says. I get the feeling that he doesn't often stand up to his brother that way.

Jackie clears her through, and I can hear footsteps on the wooden floor. "I think you all need to get to bed. None of this needs to be decided immediately. Sleep on it. Things have a habit of appearing much simpler in the morning."

"I'm not changing my mind," Samuel says.

"Well, in the end, that's your prerogative," Jackie says. "But I think you need to open up, Samuel."

Chairs scrape the floor, and I can hear the Jackson brothers coming close to the bottom of the stairs. I scramble to my feet and dash back to my room, closing the door as softly as I can.

I dive into bed, my heart beating fast. Nothing's been resolved, but I still feel heartened. Zack spoke up for me, and I feel so happy that he's seen me for what I am.

As for Samuel, I have no idea what his problem is, but I'm determined to find out.

I'm just about to drop off to sleep when there's a rustle at my door. I turn and see a slip of paper sliding underneath. I hear the soft pad of steps as whoever was there retreats. Only when there's a click of a door closing, do I get up to read the note.

Danna, you're coming out with us tomorrow. Don't forget to set your alarm. Xsander and Xane.

Well, I guess I'm here for at least another day.

21

When my alarm goes off, I'm in such a deep sleep that my heart rushes, and I'm so stunned I knock my phone from the nightstand in panic. It's only when I finally manage to turn it off that I remember where I am.

This really is the ass crack of dawn.

Maybe Samuel is right. Maybe I'm not rancher's wife material.

It takes a quick shower to unglue my eyes, and I'm in such desperate need for coffee that I'm almost in the kitchen before I remember what I'm about to face. There's a rumble of male voices, but it definitely isn't as loud as previous mornings.

As I enter the room, a hush settles. Oh, God. This is so embarrassing.

I keep my eyes down and slide into my spot, quickly taking some toast. Each bite is like sand in my throat. Jackie passes me a coffee and gives me a smile that looks apologetic. I don't want her to feel guilty about this anymore.

Some of the boys start to leave, saying mumbled goodbyes. I glance up and catch York smiling as he passes. Walker, Wade, and William smile too. Zack is opposite me, but he's also keeping his eyes down.

This is the most awkward situation I have ever found myself in.

I'm taking final bites of breakfast as the room empties except for Xsander and Xane and Jackie.

Jackie sighs loudly. "Well, I'm glad that's over," she says, beginning to clear the dishes.

I glance between Xsander and Xane, but their expressions don't really give anything away. "You ready to go?" Xane asks.

I nod, swigging back the last of my coffee.

"We're going, Mom," Xsander says, heading towards the mudroom.

"You boys look after our guest," Jackie says sternly. "You make Danna feel right at home, you hear me?"

I follow them feeling like the new girl at school with the two popular kids who would rather be anywhere else than showing me around. At this rate, the day is going to be a washout of uncomfortable silences and unease.

But when we get in the truck, it isn't like that.

"Danna, we're sorry about...last night and this morning," Xane says softly.

"It's just, nobody really knows what to say," Xsander adds.

"You mean now that you know I'm here to interview

you as husbands," I say with a totally straight face. There's a classic moment of silence, and then I burst into laughter. From the backseat, I can see their shoulders relaxing. "I got you, didn't I?" I laugh.

"Yeah…the word husband isn't something I've ever applied to myself," Xsander says.

"Or me," Xane agrees.

"Shall we just start with seeing if we get on," I say. "And if we do, we can move on to whether we find each other attractive. And if that goes okay too, then we can see if that attraction leads to the right chemistry and then…"

"Yeah, maybe just leave it there," Xsander says. "Or I'm not going to be able to get out of this truck any time soon."

Xane chuckles and his brother puts the truck into gear.

"So, what is it that you guys do?" I ask.

"We oversee crop production," Xane says. "We grow all our own feed for our livestock rather than buy it in."

"And we also grow some produce to sell."

"Wow," I say. "So you're the green-fingered ones."

Xane laughs. "More like brown fingered." He holds up his hands and wiggles his fingers.

"Everything's very industrial these days," Xsander says. "We just follow a plan."

"Wow," I say. "I'm looking forward to seeing what goes into it all. The closest I've gotten to growing anything is some beans and tomatoes in the yard, and to be honest, my momma did most of the hard work."

"Our momma has a garden too. She likes to grow what she can for us to eat."

"Your momma's a superwoman. I don't know where she gets all her energy from."

"Neither do we," the boys say in unison. It seems they are agreed on something.

We spend the morning inspecting crops, and I get left to my own devices quite a lot because Xsander and Xane have to have long and in-depth discussions with their workers, checking on what's been sprayed and watered, and how much growth has taken place since the last review.

I lay on the grass in a quiet spot, listening to the calming rustle of the cornfield next to me and soaking up the sun. My day with Zack was active, and I enjoyed it, but after last night's drama and my restless sleep, I'm feeling completely exhausted and in need of some rest.

By the time it's lunchtime, I am absolutely famished despite my lack of physical exertion. Xsander opens the back of the truck and then grabs the paper bags that Jackie handed to him on our way out.

We sit in a row, me in the middle, eating our doorstep sandwiches like we're in grade school. The sun is shining, and the birds are singing, and even though I'm probably eating dirt from my hands right now, I can't remember feeling this content.

"Your mom makes a good sandwich," I say with my mouth still half full. The cheese is tangy and mature, and the ham is thick and salty. There's pickle too; probably something homemade.

"Everything tastes better if you eat it in the open air

after a hard day's graft," Xsander says.

I nod even though they're the only ones who've actually done any grafting today.

"So, you gonna explain this thing to us," Xane says out of the blue.

"What thing?"

"The ten men thing." He takes a small bite of his sandwich. For some reason, his lunch looks different from mine.

I reach for the paper towel in my lap and dab my lips. "What do you want to know?"

"Why so many?" Xsander says. "I would have thought that part of the question would have been obvious."

I shrug. "We look at monogamous partnerships like they're the only way to live. In the western world, I guess that's all we really see, outside of the odd faith that advocates one man to more than one woman, but in other societies, there are other ways to live, and there have been throughout history."

I turn from side to side, trying to read their expressions. What did they think I was going to say? That I have a thing about gang bangs! Well, that's something to discuss another day, me thinks!

"You know that there is a tribe where all women have more than one husband. I can't remember where it is, but they live on the side of a mountain and need more than one man working to support each family unit."

"So is that what you're looking for. Multiple men for security."

"This is not financial," I say. They really need to understand that because the last thing I want is for them to think that I'm after their ranch. "I'm an only child, and I've always felt like there needed to be more noise, more fun, more love."

"But ten. That's a pretty big increase," Xane says.

I nod and shrug. "I guess, and I probably never would have considered it if it wasn't for my friend."

"The friend on the show?" Xsander asks.

"Yeah."

Xsander grabs a beer from the back of the truck, flicks off the lid and passes it to me. I pass it on to Xane but shakes his head. "I can't drink," he says. "I'll just have water." Xsander is already passing his brother a bottle of cool, spring water.

"How come?"

"I've got Crohn's disease," he says. "I just have to be careful."

"Is that why you have the different bread?" I point to his half-eaten sandwich.

Xane nods. "Mom bakes gluten free bread for me. It's better for my gut." He sips the water and goes back to eating his sandwich slowly, chewing every bite.

"But you don't have it?" I ask Xsander who's drinking his beer like it's the last one on the planet.

He shakes his head. "Who knows why. We're identical except for that."

"He could get it," Xane says. "I keep telling him to

look after himself."

"If I do, I do," Xsander says flippantly.

Xane shakes his head. "You see…we need a woman around to keep Xsand in line."

"I think you do," I say. "Seriously, dude. Why are you doing stuff that could make you sick?"

"We only have one life," Xsander says. "I want to live mine to the full."

Xane shakes his head. "You see this is where our identical twinness just doesn't sync. Drinking beer and eating normal bread isn't my idea of living life to the full."

"Or mine," Xsander says. "Not really. But what chance do we have to do the things we want. We're tied to this ranch with leashes, and we're never getting away."

For a moment I'm shocked at what Xsander said. I don't know why I assumed that all ten of the Jackson brothers would be happy to continue the legacy their father built here. I know that some of the McGregor brother didn't want to work in the management team of McGregor corps. Donnie wanted to be an artist, and Elliot wanted to be a personal trainer. I also know that Laura has done her utmost to encourage them all to pursue their outside interests as much as they can. The day job doesn't have to be all there is, although I guess living on this ranch is more inhibiting than living in the city.

"What would you want to do if you could?" I ask.

"Football," they both say in unison. It seems that they can agree on that.

"You play?" I ask.

"Used to," Xane says. "It's difficult for me. I don't have the physical strength that I had in college."

I look Xane overtaking in his broad shoulders and muscular chest and arms. Yes, he's a little leaner than his brother, but he's still packing some power in that gorgeous body of his.

"Xane was being scouted before he got sick," Xsander says proudly.

"So were you," Xane says.

"I know. But I wasn't going to go anywhere without you, and you know it."

There are moments when I feel a real ache for a sibling bond, and this is one of them. To see two brothers who are so dedicated to each other, even in the face of adversity and disappointment, is heartening and sad all rolled into one. Xsander had a chance to do the thing he loved, but he stayed with his twin. I don't see any resentment there either. Just frustration that they're not both doing what they really love.

"So you just quit?" I ask.

Xane nods. "For a while, I was in the hospital. Then, when momma sorted out my diet and supplements, I started to get better. I'm as strong as I've been since my diagnosis."

"And you?"

Xsander shakes his head. "I still play for a local team, but it's just to kill time and keep fit."

"Well, that's great. At least it's still a part of your life."

"I guess."

We all sit staring out over the landscape, watching as the clouds pass overhead driven by the wind. The sun warms my skin like a balm, but beneath the calm, I'm restless. I need to know where these boys stand on being part of my harem. I jump down off the truck and turn to face them both. Being able to see their expressions is essential when you're discussing a topic that is so out there.

"So, what do you think of the reason I'm here?" I say.

Xane smiles. "You don't beat around the bush, do you?"

I shrug and shake my head. "Doesn't seem much point. We're all adults. We all know the score."

"I think you're crazy," Xsander says. "I mean, these guys are my brothers and we've all grown up together, so I love them more than I love myself, but why anyone would want to put up with all of us I have no idea. You're a glutton for punishment if you're seriously considering this."

Xane chuckles. "Do you know how much washing needs to get done in this place? How much food needs preparing? How many beds need changing?"

"That's not something that's gonna put me off," I say.

"And do you have any idea how much sex you'd need to be partaking in?" Xsander says with a wicked gleam in his soft gray eyes.

"Xsand," Xane says. "Chill out. You can't say shit like that to our guest."

"Why the hell not? Danna wants to get real, so I'm getting real. You think you could take ten men's physical needs."

I put my hands on my hips and cock my head to one side. "Are you asking me if I have a high sex drive?"

Xane eyes drop, a flush spreading over his caramel skin. Xsander, on the other hand, meets my gaze and doesn't look away. "That's exactly what I'm asking you?"

"I'm horny pretty much twenty-four-seven," I say. "Now as to whether I could physically take you all one after the other, I have no idea. But I want to try and I'm pretty sure it's something my body would get used to after a while."

Xsander's grin gets wider with every word. "You know, in college, me and Xane used to get all these freaky girls wanting us to double team them. I think it must be a twin thing."

Xane looks at his brother. "You seriously going to share now?"

"Well, it's kind of relevant, don't you think?"

Xane shakes his head. "You know you're unbelievable sometimes."

"So you got a thing for twins too, Danna?" Xsander's grin is now megawatt, his beautifully straight, white teeth glinting like in the toothpaste commercials.

"Who knows," I say. "I like what I see but I the proof of the pudding is in the eating."

"Hell yeah," Xsander says.

He jumps down off the truck and comes to stand close to me. I gaze up at him, the sparkle in his eyes making me wet between my legs. I don't know what it is about cheekiness in a man that has me reeling. Xsander is cocky to the bone.

"I wanna taste," he says, leaning in as though he gonna kiss me. Just before his lips touch mine, he pauses. "Why do I get the feeling that you're trouble, Danna?"

"I don't know. I get the same feeling about you," I say.

"Well, you're definitely right about me," he says, his lips brushing mine as his hand finds my waist. "Am I right about you?"

"You'll have to wait and find out," I say, brushing his lips with mine. It's the most teasing kiss I've ever had, as though neither of us wants to show that we're too interested.

"Fuck," Xane mutters from behind. "You guys seriously gonna do this out here?"

Xsander doesn't seem to hear, though. His hand is sliding up my side, his thumb caressing the softness of my belly as it travels higher. I shiver as his palm cups my breast, squeezing gently before he finally deepens the kiss. I get lost in the sensation of his tongue sliding over mine, marveling at the mesmerizing rhythm of his hand and mouth. Knowing his twin is watching too just adds to the heat. I'm not expecting Xane to join in. Up until this point, he's been pretty reserved, but I guess seeing his brother making a move has motivated him to do the same. I hear his feet thud on the ground and the heat of his body as he closes in behind me. His cock is already hard as he presses against my ass, his hand sliding under my top to find the nub of my nipple through the sheer fabric of my bra. I moan against Xsander's lips, and that seems to be all the permission he needs to cup my pussy over my jeans and press. Oh god, that feels good. I'm so wet and achy there, my mind imagining his fingers slipping over my clit and then deeper inside me. But we're outside, and this isn't the place...or is it.

It could be. The cabin of the truck is big enough for sure.

Shit. Even thinking about fucking these brothers out here has me panting.

"You wet, baby?" Xsander asks, his soft lips tugging my bottom lip tantalizingly.

I nod, and Xane groans from behind. "You see what you've gone and done."

"You want us to fuck you?" Xsander asks. I open my eyes and look between him and Xane. They both have the fire in their eyes that only comes with sex, and a heat to their bodies that's making me sweat. I know exactly what I want to say. YES! YES! A thousand times, YES! And I can tell from the hardness of their cocks and the way their chests are rising and falling fast that this is exactly what they want, too. But is it the right thing to do?

There's always that question about sex, even when you're in a relationship that's building towards love. Sex isn't just a physical act. It holds emotional risk and an element of power exchange too. My momma told me that women feel differently about sex than men. Her theory was that because we have to accept a man inside ourselves that we feel the impact of sex more. Her most significant warning to me about sex was to always think carefully about what I was hoping to achieve through doing it.

I know what I want to achieve here; physical closeness

with these men, pleasure, and connection. I want it to show them that we can work together and that my idea has a chance to bring them what they need from a relationship with a woman.

But is doing it in the middle of a field in a dirty working truck the right thing?

I have so few days and who knows if I'll get another opportunity.

My momma also told me to seize every day and suck all the life out of it that I can. She was close to the end, and I suppose she must have been thinking about the things she didn't do in her life.

Will I regret taking this step with Xsander and Xane?

I don't think so. This could be the start of our life together, or it could be a holiday interlude. Who knows? Either way, it'll be a hot memory to warm me up on colder days in my future.

I take hold of both of them by the t-shirt and nod towards the truck. "Maybe with a little more privacy," I say.

The twins waste no time. Xsander picks me up and tosses me over his shoulder, striding towards the truck faster than anyone should be able to with my weight in their arms.

Xane shakes his head and tuts. "Always with the grand gestures," he says. I'm grinning from ear to ear, loving the way they relate to each other and to me.

"Haven't you learned yet that women love grand gestures?"

There's another eye roll from Xane, but he's already tugging his tee over his head, revealing tight pecs and what looks like an eight pack. I mean, is that even a thing. There's a large scar across his abdomen too, maybe surgery for his condition, but it doesn't detract from his sexiness. In a way, it just makes him hotter. When you hit an obstacle and survive to tell the tale, you become a stronger and more rounded person. Xane has a maturity which I love and is a perfect contrast to his twin's impetuousness.

Xsander throws the door open and drops me to my feet.

"In the truck, missy," he says patting my ass. I scramble in, barely getting time to adjust before they're either side of me, slamming the doors closed. The truck's seats are thrown back. "Who do you want to ride first, baby," Xsander says lazily, his eyes heavy-lidded.

"You want me to pick?" I say.

"It should be easy," he says. "We're pretty much identical."

"That's not the point," I say. "I'm not down with showing favoritism."

"How about you toss a coin?" Xane says, fishing around in the pocket of his jeans.

"Good idea," I say.

"How about you toss me," Xsander says. His jeans are open, and his hand is already wrapped around his cock. And what a cock it is. Damn. It's a thing of wonder. Thick and straight and big enough to hurt just a little.

"Guess correct it's him, guess wrong it's me," Xane says.

As he tosses the coin, I wrap my hand around Xsander's cock and stroke it. His eyes drift closed, the heat of his cock warming my palm.

"Heads," I say.

Xane shows me the coin. It's tails.

"Looks like you need to drop that cock and hop on this one," he says, unbuckling his belt and pushing his jeans and boxers down just enough to reveal it. These twins are as identical between their legs as they are everywhere else. I push down my leggings, toeing off my boots at the same time. I don't even get my panties off before Xane is hauling me into his lap.

"If you were looking for lovey-dovey romantic sex, this is gonna be a fucking disappointment," he says, tugging my hips, so I'm pressed against his cock. His eyes drop closed too as I move back and forth, the pressure through my panties just perfect to get me hot. I know that I'm going to need to be pretty wet to take them both without making myself too sore to sit down for dinner later. Xane's hands slide beneath my top, and he undoes the front clasp of my bra, allowing my breasts to spill free. Hot, rough fingers tease my nipples. I lean in to kiss him, and warm lips tease against mine too. It's lazy and slow and tortuous, and it doesn't take long for him to put his hand between us and yank my panties to the side.

"Fuck," he says, staring at where I'm pink and wet, sliding the head of his cock over my swollen clit.

"You gonna fuck her or what?" Xsander asks.

"You're just a sore loser," Xane says grinning. His finger presses inside me, testing. "She's tight, bro. I've gotta give her time to warm up."

"She's warm," Xsander says. "She'll slide onto your cock like a glove onto a hand."

"Nice analogy," I say, raising myself up until I'm poised over the tip of Xane's big cock. "Let's see who's right."

I let my weight do the work, pressing me down slowly. I can feel my pussy spreading to take Xane's girth, that delicious feeling of penetration making me want to grunt. "Fuck," I mutter.

"You struggling, baby?" Xsander asks. He shifts closer, lifting my top and latching onto my nipple with his hot mouth. He sucks hard, his eyes fixed on mine as Xane's finger finds my clit and circles it maddeningly slow. I hold onto Xane's shoulder for stability, raising up and dropping down again. Each time I do this, Xane gets a little deeper, and I get a little wetter, and between us all, I finally get him deep enough to count.

"Fuck," I say again. "You're really huge."

"That's what all the girls say," Xsander laughs.

"Dude, it's not the time to be talking about other girls, right now," Xane says.

I lean in to kiss him for that, even though I know they are both messing around. I move slowly at first, grinding my clit against the rough patch of hair surrounding Xane's cock. It's perfect stimulation.

"There's only one girl for you to think about now," I say grinding my hips.

"Yeah," Xane says.

"That's it," Xsander says, his hand on my ass. "Fuck my brother good."

"I'll fuck you good too," I say, sliding my hand over his face.

"Yeah you will," he says.

There can't be anything sexier than fucking Xane while Xsander talks dirty and guides me into a rhythm he believes will please his brother. Around us, the birds are still calling, and the wind blows softly through the open windows of the truck, and I feel free in a way that I haven't in a long time. What I'm doing might appear foolish to some, but it doesn't feel that way. These boys are good men with so much love for each other and for their family. They've made sacrifices to stay on this ranch and leave behind their dreams for the greater good. They're fun and sweet and cheeky in all the best ways, and my actions feel right.

Absolutely right.

Xane's hand's snake to my hips, tugging me harder and faster. I can feel his cock swelling inside me, his cheeks flushing in that way that shows me he's getting close. The deeper penetration and increased friction are good for me too. I arch my back as Xsander pinches my nipple again, the nerve ending connecting to my clit in a way that has me moaning. "Oh…" I gasp. "Don't stop. I'm gonna…"

I don't manage to get the words out before I'm coming, my pussy clamping down in waves on Xane's huge cock. I'm momentarily paralyzed with the ecstasy, my body too rung out to continue. Xane pulls himself from inside me and in three strokes he's coming in thick ribbons across his belly. The groan he makes is too much; deep guttural pleasure that comes from a place deeper than you can find in any way other than through sex, and watching him come like this is so intimate.

"Fuck," Xsander says. "That was hot."

Xane doesn't move. With his eyes tightly shut, he's locked inside the moment.

"Come on then girl, let's have you." Xsander pats my leg and takes my hand.

Moving from Xane's lap to his brothers isn't easy in the confined space, but I manage it. He pulls me close and kisses me hard, his arousal and frustration are evident. "Did you like fucking my brother?" he murmurs against my ear. I nod, and he chuckles. "Are you ready to fuck me now?" I nod again and feel him shiver at my response. For all his bravado, Xsander isn't as in control as I was expecting.

He does the same as Xane, taking hold of his cock and sliding it over my clit and through my wet folds. I'm practically dripping by the time he notches into my entrance.

"Look at me," he says. He takes my hands and places them on his shoulders. His hands take me by the waist. He holds my gaze as he slides inside me, taking full control of my body even though I'm the one on top. "That's it," he says as I slide down his huge cock. I know I've just fucked a cock that's almost identical to this one, but it's still a struggle to get him deep inside me. He watches the penetration. "Your pussy feels so tight."

"You thought I would have fucked her open," Xane says lazily. He's smiling when I turn to him.

"Pretty much," Xsander says.

I clamp down my pelvic floor, grasping his cock as hard as my pussy can and Xsander groans. "Fuck, do that again."

I pulse my pussy, and he closes his eyes. "Damn," he mutters. I start to move, and his fingers dig into the flesh of my hips, grasping me to come close with each thrust. "That's it," he says. "That's it."

I roll my hips in the way that Xane seemed to love, and Xsander moans like his brother. I'm getting close when Xsander has other ideas.

"Hang on a minute," he says. "Flip over."

I scramble off him into the space between him and his brother and Xsander somehow gets on top of me. He pushes in deep and fast, hooking his arms beneath my knees and spreading me wide. It's sexy as fuck to be beneath such a big and powerful man. Sexier still when Xane takes my hand and wraps it around his cock. He's hard again, his eyes rolling as I stroke while his brother pounds into my pussy.

"Oh," I gasp, the reality of a second orgasm almost too much for me. Xane's finger slides between us, finding my tender clit and circling tantalizingly slow.

I'm going to be ruined forever after this week. If these brothers decide that my plan is ridiculous, how would I ever go back to regular vanilla sex again?

Sex with one can be good, but sex with two is fantastic. Laura tells me sex with ten is mind-blowing, and I really hope I get to find out before I have to return to normality.

"You gonna come on my big cock?" Xsander asks. His breath is coming in pants, his abs rippling with every undulation of his hips. My free hand goes to his ass, tugging him into more aggressive thrusts that hit me just right inside.

"I'm gonna come so hard," I say because I am. I really

am. "Oh my…"

This orgasm comes from a place deep inside and hits me like a ton of bricks. Xsander doesn't stop, though, using the pulses from my orgasm to trigger his own. Like his brother, he doesn't come inside me but withdraws and covers my stomach. There is something so unbelievably sexy about this. The heat of it. The sheer release. And the weakness in a man at this moment. Xsander's hand trembles, his thighs quivering. Xane groans too.

It's a moment of pure surrender.

I don't know what I imagined the aftermath of this would be. The surroundings are hardly romantic or comfortable, but Xsander and Xane clean me up, help me find my clothes and spend time telling me how amazing I am. There are kisses and affection and laughter too.

But work is calling.

One thing is for sure, this will go down as my best lunch break ever!

22

The rest of the day passes quickly, but I'm dead on my feet. I don't know how these boys can keep going after the sex we had. All I want to do after is curl up and sleep.

On the way back to the house, Xsander squeezes my knee. "You're alright," he says.

"What does that mean?"

"It means you're cool. On a level."

I put my hand over my heart. "Why thank you, Xsand. I'm so happy that you think I'm cool."

"That's high praise from him," Xane says.

Xsander laughs. "It is actually."

"But what does it actually mean?" I ask.

"It means, I'm game for giving your crazy plan a shot," he says. "You handled us well. You're funny and cute, and you've got enough sass to keep me on my toes. When I think about getting back inside that hot, sweet pussy of yours..."

"All the necessary traits then," Xane laughs.

"I'm not a complicated man, as you know, bro."

I'm grinning from ear to ear. "What about you, Xane?"

He throws his arm around my shoulder, tugging me against his chest and planting a firm kiss on my head. "I'm not a crazy man," he says. "I know something good when it drops into my lap, and I'm not about to pass you up no matter what anybody says."

"Guys!" I squeeze both of their thighs in happiness. "This has been the best day ever."

"Better than the one you spent with William, Walker, and Wade?" Xsander asks. He turns away from the road for long enough for me to see that wicked gleam back in his eyes.

"You know about that?" I don't know why I'm surprised. Boys talk, especially about sex.

"Fuck, yeah. They've been singing your praises ever since."

"Ah, so you already had a review and recommendation," I say.

"Pretty much, but I only take those with a pinch of salt."

"You should trust your brothers more," I say. "That'll be important if I manage to convince the rest of them to give this a go."

"Don't forget you have mom on your side," Xane says. "Never underestimate the power that a mother has over her sons."

"Well, I wouldn't want to think that you were bowing to pressure from Jackie," I say. "I want you to get into this with your eyes firmly open."

"And our jeans, too," Xsander laughs.

"Well, that helps," I say.

We're pulling up at the front of the house, but the boys don't get out immediately. Xsander takes my hand and brings it to his lips. "Danna, baby. This has been a day that I won't forget in a hurry."

Xane moves my hair from my shoulder and kisses my neck. "It was pretty damned special," he says.

It was, and it is. These men continue to show me just how lucky I could be if only the rest of them can see how fantastic harem living could be.

Just as we're about to get out of the truck, William, Walker, and Wade pull up next to us.

"Hey," Walker calls through the window. "You have a good day with these reprobates?"

"They know how to show a lady a good time," I say, not missing the raised eyebrows and questioning gazes.

"Well, that's…great," Walker says.

We all slide out of the trucks, and the boys usher me first. I'm not sure if they're being gentlemanly or they want to exchange hand signal and winks behind me. I guess I'm going to need to get used to being discussed with so many men around.

I've never been so grateful to be handed a cup of

coffee and presented with a delicious homemade blueberry muffin. Jackie really knows how to look after her boys and her guests. She's going to be a tough act to follow for sure.

"So how was your day, sweetie?" she asks.

"Great," I say. "We achieved a lot." I give her a quick wink, and she looks so pleased I want to hug her.

"And my boys looked after you?" she says, handing muffins to Xsander and Xane.

"They were brilliant," I say.

"I'm sure they were," a voice says from the corner. Samuel is sitting there with a stack of paperwork in front of him.

"Less of that," Jackie warns.

"Is it okay if I take this up?" I ask. "I want to clean up and make a call."

"Sure," Jackie says.

So I wave my bye's to the boys and head to my room. I devour my muffin while responding to Laura's message. I tell her 'two more down' and get a smiley face in reply. After a speedy shower, I dress and finish my coffee, catching up on some email notices from college. The reality of how little time I have left before I need to return to normality hits me.

When there's a knock on my door, I'm not worried about who it might be. I know I can handle whoever might be out there. When I see that it's York, I decide to take the bull by the horns, grabbing him by the shirt and tugging him into the room. I don't even let him speak before I kiss him. His hair is still damp from the shower, and he smells too deliciously fresh for me to let him go. He allows me to lead for a while, but then he takes control, backing me towards the wall and grabbing hold of my wrists. When I'm pinned, he pulls back, his piercingly blue eyes scanning my face.

"Danna," he says. "We don't…" He pauses, his chest rising and falling rapidly.

"We don't what?" I ask.

"We don't have to move so fast," he says.

I'm momentarily stunned because speed hasn't seemed to be an issue for any of his brothers. In fact, they seemed to have loved the pace. "You don't want to?" I ask.

"It's not that," he says. "It's definitely not that." York takes one of my hands and presses it against his huge erection. No, there is certainly no problems in that department."

"So, what is it?"

"I just…want to hang out a bit first."

"Oh," I say. "Okay."

He releases my wrists and takes a step back. There's a moment of silence that's awkward as hell, then he asks if I wanna watch some TV with him? Well, I wasn't expecting that, but it turns out that he likes the same shows as me. We settle on my bed, and I let him have the remote. We laugh at the same jokes, and I love that we share the same humor. We start off sitting with a little gap between us then slowly his fingers wrap through mine and then a little later his arm goes around my shoulders. When he strokes the sensitive skin of my neck, I can't help but shiver, and when he turns to kiss me, I'm so relaxed and ready that it's bliss.

"I don't want to rush things with you," he says, between gentle kisses that make me melt.

"I know," I say running my fingers through his hair and kissing the soft skin above his cropped beard. "But I'm not here for long."

He sighs. "Time is the worst kind of pressure," he says.

"And the best," I say. "If we didn't know that time was ticking, we'd never have any pressure to move forward."

"That's true." He strokes the soft waves of my hair that have fanned out over the pillows. "I just wish we had more."

"I know…but I'm trying not to think that way. I'm trying to seize the day, make the most of every moment. We never know when it could be our last."

York nods and his eyes seem to glaze a little. Is he thinking about his parents? I know I'm thinking about momma. He trails his hand over my shoulder and upper arm, then back, glancing the top of my breast. "You're intoxicating," he says. "Clever and funny and full of life. When you're next to me, I feel like anything's possible."

"It is," I say. "All we have to do is hope and try."

His mouth finds mine again, the softest ghost of a kiss that he deepens slowly until my toes are curling. When his hand finds my breast, it's with a gentle squeeze. I'm the one who tugs him on top of me, relishing the weight of him, the solid press of his muscular body against my soft, femininity.

His cock is rock hard between my legs, pressing where

I'm hot and wet and aching. The sex I had earlier with York's twin brothers only serving to make me want more. I wonder if he knows about the others, and if he does, how does he feel about it? Jealous enough to want to claim me for himself. Turned on at the idea of pushing his cock inside a place that his brothers have already been. There's a definite edge of taboo here, increasing with every Jackson brother that I fuck.

I can't imagine what it would be like to have them all at the same time. The eyes on me. The sheer number of men who'd want me to serve them their pleasure. My pussy flutters just thinking about it. How many times could I come? It was never a question that I asked before this week, but now, I can't stop thinking about it.

"You're beautiful," he says between kisses, then he pushes himself until he's kneeling between my legs gazing down at me. My skirt has shifted up and over my thighs, revealing the black lace panties, I'm wearing. His eyes are fixed between my legs.

"You can take my panties off," I say.

York's eyes meet mine. "You take them off," he says.

I don't hesitate, tugging them over my ass and past my thighs. When they get to my knees, he takes over, then frantically starts undressing, unbuttoning his shirt and removing his jeans in record time. I'm practically salivating by the time he's revealed himself; gorgeous tan skin and a dusting of light brown hair over his chest and down in the happiest of trails into his boxers. "Everything," I say. "No point leaving those on when the good stuff is behind them."

York grins. I think he likes my cheekiness, which is good because I'm not planning on changing for anyone, but he's definitely a little shy which is sexy as hell.

There are definite benefits to having multiple men in your life, each one able to fulfil a different fantasy or need.

York certainly doesn't have anything to be shy about. His cock is perfect; long and thick with just the gentlest of curves. I reach out to stroke him, loving the way his eyes drop closed and his hands fall to his thighs. He lets me have complete control, his pose one of total surrender.

I touch myself at the same time, and when he finally opens his eyes, they flash with fire. "Can I taste you?" he asks, ever the gentleman. I nod, and York looks like I've just given him a free pass to heaven.

Oral sex is such an intimate thing. Our private parts aren't exactly the most attractive things, and I used to be so conscious of the way I smell and taste, but something I've learned is that most men love getting up close and personal with a pussy. York is no different. I catch him inhaling before he licks and it's such a turn on. The first swipe of his tongue over my clit is bliss. I let my legs fall open wide, watching him pleasure me, enjoying the innocence of his expression; eyes closed, eyelashes casting a fanned shadow over his sharp cheekbones. I run my fingers through his soft hair, gripping just a little. I can tell he likes it by the way he buries his face a little deeper. York knows how to get me close, but never entirely takes me far enough to come. When I'm close for the third time, I wriggle my hips, and he looks up smiling.

"I think it's time you fuck me," I say.

"I think it is too." York searches his pocket and expertly rolls a condom over his length. By the time he's done, I'm panting. He settles over me, resting on his forearms and kisses my face tenderly, the weight of his cock heavy on my pubic bone. "You ready?" he asks me.

I nod, the intensity of the moment stealing my words. His hips pull back a little, the head of his thick cock, finding my entrance quickly. York works his way inside me slowly, relishing each push and pull until he's fully seated, then he pauses to kiss me long and deep.

"You feel good, Danna," he says, and I love the way my name drips from his tongue.

He moves slowly with a delicious grind to his hips that has me mirroring. It's less about fucking and more like making love. I know that sounds stupid because I've only known York for a short time but the way he is with me, the connection we have, tugs at my heart as he possesses my body. I open my eyes because I want to see him. He's gazing down at me, his blue eyes like a summer sky, pupils wide with arousal.

"York," I gasp as I feel my orgasm starting to build. My hands instinctively find his hips, tugging him against me in a rhythm that I know will get me off. It's bliss; intimacy mixed with a passion that is pure contrast.

"Are you close?" he asks.

I nod, frantic with the need for release. "Please," I beg.

His hips speed, each thrust pushing upwards against the bundle of nerves inside me that's capable of sending me to paradise. "Harder," I say, "don't stop."

The bed thumps the wall, but I don't care. I'm clawing and desperate, hips surging for my release.

And then it happens. White light and pure pleasure, sin and hope and the beginnings of a love which aches inside my chest. My heart hammers like the thump of horse's hooves against hard ground, and York seizes too, his cock swelling and releasing inside me.

He buries his face in my neck, hot breath gusting against my skin as we take our time to come back from oblivion. He strokes my arm gently, then wraps his hand into mine.

"Hey," he says, smiling as though he's just woken up to find me beneath him.

"Hey yourself." I smile back as a big bubble of overwhelming happiness surges inside me.

York's joined Xsander and Xane in confirming he'd be happy to give my crazy plan a go. And best of all, I'm starting to see that this has a chance of working.

Maybe.

Just possibly.

23

The bell for dinner rings pretty much immediately, and York looks awkward. "We should go down," he says.

"Sure. Of course." My belly rumbles right on time, and he chuckles.

We gather our clothes and dress, occasionally exchanging shy smiles. We hear the thump of feet on the stairs as York's brothers make their way down too. As we're about to leave the room, he puts his hand on the handle and pauses. "So…this was…" He grins, and I want to pinch his cheeks, he's so cute.

"I know," I say, grinning back.

"But…I'm not sure how we should be…downstairs in front of everyone else."

"Are you planning on telling your mom and your brothers…not now I mean but…"

"Yeah," he says quickly. "Of course."

"Then I guess that we go down as friends and when

you're happy to be 'out' about us then you let me know."

York smiles, dropping a kiss on my lips that has me melting. "Sounds good. There's just a lot more politics here than usual."

"YORK." There's a bellow from downstairs. "DANNA."

I guess we're late. I smooth my rumpled hair as we make our way downstairs, and as we enter the kitchen, all eyes turn to us. I don't know what York's facial expression is saying, but I can't stop myself from smiling. Xsander winks and so does Xane. Samuel looks angry. Zack is concentrating on serving his food. Tommy and Trent both seem amused. And the W triplets, well, they look like they need some love. I take my usual place at the table and smile at Wade, then Walker and William. Their expressions seem to brighten. I guess I need to find a moment to talk to them. They were so kind after Joe's, and I want to know what their thinking now things are developing with their other brothers.

We eat and rather than the discussion revolving around me, they keep it about ranch business. Jackie has a lot to say about the town fair that is happening in two weeks. She's got jam and pickles to sell and is entering a baking competition too. It sounds like a lot of fun, and I'm sad that I'm going to miss it. Thinking about going home doesn't make me happy. I love pop, but our house is so quiet, and we can go days without a visitor. We eat with the television on. I'm going to miss the hustle and bustle and noise of this dinner table. I'm going to miss the warmth of this enormous family.

"Can you bake?" Jackie asks me, jolting me from my thoughts.

"My momma taught me how to bake some," I say.

Jackie looks pleased. "Everyone should know how to bake. There's nothing that brings joy to people's faces more than delicious cake."

"I don't know about that," Tommy says. "I can think of plenty of things that would bring more joy to my face than cake." He nudges me under the table, and I want to laugh, but feel like I shouldn't. This is obviously Jackie's passion, and I wouldn't want her to think that I wasn't taking her seriously.

"Tommy," Jackie says in a warning tone. "I don't know how many times I'm gonna have to remind you of your manners."

"Probably until one of us isn't here anymore," Tommy says. Jackie gives him a withering look. I'm just about to say something more about baking when my phone starts to ring.

Ugh. I should have put it into silent mode. It's really rude for this to happen and I don't want Jackie thinking that my manners are poor too. "Sorry." I fumble for the phone in my pocket and see that it's Dad. I switch it onto silent and let him ring out. I can talk to him later. As the conversation continues around me, I see him call again. Then a message pops up.

Dad: Where are you? I bumped into Nora in town, and she said you weren't staying with Laura.

Oh shit. Dad's caught me in a lie, and I feel terrible.

What the hell am I going to tell him? Now anything I say to him is going to sound suspicious. He's going to suspect I'm with a man, for sure. I know I'm a grown woman, and I should be able to do what I want, but living

211

under his roof makes me feel as though I owe him explanations whenever I'm away.

"Everything okay?" Jackie asks. I guess she's seen my gray face and panicked expression.

"Yeah," I say. "I just need to make a quick call if that's okay."

"Of course," she says.

I'm not very coordinated as I get up from the table and stumble over the bench leg. Tommy grab's my arm and catches me before I fall. "Easy," he says.

I mumble a quick thanks and head for the den, closing the door behind me.

Staring at the phone, I consider my story. I can't go into another full-blown lie now. It just won't wash. I know my dad, and he's going to be seriously suspicious, but telling him the truth while I'm still not sure of anything here would be foolish too. As I dial his number, I settle on a halfway option.

"Danna," he says. "Thank goodness." I hear him exhale what sounds like a shaky breath, and I automatically feel hideously guilty.

"I'm fine, dad."

"Well, I'm not," he says. "You don't know how worried I've been."

I perch on the couch, as shame wells inside me. Dad has been through so much losing mom, and I shouldn't be putting him through worry about losing me.

"I'm sorry. I'm...I'm in Broadsville, staying with

friends."

"Broadsville? Who do you know in Broadsville?"

"You don't know them," I say. "I didn't want to worry you, so I told you I was with Laura. I knew you'd be fine with me being there."

"Are they college friends?" he asks.

"No," I say. "But I'm fine, Dad. I'll be home at the weekend."

"Can you send me the address, Danna? I want to know where you are in case anything happens."

"Laura has the address," I say. "And I'm fine. Everything is fine."

"Danna. This is no way to behave. You have no idea what it feels like to be a parent. You're all I have…" Dad trails off, but I know what he was going to say. I'm all he has left of mom. My heart aches for her and for him. Loss is so hard to bear, especially when you see the pain in someone you love too. Somehow, my own grief is easier to cope with than my fathers.

"Everything's fine, dad. I'm safe and having a break from college stress. It's nice here. Rural. Lots of fresh air and outdoor activities. I'm getting some sun on my skin and some wind in my hair."

I know how much dad likes the great outdoors. He'll be happy to hear that I'm indulging in one of his passions.

"Well, that all sounds lovely," he says. "Just message me every day to put my mind at ease, okay?"

"Sure," I say. "And dad…I'm really sorry if I worried

you."

He sighs gently. "I...I just want to know that I can trust you, honey. I feel so responsible for you, now it's just me here to worry about where you are and who you're with."

"I know. I should have just been honest," I say. "Is everything good with you?"

"Same as usual," he says. "The house is quiet with you gone."

"It's quiet with me there," I laugh.

"True," he says.

"I'd better go. I was in the middle of dinner."

"Okay." There's a pause. "Be safe," he says. It's like he knows that for all my reassurance that there's something not quite right.

"You too," I say, waiting for him to hang up first.

I stay in the den for a couple of minutes to get my equilibrium back. I'm about to stand when there's a knock at the door. "Come in," I say, getting to my feet. It's Tommy.

"Mom asked me to come and check on you," he says. "Everything alright?"

I don't know why, but as soon as he asks, I burst into tears. It's as though all the worry I've had about dad over the past few months spills out in one massive avalanche. Tommy looks momentarily petrified and then strides across the room, tugging me against his chest. "Hey," he says. "What is it? What's happened?"

I bring my hand to cover my face, sobbing, my shoulders shaking as Tommy tries to soothe me. "Shit, Danna," he says. "Did something happen to your family?"

I shake my head, wiping my tears away, and hiding my face. I must look so blotchy, and I'm sure my mascara is all over my cheeks by now.

Tommy is solid and strong, his arms a welcome place for me in this moment of grief, even though I suspect he'd rather be anywhere else right now. I can't find words to explain why I'm so upset, so I just cry until my tears have dried up and my heart feels less heavy. By the time I'm ready to pull away from Tommy, there are more footsteps in the room.

"Hey," Trent says. "Is everything okay?"

I bury my head in Tommy's chest again. "She's upset, but she won't tell me why."

Trent comes close and strokes my hair with his big, rough hand. "Hey, honey. You gonna tell us what happened?" I shake my head, but he keeps on stroking. "You know we can't help you unless you tell us."

I shake my head again. "I don't need help," I say. My voice sounds choked, and my words hollow as a result.

"Yeah you do," Tommy says gruffly. "We all need help when we're feeling upset enough to cry."

I start to sob again because his words are so sweet and I would never have expected him to say something like that.

"Talk to us," Trent says. "I know you don't know us very well, but we'll do our best to make you feel better." His hand continues to stroke, his fingers finding their way into my hair. My scalp tingles with the sensation. They're so close around me, Tommy at my front and Trent almost behind. Even though my worry and anguish, I feel protected and safe between them. I swipe at my eyes again, starting to pull back from Tommy.

"I don't want to go back to the kitchen," I say. "I'm too blotchy."

"You look fine," he says, tipping my chin. I gaze up at him, his green eyes shining with concern. "But worrying about what you look like right now isn't where your head should be at."

"Tommy's right," Trent says. "But if you want to stay here you can. I can go back and tell the rest that you need some time and space."

I nod, feeling so grateful that they are so understanding and kind. "That would be good."

Trent takes my hand and squeezes it. "I'll be back," he says.

"I'm gonna sit," I say to Tommy, and I slump into the corner of the biggest couch, curling my legs up and covering my face. I hear rustling and Tommy places some tissues on my lap, sitting next to me. His arm comes around the back of the chair reassuringly, like he's trying to let me know he's available to comfort me without invading my space. He doesn't ask me to tell him what's wrong again either, giving me space to just get myself together.

Trent comes back and closes the door behind him. He grabs a chair and pulls it close, so he's sitting in front of me, leaning forward.

In the end, after I've wiped the makeup from around my eyes and blown my nose, I feel like I need to fill the silence.

"My mom died last year. It's been really hard, for dad and for me. I...I didn't tell him where I was going this week...I told him I was staying with a friend, but he found out...he was just really worried and I felt guilty."

"I'm sorry," Tommy says. "About your momma. That must have been really hard to go through."

"It was," I say.

"You feel guilty for lying?" Trent asks.

I nod, twisting the tissue around my fingers. "And for worrying him. He's had enough to be upset about, he doesn't need me making things worse."

"He's worried because he loves you. Maybe you shouldn't have lied to him, but you're a young woman of an age where you need some independence and privacy. I don't think it's too much to ask for."

Leaning back in the chair, I sigh. "It's hard. I feel like I need to be something different for him now my mom's not around. Less of a daughter and more of a..." I don't really know what to say next. A confidant? Not really. A support? It's hard to identify what my dad needs from me now.

"An equal?" Trent asks.

"I suppose. It's as though our relationship has shifted and I don't really know how to be what he needs."

Tommy drops his arm around my shoulders and tugs me towards him. "You just need to be yourself," he says. "Too many women think they need to mold themselves into something they're not just to be what's good for men."

I'm surprised to hear something like that coming out of Tommy's mouth. He never struck me as a feminist. To be honest, I would have assumed the exact opposite. Trent must see my stunned expression and starts laughing.

"You've stunned her into silence," he says.

"Why?"

"She thought you were a misogynist pig," Trent laughs, and Tommy shakes his head.

"I don't know why women assume that about me."

"Could be the way you look at them like you want to strip off their clothes and fuck them on the sidewalk," I say.

"Just because I have an appreciation of the female form and love sex doesn't mean that I want to treat women as second class citizens."

"I'm impressed," I say. "Your mom's done a good job."

Trent and Tommy look at each other. "Jackie's been brilliant," Trent says. "The best adoptive momma we could have hoped for."

"But it's not so much what she did," Tommy says.

"When we were thirteen we wanted to find out more about our birth momma," Trent says. "When we asked Jackie, she explained that our momma had to give us up because she was thirteen years old when she had us."

"We couldn't believe that she'd had us when she was so young. When we asked about what happened, Jackie told us that our momma had been having a relationship with a much older man. He went to jail after we were born and it was proven he'd been with a minor."

"Oh," I say. "That's so sad."

"It is," Trent says. "From what we understand, she was in love with him…as in love as a girl that age could have been, and he took advantage of her."

"And that's what makes me feel like this about women," Tommy says. The twins are blunt in the way they've explained something that's obviously been very difficult for them to come to terms with, something that must have made them feel different about themselves too. I think about my mom and dad and the secure home that I grew up in and imagine what it would be like to think about a strange girl having terrible life experiences and you being the result.

"Your poor momma," I say gently. "Thirteen is so young, and there's no way she would have been ready to have a relationship at that age, especially with a much older man. I can understand why you'd feel the way you do."

Tommy squeezes me again. "So you're hearing me, then. All you need to be in life is yourself. I'm not saying you need to go around being a bitch, but you don't need to change yourself to fit in with anyone else's expectations or needs, no matter who they are or how much you love them."

Trent nods. "Your dad loves you, I'm sure. And you just want to make things easier for him, but it shouldn't be at the expense of making things more difficult for yourself."

"I…I feel like I'm going to disappoint him, and I don't know how to do that and still feel okay about myself."

"How do you think you're going to disappoint him?" Trent asks, then his eyes widen as he realizes I'm talking about why I'm with them. "You mean by wanting this alternative life?"

"Yes, I say. "My dad is a Sunday churchgoer. I can't imagine what he'd think."

"I hope he'd think we were good men who were going to look after his daughter," Tommy says.

"He'd be happy with one of you, maybe," I say. "But ten will push him over the edge."

"Maybe," Trent says. "But eventually he'd see you were happy and he'd have to be happy for you. Isn't that what happened with your friend."

I shake my head, the image of my dad's crestfallen face flashing through my mind. "It turned out okay for Laura, but I think there are things we can do as children that would be unforgivable in the eyes of our parents." I glance between them, marveling at their identical concerned faces. Of all the brothers in this family, these two are definitely the most alike. "And anyway, I don't think it's going to happen. No point in worrying about it."

"What do you mean," Tommy asks.

"Well, I think that York, Xsander and Xane are happy to try, and maybe William, Walker, and Wade but I have no idea about the rest of you."

"I'm happy to try," Tommy says. "Anything to get in between those sweet thighs of yours."

I burst with laughter, shocked at his ability to move between deep and lighthearted conversation so fast. Trent rolls his eyes. "My brother is such a romantic."

"What?" Tommy says, exasperatedly. "Women love the cocky, dirty talk, don't they, Danna?"

"Sometimes," I say.

"Would you like me between your legs?" Tommy asks.

Trent leans forward at punches his brother's shoulder. "Shit man, the girls upset and your mind is in the gutter already."

"It's called lightening the mood," Tommy says. "You should try it sometime."

I put my hands up to stop their bickering. "I'd love you in between my legs," I say. "Both of you."

Tommy and Trent's eyebrows rise with identical shock. I guess they weren't expecting me to be so blatant.

"What the fuck are we waiting for then?" Tommy says. "Let's do this."

24

You're probably thinking how can I go from crying to fucking in such a short space of time. I'll admit my emotions are all over the place, and if I were advising a friend, I'd be telling them that now was not the time to be making more emotional connections. But we often don't think as clearly for ourselves as we do for others and so I find myself creeping up the stairs with Tommy in front and Trent behind me. The noise from the kitchen is loud enough to cover our movements, and all I can think about is masking my sadness and concerns with these gorgeous men.

Tommy passes my room, and I almost tell him to stop, but then I realize he's taking me to his place and I follow him. It'll be good to see his space. I want to know everything I can about the Jackson brothers, so my decisions, later on, are based on as much information as I can gather.

Tommy throws open a door at the end of the hallway, and we enter a bright, modern space. He's neat and organized, something that surprises me no end. Then I notice that there are two beds and that the twins share this space.

"Welcome to our casa," Tommy says. "It's not quite the penthouse apartment I wish I owned, but it'll do."

"Very nice," I say. Their beds are dressed with matching comforters and pillow in dark blue. There's a large sofa on one side and a TV complete with games console. Beside each bed, they have nightstands, and I'm surprised to see books. They didn't really strike me as bookish types. When I get closer, I see they're reading agricultural non-fiction. I guess that fits a little more with the demands of ranch life.

Trent closes the door behind us and flicks the lock. Just the sound of the clunk of metal on metal and the idea that I'm now shut in their space sends heat to my pussy. There are a few seconds where we all stand around politely, then Tommy seems to sense that it's time to start what we were talking about downstairs.

He tugs off his shirt, his hair ruffling in the process. When he gets nearer, his eyes seem to darken, the green irises getting swallowed by his widening pupils. Tommy stands close, the heat of his body radiating even though I'm not touching him. He's all man with his broad chest, defined pecs, and flat stomach. With smooth, sun-kissed skin from outdoor work, he's absolute perfection. I put my hand out to feel what I've only been able to imagine up until now. Tommy lets me explore his chest, shoulders, and arms, fingers trailing, palms searching out the solid strength of him. Trent comes closer too, his hands finding my hips, his lips seeking the tender flesh at the side of my neck.

It's Trent who lifts my shirt, revealing my breasts to his brother. It's Tommy who undoes the front clasp, allowing them to spill free. Tommy's eyes are hooded as he palms them, tugging the nipples with his work-roughened fingers, making me shiver. It's Trent who kissed down my spine, dropping to his knees behind me and pulling down my skirt and panties. His lips kiss my hips and ass as his brother drops to his knees too. It's Trent who nudges my legs open wider so his brother can lick me. Trent strokes his hands up my calves and thighs as Tommy's hot, wet tongue finds my clit and circles it.

My legs are shaky, and my mind is scattered. Having two gorgeous men worship me this way is overwhelming, but it's not only my body that's falling, it's my heart too. "Fuck," Trent mutters, moving so he can watch his brother feast on my pussy.

"I need to sit," I say, steadying myself on Tommy's shoulder. The twins don't hesitate, moving me back so that I can perch on the edge of one of the beds. I lay back, my feet on the floor and my legs spread wide as Tommy takes back his position and Trent removes the rest of his clothes.

I've seen a lot of dick this week. Gorgeous thick cocks that have blown my mind and wrecked my body. Trent's is just as overwhelming in size. He approaches the bed, holding himself and stroking. He comes to kneel next to me, and I replace his hand with mine, caressing him up and down, and weighing his balls in my palm. He groans, balancing back on his hands which are behind him, his muscular thighs spread to give me easy access. I turn, bringing my mouth close so I can taste him, relishing the salty-sweetness of his arousal. Trent groan's again, sliding one of his hands into my hair and gently guiding my mouth deeper onto his cock. It hits the back of my throat but not in a violent way. Trent is gentle, even when he's demanding more. I swipe my tongue around the tip, teasing him until his legs are trembling. When I open my eyes, I find him watching me. "You're so fucking sexy," he says.

"Her pussy tastes so sweet," Tommy says, licking me from my clit to my wet entrance, forcing my legs wider.

"I wanna taste," Trent says, so Tommy rises to his feet and gives his twin a turn. They might be identical, but there is nothing similar about the way they eat pussy. Tommy is measured and gentle while Trent feasts on me like he's starving.

Tommy strips too, taking Trent's place so I can take his cock into my mouth. I know I shouldn't be surprised that they smell and taste the same, but I am. "That's it," Tommy says. He doesn't control me like his twin, just lets me take things at my own pace. I can taste when he's getting close, and he pulls out before I can take him over the edge. "Not so fast," he says.

My pussy is so swollen and wet that when Trent pulls back to find a condom, I almost beg him not to stop. He finds a foil packet in the nightstand and is wrapped and ready in seconds.

I've had a lot of sex this week too, but I'm still filled with anticipation. The thing that I've learned is that no two people are the same when it comes to sex. Their approaches and methods, the way they make you feel with words and touch, it's all so different. I don't know what I'm expecting from Trent and Tommy, but when Trent sits on the sofa and encourages me into his lap, facing away, I'm excited. He supports me while I work his cock inside me, his thighs spread wide and my legs in between. I grip the edge of the sofa for stability and to help me rise up each time. Tommy comes forward and teases my lips with his cock, encouraging me to open and take his length. I release the sofa and hold onto him, gripping his tight ass so that I can move on his brother's cock and suck him too.

It takes more concentration than I'm used to, but the resulting sensations are out of this world. Knowing that Trent can see me sucking his brother's cock and Tommy is watching me fuck Trent is so damn sexy. Feeling so full in my pussy and mouth is overwhelming in the best possible way.

This feels different too because I know that Tommy and Trent understand why I'm here and their eagerness to connect with me is based on that knowledge rather than just physical attraction. This feels like a stepping stone towards something bigger and deeper, and their attentiveness and care, even during passionate sex shows me how just how right we could be together.

Tommy's hand in my hair guides me to give him exactly what he needs; short, shallow licks then longer, deeper sucks. Trent's fingers digging into my hips do the same. I'm getting close, the push and pull of Trent's huge cock hitting all the right places but I need more. His finger, moistened in his mouth and pressed to my clit, is exactly what's missing, and he gives it to me. Oh boy, he gives it to me.

I moan around Tommy's cock, wanting to tell Trent to fuck me harder, to pinch my clit with his fingers, to slap my ass and own my body but I can't. I'm too stuffed by Tommy to say a word, but he knows without me having to say a word.

When he spanks me for the first time, my hips buck faster. It stings at first, warmth spreading deliciously over my ass and between my legs. "Fuck me faster," he orders, and I do, forcing my hips to buck, even as I'm my muscles are getting tired.

Tommy strokes my cheek, his hand trembling as he gets close. I can taste his arousal, and I suck just a little harder using my fingers to stroke him too. It's Tommy who comes first, filling my mouth with salty-sweetness and groaning as though he's in deep pain rather than overwhelming pleasure. His legs give way, and he drops to his knees, hands on his thighs as he pants through his orgasm. Trent's hand tugs at my hips, making me speed even more as his finger presses and flicks my clit.

"Oh fuck," I say as Trent's cock starts to swell. "Don't stop."

I'm close, but it's not until Tommy's mouth latches onto my nipple and he bites down hard that I finally come.

I know I sound desperate – the sound of my release a loud and ugly thing – but I don't care.

Trent is there, groaning with me, his cock pulsing as my pussy clamps down in pulsing waves.

We're sweat-slicked between us, and I know my lips are swollen and my hair mussed, but I don't care because I feel amazing. I'm eight brothers in, and they all know how to make me come as I've never come before. They all know how to make me feel relaxed and safe enough to let all my inhibitions go. They've all managed to touch my heart, even in this short space of time.

Tommy kisses me tenderly as his brother strokes my back and arms. I turn into his embrace and kiss Trent too.

"You were amazing," Tommy says.

"Perfect," Trent says.

"Fucking mind-blowing." I laugh because Tommy's eyes are bright and filled with glee. With his rumbled hair he looks like a naughty kid version of himself.

"That was…" I'm lost for words, but they wait for me to finish. "Awesome!"

There's lots of laughter from us all, driven by the perfect after-sex euphoria that has so much happiness bubbling inside me that I think I could burst.

I'm about to suggest we all get into bed for a cuddle when there's a knock on the door.

Damn, people in this house really need to be more considerate!

25

I should be getting used to interruptions. With so many people in this house, it's a miracle we got through the sex before someone came knocking.

"Tommy," a voice calls. I think it's Wade. "Something's wrong with Ruffles."

The twins look at each other, then start to gather their clothes and dress frantically. I do the same, a little shocked at the urgency. I know Ruffles is important to Zack, but I didn't expect Tommy and Trent to be panicking like this. Tommy tears open the door and Wade is outside. He glances into the room and sees me still fixing my top. His eyes widen for a second, but then he smiles.

"My brothers' treating you well," he asks.

It's tough to know what to say. Yes, is the obvious answer but I don't want Wade to think that I wasn't happy with how he treated me too. There is going to be so much emotional politics with ten involved!

"Yes," I say. "Just like you did."

Wade grins, and Tommy and Trent snort with laughter. "It's a Jackson thing," Tommy says.

"What's going on with Ruffles?" Trent asks as he's ready to go downstairs.

"York's with him, but it isn't looking good. Zack's a mess. He found Ruffles after dinner...the poor thing couldn't stand."

"Shit," Tommy says.

They start off down the hallway, and I trail behind, feeling like an intruder into what is obviously a very upsetting family situation.

The kitchen is quiet, despite there being so many people. The air of anxious anticipation is palpable. In the corner, York and Zack are kneeling on the floor next to Ruffles. Tommy, Trent, and Wade come to an abrupt halt, watching and waiting to see what is going to happen next. York is speaking slowly and quietly to Zack, who is shaking his head like he doesn't want to believe whatever his brother is telling him. Ruffles' chest is barely moving, his eyes closed and tongue slightly protruding from his mouth. He looks smaller somehow, and I know this is the end for him. I remember when our dog Samson died, and it was the same. For a time, the body seems to remain even as the soul and spirit of the animal are moving on.

Jackie kneels next to her sons, stroking Ruffle's gently behind his ears.

Zack doesn't touch Ruffles at all. He's not even looking at him now. My heart breaks as I see Zack fall apart. It's not the movie style of grief involving tears and whys? Instead, he goes absolutely still and rigid, his eyes closed as though he can shut out the world.

I'm standing back, not feeling like it's my place to step in, but no one is going to him, and he needs it. I can see how much he needs it, and I can't just leave him to suffer. As I move through the room, the Jackson brothers watch me. I don't look at Ruffles because as much as I'm sad that he's close to passing, it's Zack who's my main concern. I kneel next to him, placing my hand on his leg. "Zack," I whisper, then a put my arms around him and hold him tight. He's like a statue for the first few seconds, and I start to panic that he's going to push me away, then he seems to crumble into my embrace. His head rests on my shoulder, face buried into my hair, and he cries.

And my heart bleeds with his tears.

I remember hugging my dad when mum passed. We were both sobbing then, so his sadness didn't affect me as much because I was drowning in my own. With Zack, his pain is overwhelming.

I don't know his history or the story of his relationship with this dog, but anyone can see that he's relied on Ruffles for support and consistency. They had a quiet bond and a level of trust that is hard for some people to find with other human beings.

I hold him closer, needing for him to feel as secure as possible, wanting to give him a safe place to express his grief, and as Zack cries, I watch York and Jackie stroke Ruffles until his chest stops rising and falling. "He's gone," York says gently, resting a hand on Zack's shoulder.

"Fuck," someone says from behind us. The room is silent as each member of this family comes to terms with the loss of a truly loved animal. Eventually, footsteps signal the other Jackson brothers dispersing, giving Zack the privacy that he so obviously wants and needs.

"You need to say goodbye," Jackie says to Zack, but he shakes his head.

"I can't." He pulls away from me, getting to his feet and swiping at his face as though his own tears disgust him, then he storms outside.

I rise and follow him, worried about what he might do next. Grief can bring a person so low, and no one in such a distressed state should be left alone. I scramble to find some work boots that will fit, and by the time I've tugged them on, Zack has disappeared into the night. I stagger around in the dark, unsure of which direction to take, but remember the route that Zack would take to walk with Ruffles each evening. I follow the path around the house and then further, seeing a shadowy shape ahead. I start to jog, wanting to catch up with him before he gets too far. The light from the house is dim and doesn't spread extensively, and I'm not used to being out in such pitch blackness.

Zack must hear my feet pounding the dirt, and he turns. I call his name, but he keeps on walking. By the time I reach him I'm panting and have to grab his arm to get him to stop.

"Leave me alone," he shouts. "I don't want you out here."

"Zack," I say. "It's okay. I just don't think you should be alone."

His dark eyes flash angrily at me; fury masking the anguish he's feeling in his heart. "Just leave me alone," he says.

"NO!"

For a moment he stands totally still, obviously utterly

shocked at my determination.

"There's nothing you can say," he says. "Nothing, anyone, can say that will make any difference."

"I know that," I tell him. "I know what it's like to feel like your heart has broken and will never repair unless the person you've lost comes back to life. But being on your own when you're suffering isn't right. Just let me come with you. I'll feel better for knowing you're okay."

He doesn't say yes, but when he starts walking away, it's at a slow enough pace that I can keep up.

The night is so still. No wind to disturb us. A sliver of a moon to light our way, but Zack knows his land well, and he keeps us to a well-trodden path. We're silent for what feels like hours and when we get so far from the house that it's a struggle to see anything at all, Zack stops and sits down on a rock, resting his head in his hands. I sit too, putting my hand on his back for comfort.

"He was just a puppy when I got him."

"How long ago was that?"

Zack doesn't look up. "Fourteen years."

"Wow. So you guys grew up together."

He nods. "My dad bought him for me."

"That's nice," I say. "They're good company, dogs. I had one when I was growing up. He died four years ago, and I still miss the smell him."

Zack raises his head. "What was his name?"

"Samson. He had such a thick coat, and the rescue shelter warned us that he hated being groomed."

Behind us, I can hear the soft murmur of sheep stirring in the darkness. The air is scented with the dampness of the night. I don't think it's going to rain, but it feels that way; close and oppressive. Or maybe that's just because of the sadness that surrounds us.

"I don't know what I'm going to do without him," he says.

"I know. I felt that way too. Losing someone is never easy, but time will make it feel less raw."

"I just...he was..." Zack trails off and doesn't finish his thought. I don't need him to because I know exactly how it feels.

The night chill begins to permeate, and I fold my arms to try and keep warm. Zack must notice me shiver. "Come on," he says. "You need to get back...you haven't even got a jacket."

Shaking my head, I put my hand on his arm. "If you want to stay, I'll stay. It's okay."

Zack pulls his sweater over his head and hands it to me. "Wear this," he says. I guess that means that he's not quite ready to go back, so I do as he says. The fabric is so warm from his body heat and smells of whatever scent he must wear. I feel instantly better, but I'm worried about him sitting outside in just a tee. It doesn't feel like the time or the place for me to fuss about something so relatively trivial, though.

We sit in silence for a while, then I hear footsteps coming from the direction of the house. A figure looms in the darkness, and it's not until they're almost on top of us that I see it's William.

"Hey," he says. "I thought I'd come to check on you

both."

Zack nods at his brother. "I'm okay," he says, but his voice is gravelly with emotion, so it's pretty apparent that he isn't.

"I think you need to come back to the house," William says. "I know it's hard, but you need to say goodbye before he's buried."

Zack shakes his head. "I can't," he says.

"You can." William is very definite in his tone, and maybe that's what Zack needs because he stands.

"Danna's cold. We should get her back," Zack says. If he needs to use me as an excuse, then so be it. I can see Zack take in a deep shaky breath as he attempts to stabilize himself enough to face saying goodbye to his childhood friend. I just wish there was something I could do to make this easier for him, but there isn't. We all have to face our grief alone.

We start to make the short walk back to the house, William slightly ahead.

Jackie is waiting at the door, her face marred with worry. She glances between William and me as though she's hoping to be able to read Zack's state of mind from our expressions. When Jackie sees Zack, she's watchful rather than smothering. I guess I expected her to throw her arms around him; to be the comforting mother that she seems to be, but she doesn't, and I think she's right not to.

"We've put him in his bed," Jackie says softly.

In the kitchen, only York remains. He's seated at the table with a mug in front of him, and he doesn't say anything to us, just watches as Zack walks slowly towards the corner where Ruffles is laying peacefully. It's so hard to watch, knowing that Zack is so close to falling about but is desperately trying to hold himself together. It feels wrong for me to be here, but I don't want to leave either. William stands next to me, and I glance up at him. Our eyes meet, and he smiles, filling my heart with momentary relief. "We should..." He nods towards the door to the hallway. He's obviously feeling as though this is a private moment too.

I follow William out of the room, glancing back at Zack one more time. He has his hand on Ruffle's body and, although it must be hard, it's definitely the right thing for him to say goodbye this way. He'd regret it later otherwise, and they'll be no changing it when Ruffles is laid to rest.

In the hallway, William takes my hand and tugs me around the stairs into what looks like a small office. He doesn't say a word, just stares at me with his fierce eyes and jaw that seems tight and clenched.

"Is everything okay?" I ask.

Again, he's silent, his chest rising and falling as he takes a step closer to me. I flush, getting ready for him to shout at me for misleading him. He seems angry and I'm worried that anger is driven my jealousy or maybe just because I wasn't honest about my motives. Just as I'm about to apologize, he kisses me so hard our teeth clink. "Fuck," he says, sliding his hand up my side until he's cupping my left breast. I grasp him around his neck with relief, tugging him to me so I can deepen the kiss. He pulls back tugging at the sweater I'm wearing. "You smell like my brother," he says.

"I'm sorry." My eyes search his desperate to know what he's thinking.

"What for?" he asks. "For fucking my brothers?"

I nod, then shake my head. I'm not really sorry about that at all. "For not being honest about why I was here."

"You think things would have happened differently between us if you had been honest?"

"Wouldn't they? Are you telling me you'd have come to me that night if you knew I was here looking for a relationship with all of you."

"I came to you knowing you'd slept with Wade and Walker."

"You weren't shocked when you found out at Joe's?" I ask.

William's fingers stroke the edge of my neck, his hand resting over my throat and I feel completely dominated by his size and his intensity. "I wasn't shocked," he says. "I was relieved."

"Really?"

"I'm not good at finding relationships. The ranch and my family are my life. I was concerned that it would be impossible to find someone who'd fit in with my life and love my brothers enough. You want to take all of this on..."

"Yes," I say, resting my hand at his waist. "I want this...all of it."

He shakes his head as though he can't quite believe what I'm saying. "This isn't the easiest life, Danna. Living off the land is tough, and you only have to look at my momma's hands to see what it can do to you." He tips my chin, keeping my eyes on his. "If you're worried that one of us wouldn't be enough for you..." He trails off and looks away as though he's embarrassed. Is that what he thinks this is? That I'm not satisfied sexually by one man. He needs straightening out.

"That isn't what it is," I say. "You're more than enough man, and the sex was mind-blowing. It's ...it's more than that. It's about home and family and security ...it's about me never having to worry about..." I trail off because I found myself about to admit something that I haven't really even admitted to myself.

"Worry about what?" William asks.

"About being alone."

William's face falls, and he pulls me into an embrace, smoothing my hair and kissing my crown. "You don't need to worry about that," he says. "Not anymore."

The strength of his body against mine and his reassuring words are exactly what I need, but he can't make me sweeping promises like that. Not when at least one of his brothers is abjectly against the idea of us all being together. "But Samuel," I say. "He doesn't want this, and it won't work if you're not all willing. I won't do that to your family...be the one to exclude someone. This is about your momma knowing that you'll all stay together and that your family legacy won't be diminished."

"I know what it's about, Danna. I know what momma's been worrying about since she saw her brother torn apart by divorce. I think this idea is probably a lot further than most moms will consider, but I get why she called you."

"I just want it to all work out," I say. "But I can't force it, and I don't want your mom to either. This isn't about Samuel being made to toe the line, or indeed anyone who's thinking this isn't a good idea. It has to be about everyone really wanting this."

"I don't know, Danna. I don't see Samuel coming around. You left before he really started sharing his objections …he's adamant that it's not for him."

"Then that'll be it." I shake my head, feeling a knot fastening tight in my stomach. Half of me wants to stick to my principles, but the other half is enjoying being with the men who do want me. It's selfish, and I'm sick with it, but I can't help myself.

"I haven't had a chance to speak to him," I say hopefully. "There's a chance."

"I don't think so," William says, "but you still have time before you need to return home. I don't mean to sound defeatist, and you should definitely give it your all."

"And what about you? Will you speak to him too?"

"Of course." William nods and kisses me again. Soft lips with an edge of the passion I remember from the last time we were alone. I want this kiss to last and last, but this isn't the time, and William knows it. He pulls away, stroking my hair from my face.

"I need to go back to Zack," he says.

"Okay. I'll head up to bed."

William strokes my arm then kisses me again, and I sense his reluctance to let me go. "Can I join you after?" he asks.

"Sure," I say.

As William goes to support his brother, I head up to bed. I wait and wait for him to come to me, but he doesn't, and in the end, I fall asleep.

When I wake in the night, I find him in bed beside me, arms wrapped around my waist like he never wants to let me go. I smile snuggling back into his body, but he doesn't stir, and sleep comes to retake me.

26

We're woken by William's alarm at ridiculous-o'clock, and he groans into my hair before silencing his phone.

"Fuck," he says. "One of these days I'm gonna sleep until the sun rises."

"If that's your only dream, it's a pretty easy one to fulfill," I say.

"Only if I slack off and leave the work to my brothers," he says. His hands roam my body lazily, warm from the heat of our bodies beneath the comforter.

"Can't you agree to sleep in on rotation," I say. "I'm sure the others would agree."

"You know, that's not a bad idea." Kissing my neck and shoulder, he begins to rise. "I'm gonna grab a quick shower."

And as he did earlier in the week, he uses my bathroom, pulls his clothes and says his goodbyes, disappearing downstairs for breakfast.

I'm wrecked. The early mornings have taken their toll, and as much as I want to rush to keep to the routine, I can't bring myself to get out of bed.

I must fall asleep again because when I next look at the time, it's after 8 am. I jump up and dress as quickly as I can, then I bound down the stairs. Jackie is sitting at the breakfast table with a cup of coffee and a magazine.

"Hey," I say.

She looks up and smiles. "There's our sleeping beauty."

"Sorry I didn't make it down earlier," I say. "I guess I'm not as used to the early mornings as your boys."

"That's okay," she says. "It was a stressful night last night. I think we all wished that we could hide in bed for a little longer."

I pull up a chair and join her at the table. "How's Zack?"

"He hasn't come down yet. The first time that boy's stayed in bed this long on a workday. I think he's avoiding coming down because Ruffles won't be here to greet him."

I sigh, glancing over to where Ruffles bed was. It's an empty space now, and my heart hurts for Zack. "He's not going to get over this quickly or easily," I say.

Jackie nods, taking a sip of her coffee. "I've been dreading this for over two years. Since that dog started showing his age, it's been on my mind. He's just been such a big part of Zack's life. Those two have been thick as thieves for so long."

"The penalty of love is loss," I say.

"Don't I know it." Her eyes flick to a photograph of her late husband, and her face takes on a melancholy air as memories find their way to the surface again.

"What do you think would make things easier for Zack?" I ask.

Jackie shrugs, frowning, coming quickly back to the here and now. "I don't know. I just think he needs some time and space to grieve."

"I don't know," I say, remembering how broken he was sitting on that rock in the dark. "I had an idea."

Jackie looks intrigued. "What idea?"

"I know it's kind of soon, but I think we should get Zack, a new dog."

"I don't know," Jackie says. "There's no replacing Ruffles. He was a special character; one of a kind."

"Yes," I say. "Whatever dog we get would be a whole new character for Zack to get used to."

"Exactly and I don't think he'd like it. I think it would just remind him of what he lost."

"Maybe not," I say. "If the dog is different, it could be a good distraction for him."

"It's risky," Jackie says. "What if he rejects it outright?"

I think about that for a while. She's right. There is definitely a risk that Zack won't want to replace Ruffles, but if there is a chance he will feel happier with a new focus, I think it's worth the risk. "What about if we speak to an animal shelter and see if they have any suitable dogs. I don't think a puppy would be right. We need a dog who's already trained and ready to integrate here. We could ask them if they'd be okay with us trying the dog to check him in the new environment."

"You know, I'm sure I saw a notice in the store in town. Hang on a minute."

Jackie pulls out her phone and starts dialing. "Hey Charlie, it's Jackie Jackson. Do you still have the ad in the window about the dog?" She pauses while Charlie talks on the other end of the line. "Could you read me the details?" She jumps up to find a pen and a scrap of paper. "That's great," she says, scribbling away. "Thanks."

When she's disconnected the call, she turns to me excitedly. "There's a dog for sale over in the next town. The owner has had an accident and can't care for it anymore. It sounds perfect."

"And you got the number?" I ask.

"Yep." She waves it. "Shall we call them now?"

"Might as well. It could be the happiest coincidence if you think that this is worth a shot."

Jackie starts to tap out the number. The call is answered almost immediately, and Jackie explains the situation. Everything sounds really positive. "We could come now," she says. "Okay." She starts to scribble an address onto the back of the paper. "See you soon then."

She's beaming when she disconnects the call, all the worry about Zack replaced with a new purpose. This is precisely what I'm hoping that the new dog will do for Zack himself. "Grab your purse," Jackie tells me. "We're going to see a man about a dog."

And that's how I find myself in Jackie's truck, speeding

towards the next town. She plays upbeat country music, and I feel like singing along. The sun is shining and, despite the sad reason for our mission, I'm hopeful that we're doing a good thing.

The house we pull in front of is on a long road; one of many similar looking wooden buildings which were obviously constructed at the same time. This one is the most dilapidated of them all with a lawn that's up to my knees and bushes that are spilling over the white, wooden fences. The blue paint on the door is peeling and, at the side of the house, part of the guttering is hanging down.

I follow Jackie, who is practically power walking up the pathway. She knocks the door with all the enthusiasm of a mother on a mission.

The man who answers is young and looks very fit, not what I was expecting at all.

"Hey, come on in."

We follow him down a hallway that's as rundown as the house and yard outside. Wallpaper is peeling from the walls, and the paintwork is yellowing and chipped. We enter the kitchen hasn't been updated for years, maybe since the house was built. "My uncle has had to go into supported accommodation," he says. "He hasn't been coping well. You can see." He waves his hand to indicate our surroundings and looks embarrassed. "I've been taking care of Frankie for him, but it's hard. I'm out of town a lot and Frankie's getting lonesome."

Frankie is a beautiful reddish-brown shaggy thing. He's sitting in the corner, but as the man speaks, he rises and trots over, sniffing us both then moving to stand next to his current owner.

"He's got a great temperament. Very patient, but he

also needs to be active. He loves being outside."

"He sounds perfect," Jackie says. "My son's dog just passed, and he's taking it pretty bad. Danna thought that it might be good to get him another."

"Well, Frankie needs a loving home. I hope your son will take to him."

I bend down and put my hand out, and Frankie comes over, letting me pet him. It's a good sign. He's not yappy or jumpy, just an affectionate, well-trained dog; exactly what we're looking for.

"What do you think?" Jackie asks me.

"I think he's perfect," I say. Frankie makes a high pitched sound as though he's happy we like him.

"He really is great," the man says. "I'd love to keep hold of him in case my uncle comes home. The thing is, it's looking really doubtful, and I just don't want Frankie to feel neglected."

"And you don't want anything for him?" Jackie says.

"Just for him to go to a good home."

"Well, he will be," I say. "The Jackson's are great people, and the ranch is just the perfect place for a dog. So much freedom."

The man smiles broadly and bends down to pet Frankie. "Looks like you've got yourself a new home," he says.

"Wow," Jackie brings her hands to her mouth. "I can't believe we're actually doing this."

"I know," I say. "Sometimes, fate just puts us exactly

where we need to be at exactly the right time."

"Okay then," she says.

The man walks to a sideboard and pulls out a leash. "Here," he says. "You probably won't need it. Frankie's trained to stick with his owner unless you tell him he can run, but you might as well take it."

I bend to clip it to Frankie's collar, and he starts to wag his tail, his mouth opened with excitement.

"Come on, then boy," I say. "Let's get you home."

I head back towards the front door with Frankie, Jackie, and the man following. Jackie tells the man she hopes that his uncle gets better soon; polite talk to pass the time. At the car, Frankie turns to his owner, waiting for permission.

"Go on, boy," the man says, and Frankie jumps right in the trunk. There's no worry or fear there, just a willingness to start a new life. It's nice to see that the dog trusts us immediately. They say that animals have a sense of things like that.

Jackie continues to chat with the man, and I look around, taking in the neighborhood. It's then that I notice Samuel's truck is parked up in the drive of another run down property.

When Jackie's finally wrapped up, and we get in the truck, I point it out. "Isn't that Samuel's truck?"

Jackie squints. "Yeah, it is. I wonder what he's doing out here."

She drives a little closer, peering at the house. Just as we're about to go past, the front door opens, and Samuel comes out. A woman follows with a baby on her hip. The baby's face is covered with food and is dressed in a diaper and nothing else. The woman looks terrible; her face sunken as though she's lost her teeth and limp hair which definitely needs a wash. "What the hell," Jackie says. I'm thinking that she's going to drive quickly passed, but she doesn't. She stops right outside, and I start to panic. Is there going to be a confrontation?

Samuel is talking to the woman, but as he hears the truck getting closer, he turns, and I see his eyes widen. He definitely doesn't want us to be here.

Jackie throws open her door and stomps around the rear of the vehicle.

"This again," she starts to shout. "You found him again? He doesn't need you in his life, do you understand me?"

Samuel puts his hands up as Jackie approaches, taking hold of his mom to stop her from getting near the other woman. I'm torn as to whether to get out of the car or just stay put because this doesn't feel like something I have any place getting involved in.

"Mom," Samuel says. "It's nothing."

"So this is where you've been going. We all thought you had a girlfriend you didn't want to tell us about, but it's just her again. What's she telling you this time? That she needs money for the kid?" I can imagine Jackie's face sneering. The woman has backed up a few steps but doesn't look happy.

"She didn't have any diapers or formula," Samuel says.

"Because she shoots up all the money she gets. Don't you understand that? Haven't you learned anything at all?"

"I can't just stand by and do nothing," Samuel says.

"Did you give her money?" Jackie asks, taking a step back.

Samuel shakes his head. "I bought the things she needs for my brother."

"And you gave her money?"

Samuel hangs his head. Jackie struggles to get her arms free and rounds her son, coming face to face with the woman. "Don't you think you've hurt him enough? Don't you care how hard I had to work to bring him back from your neglect and abuse? And you just can't leave him be, can you? You want to keep dragging him back into this filth again and again."

"He's my son," the woman shouts, her cavernous mouth emitting flecks of spit which land on the dirt in front of her.

"He's my son," Jackie says menacingly. "You just birthed him and left him to fend for himself."

"Mom." Samuel puts his hand on Jackie's arm, but she shakes it off. She raises her hand and points at the woman.

"You listen to me, and you listen well. You contact my son again...you ask him for anything, and I'm reporting you. That poor child is filthy. Your house is filthy. I feel sick to my stomach at the idea that you have another child to neglect."

"My kid is fine," the woman shouts.

"This one is," Jackie says, grabbing Samuel's arm. "This one is an amazing man who can't help himself. His mind should tell him not to come here and see you after what you've done time and time again, but his heart won't let him leave you to your own devices. You're a parasite. A no good leech of a person. You can't leave my boy to his own life. You want to suck him dry and ruin him too. Well, I won't let you. When they took him away from you and gave him to me, he became my son, and I fight for my family. I don't leave them in the gutter to rot."

Jackie turns to Samuel. "I know this is hard for you. I know all your instincts are telling you to be here for her, but I'm telling you that you need to come home now."

Samuel glances back to his birth mom and then back to Jackie. Then he does something I'm not expecting at all. He walks away, gets into his truck, and closes the door.

"You forget his number," Jackie shouts at the woman. "You forget he even exists. All you ever do is drag him down. Contact him again, and you'll regret it for the rest of your life."

The woman takes a step back, and the baby starts crying. Jackie flinches, and I know she must be feeling terrible for acting this way in front of an infant. I can't imagine what must have happened before to make her so adamant that Samuel shouldn't have anything to do with his birth mom. If I've seen anything this week, it's that Jackie's a fair person and someone full of love.

Jackie shakes her head and starts towards the truck, watching as Samuel drives away.

When she's in the truck, she takes a deep breath and exhales slowly. As she starts the car and takes hold of the steering wheel, I can see her hands shaking. We drive away, and she doesn't look back, but I do. The woman doesn't go back into the house until we're rounding the bend, but what strikes me the most is that she's smiling.

27

Jackie rages all the way home. The truck seems to bump into every pothole and veer with every angry gesticulation she makes, and poor Frankie whines in the background. If I hadn't already gotten the gist of the history, I'm fully briefed by the time we get home.

In summary, Samuel's birth mom is a drug addict who manipulates Samuel into giving her money. Jackie's furious that, after the last time, he hasn't learned exactly what kind of woman she is. I want to point out that it must be a terrible position for him to be in, especially knowing that she has another child, his sibling, to care for. I want to point out that Jackie's raised a good man who has compassion despite the difficult situation, who is looking to help with an open heart despite the chance that he will get hurt all over again. It's hard, though, because Jackie doesn't give me a moment to speak, and because I know it's not what she wants to hear right now.

Sometimes in the moment, we just need to be given time to vent. Only when the anger has died down, is it worth pointing things out that don't quite fit with a person's perception of a situation.

As we pull up in front of the house, I see Samuel disappearing inside.

"You see," Jackie shouts, pointing at the door. "He's going to go up to his room now, and he won't talk to me about it."

"Maybe he needs some space," I say gently. "He didn't want anyone to know what was going on. He's probably angry that we were there, and embarrassed too. I bet he doesn't like being seen to be weak."

Jackie releases a long breath. "I don't want to make him feel weak," she says. "But he just won't accept that she's a lost cause."

"Maybe he has," I say. "Maybe, Samuel going there isn't about her but about him."

"What do you mean?" Jackie rubs her face, and the anxiety she has about her boy is written all over her face.

"Maybe he's going over there for him. We all need to be at peace with ourselves, don't we? For Samuel, knowing that his sibling could be in need...well, maybe that would eat him up. It doesn't matter if his birth mom deserves the help or not, it's about Samuel doing what he needs to do to feel right. You should be proud that he has a good heart."

Jackie shakes her head, her back slumping. "I just...I don't want to see him being used. I can't bear to see him hurt and disappointed all over again."

"Maybe it won't be like that this time," I say. "Maybe, he learned the first time what to expect, and this is just about him doing what needs to be done."

"I don't know."

I reach out and squeeze Jackie's arm. "It must be so hard to see your sons suffer. Zack with Ruffles and Samuel with this, but it's just life. We have to love to be happy, and loss and hurt are just inevitable sides of love."

She takes my hand and squeezes it. "You're a good girl," she says softly. "I had a good feeling about you from the beginning, but you can only tell so much. I trust my instincts, but the more you're here, the more I know that this plan is the right thing for my boys. You'll do right by them. I know you will."

I smile and squeeze her hand back. "I really hope that I get the chance," I say.

We share a moment of hope in the dusty truck that is eventually interrupted by Frankie scrambling around in the trunk.

"I think he wants to get out," I say.

"I think you're right."

We jump down and head round to free Frankie. True to his owner's word, Frankie stays where he is until we encourage him out. He really is a very well trained animal. "Come on then," Jackie says, leading him into the kitchen as I trail behind them. "Come and see where you're going to be living."

After what Jackie had said, I wasn't expecting Samuel to be in the kitchen, but he is. He's standing by the counter waiting for us. I can see him gear up for heated discussion with his mom, but he stops himself when he sees Frankie and me.

"Who's that?" he asks, pointing at Frankie who immediately wanders over to sniff Samuel's leg.

"This is Frankie," Jackie says. "Danna thought it would be a good idea for Zack to have a new buddy."

Samuel looks up at me quickly, his eyes meeting mine for a brief, heart-flipping second, then he squats down to pet Frankie's warm, shaggy coat. "Don't you think that Zack will think it's too soon?" he asks softly.

"Maybe." Jackie's voice is cold and reserved, and Samuel seems to flinch, his shoulders twitching almost imperceptibly. If I weren't watching him so closely, I would have missed it.

"He's lovely," Samuel says. "I hope Zack likes him."

"If not, maybe you could have him," I say.

Samuel looks up again. "Dogs are Zack's thing," he says. "If well all had one, it would be like a zoo in here."

I nod, understanding that again, Samuel is willing to sacrifice something for someone else. From the beginning, I had a view of Samuel, that he's cold and aloof, out for his own enjoyment, but now I see something else. He actually restricts his own happiness in favor of others. With Walker and Wade, he let them take the pleasure. With his birth mom, he's giving everything and getting nothing back. I can see by his enthusiasm for Frankie and the wistful sound in his voice that he'd love a dog of his own, but he's reserving that for Zack. Samuel is complicated in a way that is hard to untangle.

"We'd manage," Jackie says softly. "If you wanted a dog of your own."

Samuel shakes his head, and when he stands, his shoulders are tight. "I need to get going." He's fast to walk away, glancing at me intensely as he makes his way back to the door.

"Samuel," Jackie calls, but he doesn't turn.

"I'll be back later, mom," he calls, putting his hand up to wave, even though he's facing away from us. I want to go after him, to tell him that it's okay that he wants to help his momma, to say to him that I see him, but it just doesn't feel right. I don't want to make him any angrier than he already is with me.

Jackie gazes after her son, shaking her head. "Sometimes I wish I'd chosen to adopt girls. At least I'd get some conversation out of them, but then I think I wouldn't change a thing. For all the trials and tribulations, my boys are my proudest achievement."

"They are pretty amazing," I say. "You should be proud…and believe me, ten daughters in this house would be a whole lot more difficult than ten sons."

Jackie chuckles, starting to look in the cupboards. "You know what, Danna, I think you're probably right." She pulls out a large bag of doggie biscuits and finds a bowl too. "Here, Frankie. Let's get you something to eat."

Frankie gobbles from the bowl hungrily as Jackie finds another one for water.

"Maybe you can take him out to Zack. It might be better if the surprise wasn't here in front of all of his brothers."

"You think he'll respond better without an audience."

"I know he will. He's over where you were the other day, repairing the fence."

I'm about to ask why. We finished that section of fence when I was assisting him. Then I realize there must have been more damage and I don't want to alert Jackie to anything that her boys are trying to keep from her. "Sure," I say. "Shall I take your truck."

"I don't need it for the rest of the day." She bends to pat Frankie. "I hope Zack's gonna love you. How can he not when you're such a sweetheart?"

"Fingers crossed."

Jackie crosses her fingers on both hands. "If it helps, I'll do anything."

"I know you will," I say. "The boys are lucky to have you in their corner. Come on, Frankie."

I pat my thigh, and Frankie comes immediately. I don't bother securing his leash because I'm pretty confident he's gonna do exactly what I ask him to do. As predicted, he hops back into the trunk and Jackie hands me the keys. "If it doesn't go well, just come back. You can hang out here with me for the rest of the day."

"Okay. I think, if Zack doesn't want Frankie, I'll take him home with me."

Jackie smiles. "You like him?"

I shrug looking over my shoulder to where Frankie is panting, his tongue hanging adorably. "What's not to like. Frankie is like the world's greatest pooch."

"I think you might have a fight on your hands. I haven't seen Samuel so taken with an animal before."

"Let's see."

The truck is big and unfamiliar, but I adjust the seat a little and start it up. It's strange driving a new vehicle, but I get the hang of it in no time, enjoying the high position and the tractor-like rumble of the engine. I put the windows down, and the soft, warm breeze caresses my skin, making me think of summer days at the beach with my mom. It doesn't take me long to find Zack, and my heart starts to quicken as I get close. He's currently wielding a hammer; hair messy and shirt off.

Lord.

There is something to be said for a body crafted from manual labor. He's lean and muscular with not an ounce of unnecessary fat and jeans slung low that I can see the top of his briefs too. I swallow, uncertain how I'm going to maintain my composure with so much on show.

Zack turns as he hears the truck approaching, his brow furrowing. I park up behind his truck and jump out quickly.

"Hey," I say, taking in the damaged fence that Zack has had to remove. "They did it again?"

"Yep," he says. "It feels like groundhog day."

"You've really got to report it." I put my hands on my hips and shake my head. This is such a waste of time and resources and so damned unfair for someone to get away with such blatant harassment and vandalism.

He sighs and looks around as though he's hoping to see the guilty party in the distance somewhere. Just as he's about to reply, Frankie barks.

Zack looks at Jackie's truck, squinting his eyes to see where the noise came from. I blush furiously, my brain whizzing over all the ways I can tell Zack what I've done.

"It's Frankie," I say. "I got him today." I turn and walk over to the truck, tugging the trunk open and letting

Frankie jump down. His tail is wagging as he gazes around at all the open space. "Come see Zack," I say.

Zack is looking at me with watchful eyes. He squats down as his brother did to give Frankie a good stroke. I can see from that first moment that they're taken with each other. Frankie even goes as far as to lick Zack's cheek, and I can see a little glint in Zack's eye, although his expression doesn't change.

"I didn't know you wanted to get a dog," Zack says.

"He's for you," I say then tense as I wait for Zack's response.

Zack is still, watching as Frankie sniffs around some more. Zack doesn't look at me, just stays frozen in position.

"I know that nothing can replace Ruffles. He was such a special dog, but Frankie needed a home, and he seemed like a perfect buddy for you."

I realize after the words are out that I sound ridiculously patronizing. Perfect buddy. What the fuck was I thinking? I'm braced for Zack to get mad. He looks mad. His shoulders are as tight as mine, his face cold and unmoving as a statue. He takes a deep breath as though even thinking about Ruffles has hurt his heart.

Then he stands. "Thank you," he says softly. I almost fall over with shock.

"You like him?" I say in a ridiculously high pitched voice.

"He's great," is Zack's response. "Come, Frankie," he says and just like that Frankie is off, trotting behind Zack as he returns to working on the fence. I stand and watch this man who is still so hard to fathom, and want to squeal with joy that I did something right. I had a sense that this would work out, and I was right. I feel stupid for doubting myself now.

"Can I help?" I ask. "I don't have anything else to do."

"Sure," Zack says. "You can load that into the truck for disposal."

I start to gather the pieces of broken fence and lengths of twisted, broken wire as Zack continues his task, and Frankie trots around his now master obediently. When I'm done, Zack stops work to pull on his shirt and search out his lunch. I realize I didn't grab anything before I came, but Zack hands me a sandwich, and we share what he has, sitting on the back of his truck. We don't talk as we eat, but it doesn't feel awkward. I know this is Zack. He's quiet and thoughtful, watchful and peaceful. There's a calmness and tranquility about him that settles all my internal dramas, and I love it.

When we're done with the sandwich, Zack pulls out a giant chocolate chip cookie which he breaks in half. "Thank you," he says as he passes it to me.

"Shouldn't I be saying that," I laugh.

"I mean for Frankie."

"It's nothing," I say, but Zack shakes his head.

"It's a lot," he says.

I could ramble on about my thought process in suggesting my idea to Jackie and our journey to pick Frankie up, but I don't think Zack really cares about any of that. Instead, I just tell him how well I think they fit together and Zack nods.

"You ever just get a sense about something?" Zack asks.

I nod and smile. "I got a sense about you."

"I got a sense about Frankie. He's like Ruffles. A similar character."

"That's good," I say. "Perfect."

"You must be a good judge of character." He takes a big bite of the cookie as I take a nibble.

"Sometimes," I say. "But not always. I got Samuel pretty wrong."

Zack twists so he can see me without turning his head. I guess my statement has him interested.

"What did you get wrong about Samuel?"

"I thought he was pretty selfish and up himself."

Zack shakes his head. "Appearances can be very deceptive."

"Sometimes."

"Samuel is good at concealing his true self, so don't beat yourself up about that one."

I nod, staring into the distance. "I know he's been the one who's most against the idea of…" I pause not really knowing how to approach the subject with stoical Zack.

"He's scared," Zack says before I can continue. "He's scared you'll compare him to the rest of us, and you won't love him as much."

I turn to look at Zack who carries on munching his

cookie as though he hasn't just said one of the most observant and profound things I've ever heard. For someone who doesn't give a lot away in the emotion department, he seems pretty good at sizing other people up.

"And me? What am I scared of?" I ask.

"Of being alone. Of not being enough."

My throat burns as this strangely quiet man sums up my deepest fears in just seven words. I don't even know what to say in response, so I don't say anything. We sit together in the gorgeous sunshine, and I realize what it could be like to be with Zack. He's not out there like most of his brothers. He keeps himself to himself, but if I'm patient enough, Zack could be a thoughtful and perceptive partner, and that idea has me intrigued.

I now know eight of his brothers intimately. Eight different personalities and eight different ways of fucking. What would Zack be like? I can't imagine him sharing me with his brothers, at least not at the same time. If he agreed to the arrangement would he want alone time with me and be willing to sit on the sidelines the rest of the time. Could I make that work?

"And you, Zack. How do you feel about the idea of us all being together?"

I'm expecting him to be embarrassed, but instead, he turns to me and looks me dead in the eye. "I think you're crazy to want it, but I understand why you do. I understand why my mom thought about it in the first place."

"That doesn't answer my question."

He smiles in a small way that only affects one side of

his mouth but is just enough for me to know that he's amused. "I'm a pretty easy soul," he says. "I don't like drama. I don't like too much attention, and I like it when things come together like they were meant to be."

I think I know what he means. He's not prepared to fight for love, but a love that falls into his lap and feels right and easy will satisfy his needs. Could this be what he's looking for? Maybe. If Samuel comes around.

"So if this comes together?"

"If it comes together, then who would I be to fight it?"

I nod, understanding him entirely. "Fate, right?"

He nods. "I like to follow the easy path, not swim against the current. It makes life a whole lot happier."

It's then that he takes my hand, lacing his fingers with mine. "You're more than I thought you'd be," he says, and I know that's high praise coming from Zack.

"You're more than I thought you would be too," I say.

"And isn't that exactly the way it should be."

We sit like that as Frankie sniffs around until it's time to get back to work.

And when the day is done, we get into our trucks and drive back to a place that is beginning to feel like home.

28

The kitchen at the Jackson Ranch is undoubtedly the heart of this home. When Zack and I return from fence duty all the rest of the Jackson men are already home and enjoying coffee and home baked goods. All eyes fix on Frankie as we stroll in.

Zack bends down to pat him. "This is Frankie, everyone," he says. "Danna bought him to live with us. He's a Jackson now."

I smile as Xane and Xsander come to pet Frankie and look up at me with bright eyes. I can see how glad they are that Zack has found a new buddy. There is something extra warm about a home with a dog, and everything here seems right now, Frankie is here.

"Where'd you find him?" Wade asks.

"There was an ad in the window of the store," I say. "Your mom drove us to check him out, and we decided we liked him too much to leave him behind."

"Is he good out there?" William asks.

"He stuck with me the whole time," Zack says with pride in his voice. "He's gonna be a perfect companion."

"Well done, Danna." Walker pats me on the shoulder as he comes to see the newest member of the Jackson family.

Samuel is sitting across the table, watching all of the activity, focused on his muffin. Before today I would have taken his withdrawal as a negative thing, but now I can see how he's sitting back for others to bond. It's as though he can't find his place, and I understand it completely. This is a big family with so many personalities. It's so easy to get lost here, but Samuel's no wallflower. Zack, with his quietness, should have a much harder time, but he doesn't seem to. He's happy for things to happen around him, and he finds a way to involve himself when he needs to. Samuel isn't so sure.

It's funny how we can put up barriers that make us seem frosty and uncaring when really all we're trying to do is protect ourselves. I want to go over and put my arms around him. I want to show him how special I think he is, for all his rough edges and tough exterior, but now isn't the time or the place and I'm worried that my time left here is too short. Will I find the perfect opportunity to bond with this man who seems to need it more than any of his brothers? He's the last of the Jacksons that I need to convince and definitely the hardest.

"Danna, would you like coffee?" Jackie asks.

"Sure, that would be lovely. I just want to wash up."

I head to the bathroom to wash the dirt off my hands, and Zack follows. We clean up next to each other, Zack passing me the soap and me passing Zack the towel. We smile at each other when we're done, and Zack bends, pressing a soft kiss to the corner of my mouth. "You're lovely," he says softly. "Just what this family was missing."

My heart aches at his words, more so because they are so few and far between. I wish he'd put his arms around me so I can rest against his warm, hard chest and breathe in the scent of this hardworking, soft-hearted man, but Zack isn't about big physical gestures. Things will take time with him. Instead, he lets me pass through the door first, and we walk back to the kitchen companionably. I make a point of sitting next to Samuel, grateful that space has been left there. I have no idea if it was purposeful; the boys are all aware that it's Samuel who is objecting the most and maybe they want to give me time with him.

If anyone did have good intentions, they, unfortunately, don't amount to much.

Samuel glances in my direction and then immediately gets up. He doesn't even excuse himself, just heads to the door and walks outside. We hear his truck rev and drive away. I catch Wade's eye, and he gives me a shrug. "Give him time," he says.

"Time is something I don't have much of, unfortunately.

"I know," he says. "And it's not going to be easy."

Walker nods. "Samuel never lets anyone get close. He was the kid at school who could have had all the girls but left them all dangling. He lets someone close enough that they'd feel like they were getting somewhere, then he just freezes them out."

"Like just now," I say.

"Exactly," Wade says. "And the trouble is, most girls get so hurt by his rejection that they don't try with him again…they don't work to gain his trust."

"Well, I'm prepared to do that," I say. "But trust takes time to build."

"Just do your best," William says. "We're rooting for you."

I gaze around at the faces of these special men. Nine sets of warm eyes find mine, and I feel like crying. I'm so close to taking the first steps on the path that I've been dreaming about. There's only one more set of feet that I need convince to travel the same road, and he's gonna make it as hard as he can.

Jackie's beaming around at her sons. "You make me so proud," she says. "I can just see how amazing this is going to be for all of you."

"But what about Danna…she has to finish college," York pipes up. "I, for one, am definitely not cool with her dropping out."

"It's okay, York," I say. "I have no intentions of dropping out, but I'm happy to come at weekends and holidays until I can move down full time."

"We can drive up too," Xsander says. "Although what's your dad going to think about us all turning up on your doorstep."

Tommy looks at his brother with a warning expression, but I'm not upset by what Xsander's said. He has a right to know, after all. "My dad is going to be the final hurdle," I say.

Xsander gives me a knowing look. "Yeah. I can imagine that being a pretty big hurdle."

I grimace because he has no idea how big of a hurdle it's likely to be. I mean, dad's just wants me to be happy, but happy in a socially acceptable way, and I have no idea how I'm going to broach the subject.

There's really no point in overthinking about it while Samuel's walking away from me as I stink.

"I'll tackle that one when I have to," I tell them.

"And we'll help," Jackie says. I have no idea what she has in mind, but I can't see that a busload of strangers turning up on our doorstep is going to do anything but scare my dad witless.

"Thanks," I say. I take a bite of a chocolate and banana muffin and flop back into my chair, exhausted. Around me, the conversation moves on to everyday topics, and I soak up the chatter and laughter and warmth of this home. Tommy pours me more coffee, and Frankie comes and rests his head on my knee, whining for some attention.

After around half an hour, Jackie gets up to start putting the evening meal together. I tell her that I'm going to help and she doesn't object this time. We potter around her well-equipped kitchen while the boys disappear to wash off the toil of the day. Jackie's roast smells fantastic, and all that is left to do is prepare some vegetables. We top and tail beans, peel carrots and chop broccoli then pack heavy pots to cook them in. The kitchen fills with steam and the gorgeous aroma of roasting meat. Jackie chatters about her friends and the comings and goings of life in Broadsville, and just as we're getting the food out of the oven, a vehicle comes screeching to a halt outside.

"Tommy," Samuel yells from outside. "Trent, Xsander." He burst in the door, and he's panting and red in the face.

"What is it?" Jackie says, resting the large pan on a wooden chopping board.

"It's...it's nothing for you to worry about." Samuel heads towards the stairs and yells for his brothers. Footsteps thunder down in response to his frantic calls. "They're back," he says to Zack who's the first down. His eyes widen, and he storms outside as Samuel waits for the rest. Tommy's hair is wet, and Trent is still pulling on a shirt, but they're out the door as soon as Samuel repeats the words "They're back."

"What the hell is going on?" Jackie says, her hands on her hips as she watches her sons pour out of the house and into their trucks outside.

"Mom," Samuel shouts, the last to leave. "Just leave it."

"I won't leave it. You tell me what's going on right now."

Samuel disappears and jumps into his truck, then two vehicles speed away.

"What the hell," Jackie says. "Do you know what this is about?"

"No," I say, already thinking that it must be the men from the other ranch breaking the fences again. Or maybe worse from the look on Samuel's face. Could they have gotten to the horses or the other animals? I feel sick at the thought of the damage they could do so quickly.

"Are you sure. I'm...this isn't right," Jackie says. "This must be something serious...they know how I am about dinner. They wouldn't all walk out of here without explanation if it wasn't something bad."

"Just stay calm," I say. "I'm sure they'll be back soon."

"How can you know that?" Jackie says. "Tell me what you know, Danna. This is serious. Or I'm going to call the police."

I put my hands up, knowing the boys don't want the cops involved. If they're keeping things from their mom, the last thing they're going to want is outside involvement, although maybe that's what this situation needs. Who knows what kind of danger they could be in out there?

"Look, I'm not supposed to say anything," I say. "I just…I was fixing fences with Zack. They've been torn down by someone. We finished the job, but when I went out with Frankie, the whole thing had been damaged again."

"What?" Jackie says. "Someone's been vandalizing our property, and no one's told me?"

"They don't want to worry you," I say, putting my hand on her shoulder. "They know how vulnerable you've felt since your husband died. They wanted to try and sort this out so that you didn't stress."

"But they're putting themselves in danger. Who the hell is it?"

"I don't know. A rival ranch."

"From around here?" Jackie says. "There's never been anything like that in the past."

"When your husband was alive, you mean?"

Jackie's face goes serious. "They think they can trample all over us because of that. I've ten sons who own this land now, and we won't back down to this kind of bullying. I'm calling the police in case something serious happens."

She heads to a wooden corner cabinet and picks up the phone, quickly dialing while she moves to the window to look out. "I need to report an incident," she says. "Jackson Ranch."

The voice on the other end of the phone speaks for a while then Jackie says, "We've had some malicious damage up here over the past few weeks. One of my boys has seen something and taken his brothers out there. I'm worried that something serious could happen. If there's an altercation…"

There's another pause, and I move to stand closer in an attempt to hear what's being said. "It's a ranch. We all have firearms."

My heart starts to pound. I don't know why I didn't think of that before. I mean, I guessed they'd have guns somewhere, but not that they might be armed all the time. Do they have rifles in their trucks? Could someone get seriously hurt?

I rush to the mudroom, pulling on boots and heading outside before I've had a chance to say anything to Jackie. I still have the keys to her truck in my pocket, and I jump in, starting the engine and trying to find the switch for the headlights.

"Wait," Jackie calls, jogging towards me in her house shoes.

She rounds the front of the truck, so I can't drive away and jumps into the passenger seat. "You know where to go?" she asks.

"Only back to the western perimeter," I say. "It's where I was with Zack today."

"I guess we can start there."

I drive faster than I should, the truck bouncing over lumps and thumping into holes in the track. The beams of the headlights in front of us are small and insignificant, and I feel almost blind in the darkness. I pray that an animal doesn't spring out in front of us because there would be no way of me safely avoiding anything. Maybe I should have let Jackie drive. She knows these tracks better than I do.

"That's it," she says. "You're doing great."

It's all the reassurance I need to put my foot down harder on the gas. Ahead we start to see the silhouette of trucks parked. There are four, and my heart starts thudding even faster. Figures take shape in the low light; shapes on the ground are moving strangely against the blackness of the night sky.

"There they are," Jackie screeches as I realize that the shapes are fighting. The Jacksons must have found the intruders, but I can't make out what's happening in the dark.

"Shit," I say, slamming the truck into park and throwing open the door. I can hear the thump of fists and grunting of fighting men, and it's too much to take in.

"Stop," I shout, stumbling over to a pair of writhing figures and grabbing a shoulder. It's Tommy, and a man is struggling to get out of Tommy's grip. Tommy slams his fist into the other man's face, and I recoil as blood shoots from his nose. I step back into the path of more fighting men. Wade has someone in a choke hold and is struggling to keep a grip on him. I stumble again, my vision spinning. Jackie is crying out too. "Stop," she says hopelessly. Samuel turns at the sound of her voice, and in his moment of distraction, he catches a horrible crunching punch to the side of his head. I see him wobble, his knees going to jelly with the impact and I rush forward, throwing myself between him and the leering man who is intent on punching him again. "Get the fuck off of him," I scream. "You're trespassing."

The man laughs. "And what would you know about that?" He reaches into his jacket, and it's like slow motion as he draws out a gun. I put my hands up, backing myself into Samuel who's managed to get to his feet, shielding him from this crazy individual in an act of pure instinct.

"Gun," Jackie screams, and things around me seems to shudder to a halt as everyone, Jacksons and strangers alike, search for the weapon.

"Fuck," someone mutters.

"Put it down," someone else shouts.

"It doesn't have to go this way," I say elbowing Samuel as he tries to put himself between the man and me. Fear is a funny thing. It makes us act in ways that we wouldn't predict. It makes our minds race and our bodies feel like we're immersed to the neck in quicksand. "Just get in your truck and go," I say. "They'll be no more trouble. Just walk away."

"You think you can keep undercutting us and we're going to do nothing about it," the man shouts. "You think I'm going to let you run my family's business into the ground?"

"That isn't what we're doing," Samuel says. "There's room for us all to expand if we do it right."

"By do it right, you mean to do it cheaper?" the man says.

Samuel put his arm around my middle and slowly

guides me back two steps. I can feel the speed of his heart against my back and a tremble in his arm that tells me he's worried this is going to go wrong. Up until this point, I was running on adrenaline, but Samuel's fear creeps along my skin and into my brain.

"That isn't what I mean," Samuel says. "Look, we can't talk like this. This isn't the time, the place, or the way to have a serious discussion. My mom is here…there are women here. I'm just asking you to get off our land. If you want to talk…for us to come to some kind of arrangement, we're willing to do that. Just not now, like this."

"It didn't have to come to this," the man says, the gun waving up and down with his gesticulating hand. "This has been going on for months."

"I know, and we didn't want to make anything worse," Samuel says. He gradually takes steps around me until I'm shielded by his warm body, his arm clamping me to his back. "Just go now, and we'll sort things out. You have my word."

The man lowers the gun, so it's pointing at the ground and looks around at his companions who are all currently being held by Jackson men. He has the power with the weapon, but the rest of his group are in no position to assist him, in fact, they are currently shielding Tommy, Trent, William, and York from becoming available targets.

I hear Jackie whimpering from behind me. I quickly turn and find her being held by Wade, her face buried into his chest as though she can't bear to look at the danger her sons are currently in.

At the crunch of the man's boot, I know that Samuel's talk has worked. No one here wants bloodshed. This is about business, not about murder, but in the heat of the moment, terrible things can happen with consequences that last a lifetime.

"Come on," he shouts. "Let them go. We're going."

The Jackson's release their captives who stagger forward, their faces bloody from fighting. The man raises the gun again, moving it from side to side to let us know that he could kill any one of us if he wanted to. When all his friends are in the truck, he backs up into the passenger seat.

"I want to see you tomorrow, boy," he says. "I'm not messing around. This shit your pulling isn't going to end my business without a fight."

The tires spin on the gravelly ground and then truck speeds away over the field to the west of the Jackson's ranch, a vast dust cloud rising in the darkness.

"Fuck," Samuel says. He doesn't let me go, but his body goes slack, his breath coming in fast, deep pants. I put my hand on his shoulder.

"It's okay. You did good," I say softly.

Behind us, I hear the other brothers swearing, checking on their mom and each other. As Samuel comes around from the shock, he turns. "You did a foolish thing there," he growls. "What the hell were you thinking of acting like a human shield for me. You could have gotten killed."

"You could have gotten killed," I snap back. "He was less likely to want to kill me than you."

"So you risked your life for me," he says. His eyes are burning with rage and something so intense my instinct is to step back, but I don't. I hold my ground, keeping my eyes on his, reaching my hand out to touch him again.

"I risked my life," I say, "to try and stop things going bad. I couldn't bear it if anything happened to you, to any of you."

He searches my face, his chest still heaving. In the dark, his blond hair messy and his blue eye fiercely cold, he's fearsome and mean-looking, but I know that's not him. That's a façade, an instinct he developed when he was too young to understand why he couldn't rely on his momma to protect him. From looking at the child she has now, I can imagine what Samuel went through, and my heart bleeds. No wonder he pushes everyone away before they can hurt him again, but that won't be me. I'm here, and I'm with him for good. If he doesn't understand that now, I'll get through to him somehow. I'm not going to let him hold his heart in a cage when he needs so much love.

"I don't need your protection," he hisses. "I can protect myself."

"I know you can," I say soothingly. "But I was…I was worried things would escalate, and he had a gun. You can't protect yourself from a bullet."

"Neither can you," he shouts. "You could have died."

"But I didn't, and neither did you." I put my hand on his shoulder and move closer to him, fully expecting him to push me away. I move slowly, keeping my eyes on his. I can see the fear there, but he doesn't move. "It's okay," I say softly as though I'm reassuring a child. "It's okay."

All around us there is silence, but I'm so focused on Samuel that I don't turn to find out what's happening. I'm close enough to put my arm around him, so I do; a slow and tentative slide. He's so solid and warm, but rigid and cold too. I move closer, resting my other hand on his chest, leaning into his large frame, so my face is in the hollow of his neck. He smells good; of something alpine, of the outdoors and of himself. I breathe him in, not knowing how long he's going to let me do this for. I imagine him grabbing me by the upper arms and shoving me back, but he allows me to hold him until he starts to relax. I feel the dropping of his shoulders, the movement of his arm as he gathers me against him. His whole body curves around me like a large shield. "You shouldn't have done that, Danna," he says. "Don't you ever do anything like that again."

The word again seeps into my bones. Again means time after tonight. Again means the chance of a future. I look up, wanting to see if I'm reading this right. Is Samuel saying what I think? His eyes meet mine, and then he looks away. It's as though he wants to make a connection, but he can't. It's then there's a cough behind us.

When I turn, everyone is staring. Samuel releases me as though he's been caught with his hand in the cookie jar, and the moment of connection we had is shattered.

"We should get back to the house," Zack says calmly.

"You should never have come out here," Jackie shouts. "WHAT THE HELL WERE YOU THINKING?"

"We were trying to protect our home and our business," York says.

"No, you were acting like idiots. Do you think I care about this ranch so much that I would sacrifice even one of your fingernails for it? I don't care about any of it. You are more important. DO YOU HEAR ME?"

The boys say nothing but look pretty contrite. "And another thing," Jackie shouts. "Why don't I know anything about this? Are you keeping things from me now? Am I so feeble that you can't tell me these things? I was running this ranch with your father for years while you were all in diapers."

Again there's silence.

"Anyway, get your asses back to the house. The police have been called...they're going to arrive soon and I want you to be ready to tell them everything. We're not getting into any kinds of discussions with these lunatics."

"MOM," Samuel shouts. "Why the hell did you call the cops?"

"Because I was afraid for your life," Jackie says, waving her finger again, "and because it's the right thing to do. It's what your father would have done in this situation."

Jackie stomps towards her truck, jumping into the driver's seat. I follow quickly because she's upset and I don't want to leave her to drive back by herself. By the time I'm pulling on my belt she's already heading home.

"Fuck," she says. "Fuck."

Her hands are trembling even though she's gripping the steering wheel.

"It's okay," I say. "Everyone's okay."

"But..." She starts to cry, swiping at her tears as though she's mad with her own emotions. "What would have happened if you weren't here," she says. "I wouldn't have known anything about this...I wouldn't have known where to go."

"You can't think like that. Everything's okay. We just have to focus on the positive."

"Okay for how long." She thumps the steering wheel. "They're not going to back off. If they were prepared to pull a gun on my sons, they're prepared to use it."

"Not necessarily. People do things in the heat of the moment and think afterward." I rest my hand on her arm for reassurance, but I don't think it helps. She's so wound up with worry and anger.

"If their dad were here, none of this would be happening."

"You don't know that," I say. "And you have to just deal with things in the here and now. You can't wish for things that can't be."

"Someone's going to get hurt," she says, sobbing again. "I can't protect them. Not when they won't talk to me."

"Look, it's all out now," I say. "You can show them now that they were wrong to keep you in the dark, but you have to be in control. If you're emotional and worried, it's going to make them feel even more that you need to be kept out of stressful ranch business. That's not what you want, is it?"

Jackie shakes her head.

"I know you just want what's best for them and I understand how hard it can be to see people you love in danger. I didn't know what to do." My own hands are shaking in my lap as the adrenaline that's been coursing through my veins takes effect.

"You did too much," Jackie says. "You stood between my boy and a bullet today, Danna. I don't think I'll ever be able to repay you."

I shake my head. "I wouldn't be here if it wasn't for

you. I wouldn't have this chance to try and find the life that I want if it wasn't for you. It's me who won't be able to find a way to repay you."

We pull up in front of the house and Jackie looks around as though she's worried someone might be lurking in the bushes. The ground crunches behind as the other two trucks draw up, engines turning off immediately. The boys aren't quiet as they exit their vehicles. They obviously don't have the same concerns as their mother, simply stomping towards the front door. Walker, Wade, and William wait for us, and we all walk together.

In the kitchen, the boys are shouting. "THAT FUCKER HAS GONE TOO FAR," Samuel bellows. "HE PULLED OUT A FUCKING GUN."

"It's gotten out of control," York says. "It needs to stop here before something really bad happens."

"You mean like Danna getting shot," Samuel says. "She could have died."

"I know," York says, putting his hands up. "But no one ever got anywhere by escalating things. We need to speak to the police. There are enough witnesses to get him put behind bars."

"I don't know," Samuel says. "You think that his family is just going to lay down after that happens."

"We don't know what will happen," Tommy says. "We need tighter security. More cameras. Dogs maybe."

"They can shoot dogs," Zack says. "If they're pulling guns on humans they're not going to think twice about killing security dogs."

Tommy slumps his shoulders. "I don't know. We've

just got to do something."

"Let's see what the police say," Jackie says softly. "We can only take things one step at a time."

The boys are quiet as they contemplate their mom's words. She couldn't have chosen better. "We're sorry we didn't tell you, mom," Xane says. "We just didn't want you to worry."

"Please just don't do it again. Knowing that you've been keeping this from me is going to worry me a lot more. I need you to promise you'll always be honest; otherwise, I'm not going to be able to sleep at night."

Xane pulls his mom into a hug. "Okay, mom."

I put my hand over my mouth as my emotions start to bubble up. This family is just exactly what I need in my life, and whatever happens, I'm going to do my best to try and keep them safe.☐

29

The police arrive half an hour later. I guess that outside of a city, there is a much longer wait for emergency services. The thought scares me a little, especially after what happened tonight.

Two cops sit in the kitchen with cups of coffee. They both look like they'd have trouble getting themselves out of bed, let alone chase down criminals. The guns on their hips could be helpful, but only if they were fast enough at drawing them.

"So you know the man," he asks Samuel.

"Yes, and so do you."

The cop grimaces. "Small town," he says. "Makes hiding from your wrong doings a lot more difficult."

"I don't know," Trent says. "People still seem to get away with things that are done in plain sight."

The other cop raises his eyebrows. "You got something to get off your chest?"

Trent looks away, and I start to worry that this isn't going to get taken seriously.

"Let's just keep on track," Zack says. "We can all provide witness statements for tonight and previous damage. I have photos of the fences and the dead animals."

Jackie's head swivels. "Dead animals. They've been killing our livestock."

Zack nods, and Jackie's hand goes to her mouth before a sob can escape.

"Okay. We're going to take statements."

It takes three hours for the cops to take statements from everyone involved. By that time, we're all done, my stomach is growling. I'm feeling a little sick too, but I'm not sure if it's from hunger or nerves. The food is stone cold, but we serve it out anyway and eat in silence. There isn't much to say, and I'm so drained, I could sleep where I'm sitting.

After the dishes are cleared, I give Jackie a hug and make my way upstairs. The boys have already all dispersed, and the hallway is quiet. In my room, I close the door and burst into tears. I'm not expecting it; my body shudders, and I have to cover my mouth to silence my sobs. It's like a terrible bubble of fear and emotion has risen to the surface, and I clutch my arm around my ribs, trying to hold myself together.

We could have died tonight.

I stood in the path of a loaded gun.

The Jackson family are still targets for this crazed man, and goodness knows what the police will be able to do about it.

And Samuel.

I don't even know what to think about Samuel. For a moment I thought we'd made a breakthrough in the most difficult of circumstances, but then the connection was lost and I have no idea if we'll ever pick it back up again.

I slump into the chair, bending forward so that I'm curled around myself. I breathe deeply, trying to suppress my tears. We're all okay, I remind myself. Nothing actually happened. And just because Samuel withdrew, doesn't mean that there won't be a chance to reach out to him again.

I'm reaching for a tissue, wiping my tears and blowing my nose and then I notice my phone is flashing.

I didn't hear any messages or calls, but when I check it, there are four missed calls and a message.

Laura: Call me as soon as you can…like right now!

I feel the color drain from my face because there must be something terrible going on. She wouldn't demand a call like this if there wasn't.

My heart is thumping as I dial her number.

"Thank goodness," Laura gasps.

"What is it?"

"Fuck, Danna. The TV production company received a call from the press. Someone in Broadsville has contacted the media, and they know about you and the Jacksons."

"What?" I say. "What do you mean they know?"

"They've put two and two together and made a hundred. The conversation we had on the show about you wanting a harem too…they wanted a comment from me about it. They wanted to know if I've pushed you into finding the same kind of lifestyle…like I'm some kind of gang-bang pusher, and if they're calling me already, they're gonna be finding their way to you."

I swallow as fresh tears start to burn at my throat. I remember the drama that Laura faced when the media found out about her and the McGregor brothers. It was a shit storm that almost cost my friend everything. If that kind of attention finds its way here, I don't know what I'd do. And the Jacksons. This is exactly what Samuel was arguing. If he was worried about the townsfolk finding out about this, what the hell is he going to say when the whole state is gossiping about his family.

This couldn't be worse. Any progress that I've made with the boys will be undone, and my pop will be mortified. Even more worrying, this will put the spotlight on the Jacksons just as the cops are investigating what happened tonight. Could this put them at more risk of harm? I don't know what to do.

"What am I going to do?" I'm hoping that somehow, my best friend will have all the answers.

"I don't know," Laura says. "I was going to tell you to get out there and deny everything. It might be the best thing to do for you and the Jacksons, at least until everything blows over, but I don't know if you'll have time."

"Shit," I say. "Shit, shit, shit."

"Look, …it'll be okay. Whatever happens, it'll come right in the end. Look at what happened to me. I thought my life was over when we found out about the front page spread that day at college, and look at me now. We could never have predicted it, but I'm sure that everything will be fine for you too."

"But the McGregors wanted the harem, Laura, didn't they? They fought for you because it was their idea all along."

"Their dad's idea," she reminds me.

"Yes, but they understood the value of it. Most of them were used to the idea and were up for embracing it. This is a whole different situation."

"The Jackson's don't want it?"

"Some of them are open to trying it. They see the benefit to their business and family life in the same way the McGregor's did, but it's just too fresh, and I'm worried that this is just going to prove them right to have concerns."

"This isn't something you've done," Laura says.

"It is," I tell her. "I was recognized in the bar in town. I shouldn't have ventured out because there was always that risk."

Laura's quiet for a few seconds as she digests what I've said. "You can't shut yourself away, Danna. This isn't something that you should be ashamed of."

"But it's something other people will be. It's something other people are judgmental of. Something other people will turn up their noses about."

"You couldn't have known that anyone would put this together, Danna. Yes, we had a conversation on screen, but it was me leading you in a jokey way."

"It was enough to prompt Jackie to call me in the first place," I say. "I'm surprised that no one has mentioned anything to my dad."

"I don't think our show is the kind of thing that your dad's friends would be tuning in to on a Saturday night," she says. "And even if they did, they wouldn't want to admit watching it to anyone."

"So you think people know and just haven't said anything?" I say, feeling mortified.

"Maybe, but again, why do you care. If this is genuinely something that you want and something that you are going out of your way to finding, then you have to be ready to take some flack. It passes, and you can move through it."

"I just think this is all too soon. I need to get out of here. I'll tell the Jacksons that they can deny everything."

"I don't think that's what you should do, but it's your decision," Laura says. "Do you want me to send you a driver?"

"Yes," I say. "But they need to get here soon."

"I'll see if I can find a local company to bring you home," she says. "I'll message you with the details."

As soon as we hang up, I begin to stuff my possessions into my bag. I'm grabbing the final items from the bathroom when there's a knock at my door. I glance around the room at my packed suitcase and purse, my washbag on the bed filled with things. I could hide things in the bathroom, but nothing is zipped up.

"Danna." I'm pretty confident that it's Wade at the

door, but I can't be sure. "Can I speak to you for a moment?"

"I'm getting changed," I say.

"Please. I just want to make sure you're okay."

"I'm fine," I call through the door. "Just a little shaken, but nothing that won't be okay with a good night's sleep."

"Will you open the door?" he asks.

"I can't right now," I say, holding back my tears. I've got to leave and seeing Wade, his soft eyes and warm expression will push me over the edge.

"Please," he says, and I start to cry. I don't want him to treat me tenderly before I go because it will make this so much harder. My heart feels like it's been split down the middle and it hurts so badly.

"I'll speak to you in the morning," I say.

There's a pause as Wade contemplates my words. "Okay," he says. "I'm not going to leave this house until you do, though."

"Okay," I say. "Night."

"Night, Danna. Sweet dreams."

I slump onto the bed, more tears dripping from my cheeks onto my jeans, creating dark patches of sorrow. A message comes through from Laura.

Laura: A car will be with you in an hour. Where shall I tell them to get you from? Can they come into the ranch without alerting anyone?

Me: No. I'll have to make my way to the gates. Tell

them to meet me there.

Shit.

I'm going to have to trek all the way back to the road in the dark. At least I know my way, but after what happened tonight, this isn't exactly a sensible decision. I'm going to need to tell Jackie so that she can drop me off.

I don't know what she's going to think. Will she try to convince me to stay, or will she understand why I have to leave? Will she want me to protect her boys or come out and be honest about everything?

There's no time for me to ponder on anything. I open the door a sliver, looking down the hallway. It's quiet, so I take my chance. Jackie's usually the only one in the kitchen this late, and I'm praying it'll be the same tonight. I pause at the bottom of the stairs, straining my ears to hear if there is any conversation happening in the kitchen, and there isn't. When I poke my head around the door, Jackie's sitting at the table at her laptop.

"Hey," I say softly. "Can I talk to you a minute?"

"Sure, sweetie," she says. "I'm just catching up on emails. I need the distraction."

I don't sit because I need Jackie to realize that I don't have much time. I rest my hands on the chair, which is tucked under the opposite side of the table to her.

"My friend Laura just called me. There's been tip-off to the press, and now they're speculating about why I'm here. It must have been someone from the bar the other night. Nadine or the girl who waitresses at the diner."

"Brandy? Oh dear," Jackie says. "That's not ideal."

Her reaction is certainly more moderate than I was expecting. "It isn't. My dad doesn't know why I'm here and if he finds out like this…well, I don't know what will happen."

"He'll probably be a bit shocked," she says. "If my boys were, and they're from a younger and more permissive generation, then I'm sure your dad won't know what to think."

"I don't want to hurt him," I say. "And I don't want to bring unwanted attention to your family."

Jackie puts her hands flat on the table. "You came here to achieve something, Danna. Have you achieved it?"

I shake my head. "I…with some of the boys but not with others."

"Samuel?" Jackie says. "He was always going to be the toughest."

"But it's more than that. I just…the rest say they're up for trying but will they really be when the whole of the state is looking at them, and the press is hounding them when they pop to the general store or to Joe's. It's one thing for the local townsfolk to find out down the line when everything's stable, but a whole other thing for your sons to become a spectacle because of me."

Jackie nods. "I understand," she says. "There's a lot at stake, particularly now."

I rub my face, feeling as hollow as I've ever felt. "This…it's been amazing, but it's not the right time for any of us and I need to leave before it all gets out of hand. If the press asks for comments, you can say you've never heard of me. Say you had someone trying out for a position of a housekeeper, but it didn't work out."

"Housekeeper?" Jackie laughs. "Chance would be a fine thing."

I shrug. "Anything you can think of to take away speculation. Hopefully, it will all fizzle out before they can print anything inflammatory. My friend has been ignoring calls and refusing to comment. She's arranged for a car to pick me up from the gates. Could you drive me?"

Jackie sighs and shakes her head. "This is a mistake, Danna. I know why you're doing it, but you're so close to finding what you were looking for, and I know my boys won't find a better girl than you in a hundred years of searching."

I start to cry again, overwhelmed by her kind words and the idea of the Jackson brothers searching for a replacement for me. They were mine for a short time…well, most of them.

"Hey," Jackie says, getting up from the table and coming to give me a hug. She smells of cooking and lavender soap; a homely scent that makes me miss my mom so badly. "If you leave now, I want you to think long and hard about what happens next. I'll take you to the gates, and when you're gone, I'll tell the boys. This doesn't have to be the end, Danna. Just a little blip in the road, and to be honest I'll feel better if you weren't here right now. With everything going on with the cops, I feel responsible for your safety…particularly as your dad doesn't know you're here."

I draw back and wipe my eyes with my sleeve. "I think I should go," I say.

"Okay. Go and get your things and I'll get my shoes and coat."

Jackie bustles away, tidying the table while I make my

way upstairs. My heart is pounding as I glance around, silently praying that I'm not going to bump into anyone. The coast is clear as I dash into my room. I pull on my shoes and then grab my suitcase and purse and make my way to the door. As I'm about to leave the room, I turn around, trying to commit this place to memory. That first night with Walker and Wade happened here, and then with William and latter, York.

My throat burns as I come to terms with the fact that I'm leaving and I don't know if or when I'll be coming back.

I trudge downstairs, finding Jackie ready and waiting.

We're out the door without anyone seeing me leave, and I'm happy and devastated at the same time. Saying goodbye would have been too difficult, but leaving this way feels like a betrayal. I just hope that they'll understand why I've gone and find it in their hearts to forgive me.

30

I wake up in my own bed, and it's strange.

Strange to be home. Strange to be alone when I've been used to having so many people around. I managed to sneak in last night without waking dad, but I left evidence that I was home so he'd know. I'm expecting him to knock on my door any second, but that hasn't stopped me from crying. I slept so badly, drifting in and out of slumber so disturbed by dreams and stretches of insomnia that it's left me shaky and uncertain. I grab my phone to check to see if there are any messages, but there aren't.

I scan the news websites, but there's nothing on there about the Jacksons, and I'm relieved. Maybe, when the press found out I wasn't there, they went away without a story. At least that's what I'm praying has happened.

I grab a tissue to wipe my face and blow my nose. I'm just about to get out of bed when the expected knock happens.

"Danna, are you up?" dad says.

"I'm still in bed," I call.

"Can I come in?"

I consider saying that I'm not decent and will see him at breakfast, but I know that will only make things more awkward. My mom always used to say, 'don't put off until tomorrow what can be done today' and its good advice.

"Yeah," I say.

Dad opens the door slowly, sticking his head around it first to check it's okay before opening it more fully. "I wasn't expecting you. Weren't you supposed to be gone for longer."

I nod. "I wasn't feeling great, so I decided to come home."

He comes closer, putting his hand on my forehead like he used to do when I was sick as a child. "You don't feel hot."

I shake my head. "I'm better now. Must be the comforts of home."

"Well, that's good to hear." He smiles, his hair still standing on end from where it's been pressed against his pillow. "Did you have a good time?"

Such an innocent question, but with so many connotations that he's unaware of. I don't want to lie to him anymore, particularly as there is a risk that I could be headline news in the gossip mags any second. I remember his reaction when he read about Laura. The shock and disgust. The memory makes my stomach clench with dread.

"You know, I'm feeling a little nauseous," I say. "I'll come down and talk to you more in a bit."

He looks me over as I slide out of bed and head towards my private bathroom. "I'll bring you some water," he says, but I shake my head. "I have some. I'm okay."

When I close the door, I perch on the toilet hanging my head. Inside I want to scream at anyone who'll listen that I don't want to live a mundane life, sticking to societies norms because that just what everyone has to do. I want to tell dad that I've found ten men who I believe can fulfill all my needs, emotionally and physically. I want to ask Laura to let the press know that they're right; I was 'interviewing' the Jackson's to be my harem, and most of them decided that they wanted the position. I get a flash of Samuel's fierce eyes and the strength of his arm around me as he tried to protect me. His words were initially against my plan but his actions...well, I hope they revealed something a whole lot different.

I'm feeling sick because, back in this house, I just don't feel right. I know that this is my home, but it feels empty and lonely without mom here. I love dad so much, but it's not the same. Mom made this house a home, and that's just how it is.

I don't want this version of my life. I want the vibrant, busy one filled with family and responsibility and warmth. I want more for my dad too. He misses mom so much and imagining him growing old without anyone else here makes me so sad that I want to cry again.

For the first time, I feel that I've hit a brick wall. I'm damned if I do and damned if I don't but am I willing to put my relationship with dad on the line? He's my only family and my last connection with mom. I don't want to break his heart when it's already been shattered.

I don't want a life without the love of my ten men or the love of my father.

Choosing between my family and my future family is impossible.

I strip and shower, scrubbing away the stickiness of tears from my eyes. I dress in comfortable clothes and take another look at my phone. I search using my name as a keyword but find nothing on any news site. The relief is huge.

Making big decisions is one thing. Making big decisions with media coverage is something else. I saw the toll it took on Laura, and it is not something I want to go through myself.

I'm not hungry at all, but I make my way downstairs to make coffee. Dad is sitting at the table, looking at bills. It was something that mom always sorted out, and I can see that he's having trouble from his deep frown line showing above the glasses he has perched on the end of his nose.

"Need some help?"

He looks up and grimaces. "Is it that obvious?"

"Pretty much." I pull out a chair and take hold of the pile of papers he has. "Most of these are being paid directly," I say. "This one…we need to look for a cheaper rate."

"Well, that's good." Dad takes his reading glasses and lays them on the table. "Your mom was always so organized. I didn't realize how much she did until she wasn't doing it anymore."

I smile. "She was a powerhouse. Would you like coffee?" I get up to make myself some.

"Sure." Dad takes his black with no sugar.

We sit at the table and sip our coffee, the silence not feeling as comfortable as it should.

"So," dad says. "Doug was telling me he saw Laura's show." His eyes flick to mine as though he's watching for a change in my expression.

"Oh yeah." Heat moves from my chest to my cheeks as my fair, freckled skin turns pink.

"Yeah. He said that it's good."

"Well, Laura's an amazing person, and the McGregor's are lovely too. It shows in the show," I say.

"Yes." Dad takes another sip. "Doug saw you on there too."

"Laura asked for the support," I say. "I couldn't say no."

Dad nods. "Of course. She's been your friend almost your whole life. Doug said that you had a conversation with her about wanting her arrangement. He told me I should watch out because I might have a full house soon." Dad laughs as though it's all a big joke, but it's not his natural laugh, rather something false that makes me feel like he's trying to dismiss this before it becomes something real.

"Well, Laura's pretty damn happy," I say. "It might not be conventional, but I struggle to see how anyone could look at them and not see how right they all are for each other."

Dad's eyes narrow just slightly, and I look away. Out in our yard, the neighbor's cat prowls around like she owns the place.

"Where were you staying this week, Danna?"

The question hangs in the air. I can't look at dad now because I can feel his anger before he's even expressed any. "With friends," I say.

"In Broadsville. Yes, you told me that. Which friends…how do you know them?"

I twist my hands in my lap as my mind skips over all the options for a response.

I vacillate between lying and honesty so many times that my brain feels as though it might explode. I imagine dad sitting at the table and me with only half a head, and I want to laugh a hideous nervous giggle that will make me sound unhinged.

Just as I'm about to open my mouth, my phone rings.

On the screen, it reads 'Jackie' and, I'm filled with an immediate sense of dread.

Do you ever get a feeling in your gut before something terrible happens? A creeping sense of unease that has you wondering what's wrong. Jackie could just be calling me to find out how I am, but she knows I arrived home because I sent her a message before I went to sleep.

"I have to take this," I say, scrambling to leave the table so I can go to another room. "Hey," I say.

"Oh, Danna. It's…" Jackie bursts into tears, and my hand goes to my mouth.

"What is it …what's happened?" I say.

"It's…Samuel, Zack, and Tommy …they've been attacked." She's crying so hard, and I start to cry too.

"What? When? Are they okay?"

She sobs again; a loud wrenching sound, and I have to lean against the wall to hold myself up. I don't want to think the worst, but my mind goes there. I saw the rage in that man's eyes and heard the unhinged way that he spoke. I know in my gut that he was capable of killing a man, and that was before the Jackson's talked to the cops. What would he be like now?

Was this revenge?

"Tell me they're okay," I shout, needing to cut through Jackie's grief so I can get the answer I need.

"They're in Addison Hospital. I just...they're bad, Danna. Really bad."

I fall to my knees as my body goes into shock. With a trembling hand, I try to keep a grip on the phone. "How bad, Jackie."

"Can you come?" she asks. "We...I really need you and...I just want you to talk to them. Tell them how you feel...anything to make sure they come back to me."

I sob because Jackie sounds desperate; a mother who'd do anything to try and save her sons. I know now how serious this is and my stomach heaves. "I'll come," I say with a voice so choked that it's almost incomprehensible.

"Thank you," she says and hangs up.

I don't know what it is that gives us focus during difficult times. My heart is breaking, but somehow, I manage to get up and go back into the kitchen. Dad has gone from looking angry to looking worried.

"I need you to drive me to Addison Hospital," I say

calmly, grabbing a tissue from the table and wiping my face. I'm in no state to drive, and I'm not sure that my car would make it.

"Where's that?" Dad asks.

"I'm assuming near Broadsville. I need to look it up."

"What's happened, Danna?"

"My friends…people that I love have been attacked. They've been taken to that hospital, and I need to get there as soon as possible."

Dad nods, quickly getting up to slip on some shoes and grab his car keys. I rush to get my purse and pull on some sneakers. My hair is in a messy bun, and I've no makeup on, but I don't care. I just need to get to my boys as quickly as I can.

While dad starts the car, I look up the hospital on my phone and show him where it is.

It's well over two hours away, and even though dad drives as fast as he legally can, I still want to scream at him to go more quickly.

We don't talk for the entire journey. I worry at the skin in the sides of my fingernails until it's bleeding, then I stare out of the window, watching the world go by as the anxiousness builds in my gut. Will they be okay when I arrive? The thought of going into a hospital fills me with dread. The last time I was there was for my mom's final few hours. I couldn't cope with losing anyone else. Not now. Not ever.

Dad pulls up at the front of the hospital. "You get down, and I'll find space in the lot," he says. "But Danna…you need to tell me who we're here to see so I can find you."

"Ask for the Jackson brothers," I say.

Then I jump out of the car and start to run towards the hospital entrance.

31

Do you ever have that dream where you're trying to run, but your legs feel as though they have weights attached or that the lower half of your body is submerged in water. You know where you want to go, but you just can't get there quickly enough.

At the desk, I cannot get the attention of the nurse who seems to want to look just about everywhere than at me. I'm patient for a few seconds, practically vibrating with emotion, then I just can't take it.

"Excuse me, I'm here to see the Jackson brothers."

She still doesn't look up, typing away on her keyboard as though I'm not here at all. I don't know how some people can be so dismissive, especially in a place where people are sick or hurt, and their loved ones are desperate. Where is her compassion?

"Please," I say. "Can you just tell me where I need to go? They've been hurt really badly."

She looks up. "Please wait a moment." Her expression is withering, and I want to grab her by the hair and smash her face against the stupid desk.

"I can't wait," I say. "I...I just need to get up there. Please."

Someone from behind must see that I'm about to collapse on the floor any second with grief, and takes pity on me. "You need the ICU," she says. "Follow this corridor and take a right at the end."

I'm running before she's even finished, eyes scanning for signs for the ICU. My sneakers squeak on the linoleum, my lungs tugging in gasps of disinfectant-scented air. The corridor seems to go on forever; I pass doors and doors like in the boat scene from Charlie and the Chocolate Factory, each labeled with a name that spells out misery.

I take a right and see the double doors for the ICU at the end of a very long stretch, but I don't tire, just push on, my legs pumping, my bag slipping from my shoulder. With each stride I get closer and feel sicker because on the other side of that door are three people I love are hurt so badly they need specialist care, and when I step through that door, I'm going to have to face their injuries.

And their seven brothers who I left behind to face a hostile situation alone.

Maybe if I'd stayed.

Maybe, If I'd stayed, everything could have worked out differently.

I come to an abrupt stop just outside the door. There's a button to press to gain access, and my finger hovers by the buzzer, my hand shaking. Then the door opens, and Walker is there.

"Danna," he says. His eyes are bloodshot, his face gray

with worry. There's blood on his shirt, and I almost collapse on the floor, grabbing hold of him to steady my weak legs. He tugs me into a fierce hug as I sob.

"What happened, Walker?"

"They were ambushed on our land. The only reason we knew what had happened was that Zack still had the strength to use his cell. Samuel and Tommy were unconscious."

"Oh my god," I say.

"I'll take you to them." Walker guides me into the ICU as I swipe at my face and take a deep breath. I see them immediately, bandaged, and hooked up machines. "Samuel and Tommy still haven't regained consciousness. They're…" he pauses as though saying more is hurting him too badly. "They're in a coma. They both have swelling on the brain. The doctors are hoping that it will go down…it will need to for them to come around."

My hand goes to my mouth as I see Jackie. She's sitting at the end of the middle bed as though she doesn't want to be too far from any of them. Trent is by Tommy, doubled over like he's feeling all of his brother's wounds. Xsander and Xane are by Samuel. Wade is next to Zack.

William and York are missing from the group.

"There's a maximum of two visitors per bed," Walker says. "I was on my way down to get my brothers to swap over."

"I don't have to stay," I say.

"Yes you do," he says. "Xsander."

Xsander looks up, his eyes bloodshot. When he sees

me, he's up and out of his seat in a flash.

"Danna." He pulls me into a fierce hug that almost knocks the breath from my lungs. "Get over here." He drags me by the hand until I'm taking his seat next to Samuel.

It's a struggle to look at him like this. Outside of the bandages, Samuel's handsome face is covered with bruises. It almost seems as though someone has kicked him in the head. I lean forward and take his hand tentatively, not wanting to disturb the drip he has running into his vein. I look to the side and see Jackie sobbing, and I don't know what to do. Should I go to comfort her? Do I sit here holding the hand of a man who doesn't even know I'm here? Do I go to Zack and Tommy? How do I divide myself when there are so many people who need me?

"Talk to him," Xsander says. There's a frantic edge to his voice that tells me just how desperately scared he is right now.

I feel as though all eyes are on me, and the pressure is immense. Did Jackie call be because she was hoping that my presence would bring the boys around? If she did, I have a feeling she is going to be disappointed.

I don't know what to say or how to say it. The only thing I can think of to do is to whisper close, so I lean in until my mouth is right by Samuel's ear. He smells of disinfectant and sickness, and I swallow down more tears as the reality of his condition truly sinks in. He could die. People with severe brain injuries, especially the kind that put them in a coma, don't always recover. "Samuel," I say. "It's Danna. I'm here with your mom and your brothers."

I stroke his cheek, praying to see his eyelids flutter a little; just enough to show us that he's in there and okay.

"You need to come back to us," I say. "Listen to my voice. We just want you to come back to us. Try and wake up baby," I say. "We need you. I need you."

I smooth his hair, feeling the grittiness of dried blood left over from the attack. I look over my shoulder, and Xane has his face buried in his hands. I stroke Samuel's cheek again. "Please," I say. "Please wake up."

There's no movement, exactly as I expected and feared. This isn't the movies. Words of love and affectionate touches don't really rouse people from terrible medical emergencies. I take a step back and turn to Zack. His eyes are closed, but they open just as I start walking towards him. He doesn't smile; instead, he grimaces in pain.

I take his hand too, and lean in to kiss him. "Hey, tough guy," I say. His shoulders twitch. "I'm glad you're awake." His eyes flick to the side to where his brothers are laying. "They're still sleeping," I tell him. "But they'll wake up soon. You just have to focus on getting better."

Zack blinks slowly. He tries to open his mouth, but it seems like it's too much for him to talk. I lean in closer, trying to make it easier for him. When I'm almost close enough to kiss him, he murmurs. "You shouldn't have left us."

My eyes find his, and they're hurting, not just from the pain but emotionally too. "I had to," I say. "I didn't want anything to hurt you...the press."

Zack shakes his head, and I stop talking. "I don't give a fuck about the press." He starts to cough, the exertion of those few words too much for him. They're too much for me also. He's angry with me for giving up so easily, and if Zack feels that way, how must the others feel?

"This isn't the right time to talk about this," I say as

gently as I can, smoothing Zack's hair. I wish I could wrap my arms around him, and show him that I'm sorry.

"I want you to…" Zack stops to cough, his lungs sounding hoarse, his body wincing with every racking movement. "I want you to stay."

"I'm here," I say, but he shakes his head.

"I want you to stay…look after Frankie," he says again before his eyelids droop, and he seems to drift into an exhausted sleep. I sit beside him, wondering if he's going to open his eyes again, not wanting him to come around and find that I'm gone. His voice was so determined, even though it was hoarse and drained.

Xsander puts his hand on my shoulder. "He's weak. His injuries have drained him."

"At least he's awake."

"All we can do is pray, Danna."

I nod, knowing that prayer didn't help keep my momma here with me. How many prayers are being said in this hospital right now that will never be answered?

"Prayer doesn't work, Xsander," I say, standing to hug him. "Prayer is just hopeless."

"No, Danna." He strokes my hair and tugs me into his embrace. "Pray is filled with hope. The answer or outcome may not be what we want it to be, but that doesn't mean that our words aren't heard."

I'm still standing that way, wrapped up in Xsander's arms when my dad comes through the door and into the ICU.

32

Dad gazes around the room at everyone present, and my heart clenches. If my best friend Laura wasn't married to ten men, then I know that Dad's mind wouldn't start to tick, but I can see the moment he registers that there might be more to this than meets the eye.

I go to him immediately but have no idea what to say. My eyes are so puffy that I can barely see, and my nose is stuffed up from all the crying.

"Danna," he says and pulls me into a fierce hug, the kind he used to give me when I tripped and scuffed my knee as a child. I sob onto his chest, and he strokes my hair gently, giving me the time I need to calm down. I don't think about who's around me and what they might be thinking. I can't. There are three men who I love in hospital beds. Two so severely injured that I have no idea when or if they will recover. I'm devastated and bereft and all the feelings that I had when I lost mom rise up inside me like a tidal wave of grief. "It's okay," he says. I feel him fumbling around in his pocket, and he pulls out a handkerchief. I didn't know he still used them. He must wash and press them himself. The thought of him doing that as mom used to do is so poignant.

I use it to wipe my eyes and gradually pull away, my gaze fixed on Tommy. He seems the worst affected and I start to cry again.

Jackie rises from her seat and comes over to where we're standing. "Hi," she says, wiping her eyes. "I'm Jackie. You must be Danna's father."

"Nolan," Dad says. "I'm so sorry for what has happened to your family."

Jackie nods, reaching for a bunch of tissues in her pocket. "I just don't know how this could happen," she says. "They are such good boys. Never in trouble when they were at school."

"It's that family," I say. "They just couldn't leave it alone."

Jackie nods. "Zack confirmed it. I think they were hoping that they'd beat the boys so badly that they wouldn't remember what happened to them."

"Have you contacted the police again?" I ask.

Jackie nods, glancing back to where the boys are laying. "As soon as the ambulance arrived, the same two cops who were with us the other night turned up too."

Dad looks to me as though he's wanting an explanation. He's going to be mad as hell when he finds out how close to serious danger I was, and especially because I haven't told him anything about it. It's not the time to fill him in on the details now, though.

"And are they going to do something about it this time?"

Jackie shrugs. "I really don't know, Danna. The boys won't let me go home alone to pick up supplies. They're worried that something might happen."

"I think it's wise for you to have someone with you for now," I say, touching her arm.

"Would you like me to take you?" Dad asks. I turn around, shocked that he's willing to step in this way.

Jackie looks between us as, uncertain as to whether she should say yes or not.

"Go," I say. I turn to dad and pull him into a big hug. "Thanks," I say softly.

"I'm gonna get us into the hotel next door," Dad says. "It'll be late for us to travel back tonight and I don't think my driving will be up to much."

Jackie shakes her head immediately. "You'll stay at ours," she insists. "There's plenty of room."

Dad doesn't look sure, and as Jackie gathers her things, he gazes around the room at the Jackson brothers. There's so much love here despite the pain. I hope he sees it too because at some point, I am going to have to tell him how I feel about these men and what I want my future to be. I know it's going to be hard for him to accept, maybe impossible, but at least if he knows these are good men, he won't be so worried about me.

Dad squeezes my hand before he leaves. "We'll be back soon. Will you be okay?" I nod, even though it's not the truth. How could I be okay?

As Dad and Jackie leave the ICU, I shuffle over to Tommy's bedside, reaching to stroking his face as I did for his brother, and whispering for him to wake up. I sit on a chair opposite Trent who looks completely bereft and rest my face on the soft blankets. I can feel Tommy's body stirring with the effort of the machine that is keeping him alive. This man who was so healthy and so vital…so full of life has been so crushed. I cry gently, and Trent lays his hand on my shoulder, supporting me even though he is consumed by his own grief. I don't know how long I stay like that, exhausted from traveling last night and the long drive today. Xsander's message stays with me, and I pray for all my wounded boys to wake up and be healed.

The quiet hush of the ward is broken by the frantic beeping of machines. "Can we get some help in here." Wade is shouting, frantically looking around for medical staff and then back at his Samuel who's moving jerkily beneath the covers. People rush to his side, and all I can do is stare as Samuel's bed is surrounded by medical staff, and then a curtain and all of my worst fears seem to become a reality.

33

He's dying.

That's what goes through my head at that moment.

The worst possible thoughts pierce my heart.

I can't see what the doctors and nurses are doing. There is too much commotion, and my view of Samuel is obliterated by the backs of working medical staff and then by a curtain which is yanked quickly around his bed.

I sob into my palm, trying to hold myself together but failing. Trent's eyes are wide as he stands to try to see what's happening through a gap at the end of the bed. On the other side, Xsander and Xane are frozen like statues with identical grief-stricken faces.

"Please," I pray internally to whoever is listening. "Bring Samuel back to us. Keep him safe. Watch over him in his hour of need, and I'll do anything. Anything."

I close my eyes because watching is too much. I mutter my prayer again, everything in me pleading for Samuel's life. I prayed like this for my mom. I pleaded and begged until I was dried up inside, and still, she died, but I remember what Xsander said, and I try to find my faith again.

I hear choking, and my heart seems to stop in my chest.

Then someone says Samuel's name.

"It's okay...you're in the hospital," a nurse says. It takes me a few seconds to realize that she's talking to Samuel. She's trying to reassure him. She wouldn't be doing that if he was still unconscious or worse, dying.

I stand, flying around to the end of the bed and pulling back the curtain. I know I'm not supposed to disturb his privacy, but I need to see for my own eyes.

And I do.

Samuel's beautiful blue eyes meet mine, and I gasp into my hands.

He's awake. My beautiful boy is awake.

The tube that was ventilating him has been removed, and he's breathing by himself.

He looks shaken and uncertain, and I walk forward, resting my hand on his blanketed foot as the nursing staff continues to check his vitals and make him more comfortable. I nod at him, trying to be reassuring because he looks like he needs it.

Behind me, I hear Xane on the phone to his mom, telling her the good news. I hear her squeal and imagine how happy she must be to know that her son is awake.

But Tommy is still unconscious.

He needs to wake up too.

"Excuse me," one of the nurses says, and I take two steps back so they can carry on working. Samuel closes his eyes again, the exhaustion of what has happened to him evident in his face, but just knowing that he doesn't need that ventilator anymore is such a relief. Xsander puts his arm around me, and we embrace tightly.

"He's okay," Xsander says as though he can't quite believe it.

"He's awake," I say. "He's got a long way to go with all those injuries."

"Then we just need to pray some more. I'm so glad you came back," he says. "We…we just didn't understand how you could leave so suddenly and without talking to any of us."

I draw back, looking into his ethereal-colored eyes which are so serious. I stroke my hand over his cheek and his short, cropped hair. "I'm sorry," I say. "I thought it was for the best."

"I think it should have been more than just you who had a say in that."

He's right, of course, but I didn't know how to tell them about my concerns when they were in the middle of so much difficulty, and now the complexity of that situation has only increased.

As we stand together, Xane comes to join us, wrapping his arms around me from behind. Trent is there too, then York and the W triplets. We form a group hug that surrounds me in the best possible way, filling my heart with warmth, even in this dire situation.

As I sigh with contentment, relishing their strength, then the door opens behind us and I hear the clicking of a camera.

William is the first to shout, and he storms towards the man who's holding the camera pointed right at us. "What the fuck are you doing. This is a hospital. You can't be in here."

The man keeps snapping as though any shot he can get is golden.

Walker and Wade follow their brother, the pap stepping backward even as he continues to take image after image of our anger and grief.

"Do you have a comment?" he shouts, as his back hits the door of the ICU.

"A comment about what?" William growls.

"About your relationship with Danna Sandhurst?"

The mention of my name has all my worst fears spinning around inside me, memories of Laura's front page story flashing back.

"My relationships are none of your business," William's hand shoots out to make a grab for the camera, but the pap is too fast. His back is turned in a flash, the camera protected by his body.

"So is it true that you and your brothers are all sleeping with the same girl?" he snarls.

"Three of my brothers are in critical condition. What the fuck are you talking about?"

"Were they fighting over Danna? How does it work> Do you fuck her one at a time or all together? Does she like it when you do her like that?"

William lurches to get around him, but the pap is on the move again. "Our readers are desperate for information on Danna's hunt for a harem. Has she won you over? Have you fucked her yet?"

"THAT'S ENOUGH," Walker shouts. "You say her name again, and I'll put in you a bed next to my brother."

"Security to the ICU," A nurse yells into a phone. The pap's eyes flick over to her and then he's sprinting towards the door. The nurse slams the phone down and rushes over. "Has he gone...I'm so sorry for letting him get passed the secure door behind another family member. It's not the kind of thing that happens around here."

"It's okay," Wade tells her. "He was going to get his pictures one way or another."

She shakes her head, glancing back down the hallway to where the pap just disappearing out of sight. "These people who live off the gossip and misery of others...I just don't understand it." She walks away, sliding her hands into her the pockets of her scrubs as I stand with my face in my hands. Oh god, they've started, and it's not going to stop. I don't have the protection of lawyers and press specialists. I don't have Roderick McGregor's money or political influence. I'm just a girl who's fallen for ten men. A girl who wants more than what normal life is supposed to offer up to us. I'm just a girl who wants to be left alone to live her life without thousands of people making judgments about her choices.

"Fuck," I mutter. "Fuck...I'm so sorry."

"What are you sorry for?" Wade asks. "For that, cocksucker and his shitty attitude. Is this why you left? Because you were worried about the press?"

"Yes," I say. "My friend told me they were sniffing

around for a story…I was there when they broke the story about my friend and the McGregors. I saw what the negative attention did to them, and they had a team of people working to turn the story in their favor. With all the pressure you're under…I just didn't want to add anything else."

"But you did," Walker says. "You left without saying a word, and that wasn't what we wanted. We didn't even get a chance to talk to you properly about how we feel."

I shake my head. "This isn't the time…you need to focus on Tommy and Samuel and Zack. Their recovery has to be your priority. I'm going to call my friend and see what she says about the pap. Her PR team might have some advice on how to deal with this, but I'll be back as soon as I can."

Everything is now so complicated, but I have to deal with things one step at a time.

First, I go to Tommy's bed and kiss his forehead. I tell him that Samuel and Zack are awake and that he needs to wake up right now. I say to him that I'm sorry I left and I promise that if he wakes up, I'll be around if that's what he wants.

Tommy's eyes don't flicker, but I'm not disheartened. With renewed determination, I tell myself that he's as tough as an ox. He's going to come back to me, and when he does, it'll be time to get real.

34

"They have photo's," I tell Laura.

"Shit. Where from?"

"From the hospital. We were embracing when Samuel came around."

"All of you?" she asks.

"Most of us." When I remember the smug grin on that camera man's face as he took those pictures, I get a knot in my stomach the size of a grapefruit.

"Are you prepared for the fallout?" she says.

"No. Absolutely not. And neither are the Jacksons. And my pop…"

"He doesn't know?" Laura asks.

I want to scream at her down the phone that of course, he doesn't know. He's not like Laura's mom who was on board with the idea of a harem for her daughter. This news is going to destroy him. "No," I say instead. "He brought me here. He's with Jackie right now, but how can I tell him?"

"I know it's going to be hard," she says. "But if this is what you need in your life to make you happy, then this is a conversation that you are going to have to have."

"I know," I say. "But I just don't know how to say it. What words do I put together to explain this?"

"You speak what's in your heart," Laura says. "You don't need to work out a script. In fact, if you do, I think your dad will react worse. You need to talk in a way that he can see your passion…he can see your need. And then you have to cross your fingers that he doesn't react from his gut."

"I won't blame him if he does," I say. "How can I when I know how he and mom reacted to your situation."

Laura is silent for a while, and I hope that I haven't hurt her. I've never told her in detail the things that were said because there was nothing to gain. My dad has never been rude to Laura or told me to stop being friends with her, maybe because he knows that I wouldn't listen, even if he did. "Your parents weren't the only ones," she says. "But it's all worked out fine now."

"You mean you care less what people think and say now."

"Yes. Absolutely. It's not them that needs to share a bed with ten men. That's my choice, and it's yours too."

I sigh, leaning forward in the uncomfortable blue, plastic chair that I found in a quiet hallway in the hospital. "The choice I have right now is whether I choose to listen to my heart or listen to my father. That is not an easy choice because my heart won't be happy if pop is unhappy."

"Look, honey. We all come across a time in our life when we're forced to make an impossible choice. Our resolve is tested, and it's tough…it's uncomfortable, but it's how we respond that counts."

"I ran," I say.

"So did I," she laughs.

"When the going got tough, we got going." I remember when Laura turned up on my doorstep looking broken as though she'd left her heart behind in the McGregor mansion because of what her head was telling her to do. Splitting heart and head leaves no one happy. I have to learn from her example. I have to remember the advice that I gave my friend and try to have the courage to live by my own words.

"But I went back," Laura says softly. "And you can too, Danna. You can too."

We're quiet on the phone for a while, as I contemplate everything that has happened over the past year. Significant changes in both our lives that have affected us both, for better and for worse.

"I just don't want my dad to feel like I'm leaving him behind," I say softly.

"We all have to fly the nest at some point, sweetie. You've both had a tough year but just because you're ready to spread your wings, doesn't mean that you're deserting him, and he knows that deep down."

I wish that my friend was sitting next to me right now, rather than sitting in her suite hundreds of miles away. A reassuring hug is exactly what I need right now.

As if she can read my mind, she says, "You want me to come down there? You know, I will. The nanny can take care of the babies. I've got tons of expressed milk in the freezer."

I shake my head because she always manages to place images in my head that I'd rather not have. "I'd love you to be here, but there is just too much going on for both of us. I promise, when the boys are out of the hospital, that I'll be over to see you guys as soon as I possibly can."

"You'd better be," she laughs. "Hannah and Hope miss you, but not as much as their momma does."

"I miss you too," I tell her. "And thanks. For always being there when I need you."

"That's bestie rules," she says. "Always and forever."

As we say our goodbyes, I finally resolve myself tell dad everything. It's going to be one of the toughest conversations that I've ever had to have, but there is no alternative. It's time to face up to who I am and what I want.

I'm Danna Sandhurst, and I want the Jackson brothers to be my harem.

35

We take it in turns to sit by Tommy's bed next to Trent. He doesn't leave his brother's side except when he needs to use the bathroom. He won't eat or drink, and I'm worried about him getting dehydrated. The last thing we need is for another Jackson to end up in a hospital bed.

I hold Tommy's hand in my right, and Trent's hand in my left, and I pray as hard as I can for this good man to be healed. It's late when Dad and Jackie get back. There's so much relief on her face when she's able to hug Samuel and Zack, and she can see that they are on their way to recovering.

Dad hangs back for a while and then leaves to get everyone coffee. Jackie's bought snacks from home, but I can only nibble a blueberry muffin as my stomach is tied in knots.

It's when Dad's at the cafeteria that Tommy comes around struggling and coughing as Samuel did, fighting against his breathing tube. We're pushed out of the way again as the medical team does their thing. Tommy's bruised face is worse than Samuels, his injuries clearer now the mask has been taken away. Through the crack in the curtains, I take in his expressions of confusion and fear and sob quietly with relief and pain. I don't want to see him suffer. I want all my boys to be safe and happy, wrapped up tight in the warmth of my love.

I hug Trent because he's crying too and there is nothing more heartbreaking than seeing a strong man reduced to tears.

"He's okay," I say, patting his shoulder. "He's going to be okay."

Soon after, we're told by the staff that we need to leave. Visiting time is over, and the wrench of having to leave Zack, Samuel, and Tommy is too much. I kiss them all on bruised cheeks. Samuel is sleeping softly, and Tommy is too dazed by the drugs he's being given to really take in what is happening around him.

"We'll be back as soon as we're allowed to come," I say to Zack. He nods stoically, but his fingers lace with mine, clasping my hand tightly. "Will you let Frankie sleep with you?" he asks. "I don't think he'll like it on his own."

"Of course," I say, kissing his cheek again. "And you'll be out soon …don't worry about Frankie …he'll be fine. Worry about getting better so that you can come back to me."

"I think it's you that needs to come back to us," Zack says softly.

"I'm working on it," I tell him as hope fills his eyes. "There's just one pretty big hurdle."

Someone clears their throat behind us, and I turn to find Dad standing there. Did he hear our conversation? It would make it easier for me if he did.

"I'm coming," I say to dad, squeezing Zack's hand again. See you tomorrow."

The Jacksons all say their goodbyes, and we make our way to the lot together as one big group. There's talk of relief now Zack, Samuel and Tommy are all improving. "They're strong," I say. "They're fighters."

"They have a lot to fight for," Dad says. I glance quickly across at him, wondering what he means. "I always wanted brothers," he continues.

"They always fought as much as they loved each other," Jackie says. "Less now they're grown. You'll stay with us tonight?" She rests her hand on my dad's arm, and from the way he smiles, I can see that he likes Jackie already.

"Thanks. That's so good of you to offer, but I think you have enough on your plate right now without adding guests to the mix. I'm going to make reservations at the hotel, for Danna and me."

"You don't have to do that…" Dad puts up his hand to stop her. "Honestly, it's better this way. We'll see you back here in the morning."

"I insist," Jackie says. "The rooms are already made up, and we have plenty of space. You've come all of this way …it's the least we can do."

I can see that dad is uncomfortable, but he doesn't feel polite in refusing again and I'm glad we're going back to the Jacksons. It'll be a chance for Dad to see this family in their home environment so that when I'm talking to him about the boys, he's not imagining something abstract.

"Okay," he says reluctantly. "We'll stay but just for tonight."

I travel with dad, and we end up following William and Xane's trucks for the half-hour trip back to the Jackson ranch. I pretend to fall asleep in the car, resting my head so it's facing away from dad because having any kind of conversation about the Jacksons are going to end in a discussion that I'd rather not have while he's driving. He lets me rest for about ten minutes before he clears his throat.

"Danna."

I don't respond at first, but when he repeats my name and louder, I have to.

"Yes, Dad."

"I think we need to talk before we arrive at the Jacksons."

"I think we do, too," I say, my heart beginning to pound in anticipation.

"Is this what I think it is?" he says.

"Are you asking me if I'm here because I want what Laura has?" I say softly.

I see Dad's throat move as he swallows and brace myself for his anger. "Yes."

That one word sounds choked, and I have to take a deep breath. This must be so hard for him to deal with too. "I want what Laura has…and I came to stay here to see if the Jackson's would be a good fit." I'm speaking calmly, but inside I'm anything but.

"And are they?" he asks.

"Yes," I say. "They're an amazing family, and this is

what I need in my life to make me happy."

There. I said it.

"This isn't what your mom would want," he says in his typical way of deferring confrontation away from himself. The thing is, mom isn't here anymore, and using her this way just seems like a low blow.

"Mom's not here anymore so I'll never know what she'd be thinking right now." I turn and gaze out of the window, as the lights by the side of the freeway create streams of color as we speed past. "I know you'd both want what's best for me...and part of that has to be about what is going to make me happy."

"This is going to make you happy?" he asks. "Ten brothers?"

"Yes."

"And all the negative publicity...people poking their noses into your lives the way they do with Laura, thinking badly of you."

"There are always going be people out there who want to judge, dad. However, we decide to live our lives is always going to be different to someone out there. What's important is that me and the Jackson's want to make this work...this is going to be what makes us happy, and if I walk away from that because of what other people might think, well... I'm only hurting myself and the men that I love, and that wouldn't be right."

"You love them?" he says.

"I do. It's all new and fresh...and I know that it'll grow and change over time, but these are good men. They love their family, they're hard-working, they're respectful and caring...they have all the values you and mom instilled in me and want me to find in my life partner."

"Yes honey, in one life partner."

"It's working for Laura," I say.

"It's been just over a year for Laura," Dad says. "Let's see if she can make it to ten."

"Half the marriages in this country don't make it," I say. "And I think she has more chance of making hers work because her men all work together to keep their marriage happy."

Dad is quiet for a while, but I have no idea if it's because he understands what I'm saying or if he's angry. "I just...I always imagined you settling down and having kids..."

"And that's just what I want to do," I say. "Just not with one man."

"What's so bad about one man," he asks. "Did I not do right by you and your mom?"

"That's not what this is about," I tell him, resting my hand on his arm and giving him a reassuring squeeze. "This is about me wanting a big family. The Jacksons home is so lively and full of warmth. I need people around me...I just want something more."

"What will the people at church say?"

Up until now, Dad has been so reasonable and respectful, asking me questions and giving responses which must have been so difficult for him, but this one...well, I'm not going to let this one pass without letting him know exactly how I feel.

"All I care about is knowing how you feel," I say. "The rest of the world isn't mine to worry about."

Dad nods. "Will you do one thing for me," he says. "Will you agree to take this slowly. I know you, Danna. Probably better than you know yourself. You've always had a tendency to jump in with both feet and think after. You have college to finish, and I want to make sure that you give you time to work things out in your own mind. Laura had those babies so quickly, and once you do that, there's no turning back. Just promise me you won't worry about proving anything to anyone except yourself, even me." He reaches out and squeezes my knee, just the way he used to when I was a little girl.

"I promise," I say. "It's still so new...I need to give us all that time."

"Good," Dad says. "You know, when it first came out about Laura, I couldn't believe that something like that...so many people living together as a family, could work. But in ancient times, large families were quite a common thing. What I'm saying is that since your mom died, I've been thinking about a lot of things. We can get so stuck in our ways, but the world out there is vast and filled with different opportunities and possibilities... I'm just proud that I've raised a daughter with the confidence to try and find what is going to make her happy, whether or not it's what is going to meet the most approval."

I shake my head, not quite believing that this man is my father but being grateful none the less. "You and mom did a good job," I say smiling and he grins.

"We did, didn't we," he laughs. "So, which one is your favorite?"

I snort with laughter because I was definitely not

expecting that question. "There can be no favorites, dad. That would be about the worst thing in a polyamorous relationship."

"Ah, okay."

"And how did you meet this family?"

"They saw me on Laura's show," I say.

"So I have Laura to thank for all of this," he says with a roll of his eyes.

"Yes, you do," I laugh as we pull into the ranch. "Looks like it's time for you to meet the family properly," I say.

"You'll forgive me if it takes me a while to remember all the names," he says.

"Did I ever tell you that you're the coolest dad in the world," I say. When he puts the car into park and stops the engine, he faces me and wags his finger.

"Not often enough," he says, before pulling me into a huge hug.

"You'll always be my little girl," he says. "And I'm going to be telling those men in there that they better be treating you like a princess."

"I can't wait to see that," I say.

Isn't it funny how we build up issues in our minds, fearful of moving forward in case our imagined repercussions come to pass? We imagine the judgments of the ones we love; their angry words and disapproval so vividly that it can keep us in limbo.

But sometimes, when we dare to face our trials and tribulations, things work out so much better than we ever could have hoped.

And now my dad isn't angry with me for wanting the Jacksons to be my harem, I know I have the confidence to face whatever comes next.

36

What comes next is a long period of recovery.

Zack is released after another day in the hospital. Samuel and Tommy take another week to stabilize and heal enough for the doctors to be willing to release them.

Dad and I stay at the Jackson's one night and at the hospital for a few more hours before we have to leave, and saying goodbye is so hard.

I needed more time with them to tell them how I feel, but I don't get it right away.

Maybe that's why, when I return to welcome Samuel and Tommy home, everything feels so strange.

Jackie has prepared enough food for twice as many of us as are actually here. When Trent's truck pulls up outside, the whole house seems tense with anticipation. As they walk through the door, the kitchen erupts with whoops and cheers. The Jacksons all surge forward to greet their wounded siblings like heroes returning from war. I can see that Samuel and Tommy still have tender bruises from the wincing and gasping they do as they're pulled into embraces and slapped on the back. By the time it's my turn to join in, I'm so conscious of hurting them that I don't even know what to do with myself. It's Tommy who pulls me into a passionate embrace first. The kisses he plants on my forehead are almost desperate in their intensity. "Danna, I'm fucking glad that you're back where you belong."

"Tommy," Jackie shouts disapprovingly. "Potty mouth."

Samuel is next, and he seems warier. "Hey," I say, leaning in to kiss his cheek. It's awkward, but I know that he just needs time to get used to me. Time to get used to surrendering to affection.

We eat and laugh, all thoughts of the attacks and the arrests that have been made pushed aside for the night. There will be time to deal with that and the impending trials in the months to come, but for now, we focus on a grateful enjoyment of our time together.

Jackie is the first to retire for the night, giving me a kiss on my forehead before she leaves. "You look after this girl," she tells her sons, and they nod, most with big grins on their faces. "We intend to," Trent says, and I blush at the apparent intention behind his statement.

I've spoken to everyone except Samuel and Zack before tonight, and they all know that I intend to focus all my attention on the Jacksons who haven't yet shared my bed. There will be time for the others afterward, but now it's about setting the final seals on our bond.

Samuel isn't long behind his mom, rising from his seat and telling us all that he's beat. His eyes find mine, and they're filled with uncertainty. I've thought long and hard about how to approach both Samuel and Zack, and I think it's with confidence and for totally different reasons. Samuel isn't shy. I know that for sure. But he isn't used to getting close to girls, and that is what I want him to do with me. This can't just be about sex for us; his usual modes of operation won't work tonight. I need to show him that I'm going to take the time to be with him and him alone.

And Zack. I've always gotten the feeling that Zack is shy, but now I'm not so sure. He's been watching me tonight with intensity in his dark eyes that speaks of intention. Maybe his reserve is less about shyness and more about him needing to be sure of what he's doing, and I can see from his expression that he's sure tonight.

"I'm tired too," Zack says, standing.

All the Jacksons look between their brothers. I hadn't imagined that Zack would be up for sharing me with anyone because he's always seemed so reserved and solitary within his family unit, but he knows what tonight is about and he is giving signals that are entirely different from what I expected.

"Me too," I say. "Long journey." The grin that forms on my face can't be held back, and there are a few sniggers from around the table, but no one says anything as I lead the way upstairs with Zack and Samuel following me.

In my room, the same one that Jackie gave me when I first came to stay with the Jacksons, I close the door softly behind my boys. They both still have bruises on their faces and hands, but they are fading now. Standing next to each other, they are so different. Zack, with his dark hair and soulful eyes and Samuel with his blond hair and eyes the color of a lagoon. Inside they are different too, but tonight they're ready to walk this path towards me together, and that makes me so happy.

I reach out to stroke their faces, tracing their different bone structures. Both close their eyes with contentment. I lean in to kiss Samuel first, knowing that he's always been the one who puts himself last. His lips are soft and warm, his kiss so much more gentle than I ever imagined.

When I kiss Zack, it's just as sweet. He takes only a second to ignite, though and then his palm cups the back of my neck, as his lips moving against mine, kindling nerve endings from neck to crown. He kisses me as though he's tasting something delicious and decadent, slowly taking each of my lips between his and sucking them gently. Samuel begins to undress, moving to kiss my neck and palm my breasts. I moan into Zack's mouth and am rewarded with a squeeze to my breast as Samuel pulls me closer, the evidence of his arousal now pressed against my ass.

My hands that are against Zack's chest are restless for more contact. I want to feel his heat, the smooth texture of his skin, so I find the edge of his top, reaching up to stroke the side of his ribcage, earning a low moan in response. Zack and Samuel are as solid as men can be, packed with hard, defined muscle that has been honed by hard work. I read Zack's form like braille, each stroke of my palm soaking up the hours it would have taken for him to earn such strength.

"Are you okay?" Zack asks. "Is this what you want?"

"Yes," I say, kissing him again and then turning to kiss Samuel. I need them both to know how right this feels to me. I step back and lift my tank over my head, watching their eyes spark at the sight of my black lace bra and the promise of what lies beneath. When I reach behind my back to undo the clasp, Samuel says, "Wait." He draws nearer, his fingers stroking along my neck and across my collar bone, as soft as a feather, making me shiver. He hooks a finger in my bra strap and draws it down my arm so painfully slowly it's torturous. I watch his progress, seeing a tremble in his hand that softens my heart. It's incredible to see such a man so undone by my body and my love.

The room is silent, except for our breathing, which is fast and erratic as I wait for the moment he'll pull on the fabric and reveal what he's anticipating so much. Samuel's other hand grips my waist as if he fears I'll pull away and all will be lost. I wonder how long it will take us being together like this for him to relax and know that nothing is ever going to change. I watch his face, the focus of his eyes on my skin, the slight flare of his nostrils as he tugs the fabric hard enough to reveal my hard, pink nipple.

This isn't the first time that Samuel's seen me naked. He's watched his brothers fuck me and come and the sight, but this is the first time he's touched my nakedness, and everything feels new. His hand cups my flesh, finger, and thumb pinching hard enough to make me cry out. He pushes the other strap down with haste as though his patience has worn thin. His hands look huge against my narrow ribcage, my breasts tiny in his palms. Samuel kisses the corner of my mouth and whispers for me to turn around, then he undoes the clasp of my bra and, to my surprise, loosens my hair until it tumbles from its fastening. His hand smooths the waves over my back, to where the ends rest at the waistband of my leggings in a way that feels almost reverent.

I know he's feeling how much I'm trembling when he holds the tops of my arms and presses a kiss to the side of my neck. I move with him until my knees hit the bed.

"Hold on," Samuel says, his voice gravelly with desire, and I grasp the edge of the mattress, shivering as he kneels behind me to draw my leggings down to my ankles, lifting my feet in turn.

There is something so erotic about being undressed slowly, layers peeled away, eyes seeing private places for the first time. Zack watches his brother, his hands reaching to remove layers of his own clothing. My knuckles are white as I grip the comforter tightly. Samuel holds my calves and presses a soft kiss to the back of my thigh, high enough that his nose brushes my ass, high enough that when he inhales my pussy pulses.

"I can smell you," he whispers, kissing my skin, leaving cool wet patches where he tastes me. "I can smell how much you want this."

He's right, I do want this. So much that I can't keep still.

"Touch me," I say. "Please."

His hands slide up the backs of my legs, hot and firm until they grip the underside of my ass, his thumbs pressing between, making me widen my stance, pulling me open just enough to make me writhe. Zack moves until he's kneeling on the bed in front of me, slowing stroking each of my breasts, tugging the nipples gently. He's gorgeous naked; leaner than Samuel and darker skinned. I wonder if his birth family were Italian or Spanish because he has a Mediterranean air about him. His finger trails across my skin, following the edge of lace on my panties, skimming down the seam of my ass until I'm weak at the knees, panting in anticipation.

Fabric pushed aside, I can feel cool air against my wetness, but Samuel doesn't touch me immediately, just inhales again. When his finger finally slips between my folds, I sigh.

"You're so wet," Samuel murmurs against my skin,

finger probing the edges of my entrance, and I can feel myself getting wetter, hotter and more desperate. He slides through the evidence of my arousal until the pad of his finger finds my clit, and I buck against him, feeling so close to orgasm I'm up on tiptoes for it. "Not yet." Samuel moves to stand, kissing and licking up my spine as I arch into his touch. "Turn around," he whispers hot against my ear.

I look to Zack who nods, allowing his brother to be in control, at least for now.

"Hold me," Samuel says, taking my hand and wrapping it around the cock that up until now I'd only seen from a distance. "That's it…that's it," he says, sounding as desperate as I feel. I can't take my eyes off the size of it, but when he thrusts into the circle of my fingers, I look up, catching the wild desire in his half-closed eyes. His hand goes into my hair, gripping to tip my face up to his. "You're mine," he says. "Do you understand?"

I nod, heat spreading over my face and body.

"You belong to us now."

"Yes," I say, gasping when he tugs on my hair harder.

"Are you going to let us own you, tonight, Danna?"

I nod again, and he smiles wickedly, but his turquoise eyes are soft and happy.

"Take off your panties," he says. I push them over my thighs and wriggle out of them until they're lying discarded on the floor.

"Have you ever had two men inside you at the same time?" he asks, pushing his hand between my legs and sliding a thick finger inside me. I shake my head but my pussy clamps around his finger, letting him know just how much the idea turns me on.

Samuel looks over my shoulder at Zack. "You game?" I turn to find Zack nodding. If I had to guess, this probably wouldn't be the way he'd want to be with me for our first time, but he knows his brother, and if this is what he needs, he'll do what is asked.

"Sit on the chair, Zack," Samuel says.

When Zack is seated, he rolls on a condom and Samuel tells me to sit on his brother.

I straddle Zack's lap, leaning in to kiss him, to stroke his face and his chest, to show him how much I want him. It takes me a while to work him inside me, his cock is big, and I haven't had sex in over a week. All the while, Zack's hands explore my body, stroking my breasts and stomach, mapping all the soft womanliness of me. His thumb gently circling my clit has my hips bucking for more.

"That's it," Samuel says, stroking himself as he watches us fuck. This is what he loves; the raw, filthiness of voyeurism. He doesn't stay a spectator for long, though. "Lean forward," he tells me, pressing me down against Zack with a firm hand at the back of my neck. Zack shifts down the seat a little as though he knows exactly what to do to make this happen. Samuel slides a condom on, then runs his hand over the cheek of my ass, squeezing enough that there's a bite of hurt.

"You ready?" he asks.

I nod, but I'm not really. Who could ever say they were truly ready for something like this. I have no idea what it's going to feel like, but I'd be lying if I said that I wasn't aroused by the idea. My pussy is practically gushing over Zack's cock.

The first press of Samuel's thick cock at my entrance feels strange. I already feel full, and it doesn't seem possible that he'll be able to work his way inside me too, but the pussy is a very elastic thing, and Samuel is very determined. The first push burns a little, but Zack senses it and brings his lips to mine, kissing me deeply while Samuel pushes again.

"Mmmmm," I groan into Zack's mouth. The stretch is a mixture of pleasure and pain, made darker but Samuel's hand in my hair, gripping the way he likes.

"You're so fucking tight," he says, but it's not a complaint. He's enjoying the work it takes to get inside me…he's loving the fact that he's breaching me in this new way.

"Fuck," Zack says beneath me. This must be strange for him too, the new feeling of tightness and the movement of another cock next to his.

"You see how good it feels," Samuel says. "You see how made for us you are."

His hand comes down on the cheek of my ass in a whack that sounds like a whip cracking. It's the fast pain I need for me to forget about the stretch of my pussy, and in one hard thrust, Samuel's all the way up inside me.

And it feels amazing.

Oh god. I'm sandwiched between these two gorgeous men. There's no way that I can move…this is all down to them. As Samuel thrusts, my clit is ground against Zack, the bundle of nerves inside me stimulated until I feel crazy with pleasure.

"That's it," Samuel says. He can feel how close I'm getting from the way my pussy is gripping down. Zack is moving too, short thrusts that jiggle me a little and drive his cock more against Samuel's.

"You feel so good," Zack says, cupping my cheek, pressing his thumb against my bottom lip. I lick out, as Samuel begins to speed behind me.

Oh god. My body is buzzing with each hard thrust, the pull, and push of his cock and Zack's hitting all the right spots, but it's only when Zack grasps my breast and pinches my nipple that I finally fall over the precipice and into oblivion.

I gasp as a tidal wave of pleasure hits me, making my back arch against Samuel. He bucks into me until it's almost too much, too sensitive, then I feel his cock swell, and his body stiffen. I look down at Zack, realizing that his eyes are closed and that he's coming too. The perfect triangle of pleasure.

As I come down from the most amazing sexual experience with tears in my eyes, I'm overwhelmed by the release, but also the feeling of freedom that comes with choosing a path and embracing it. And I know one thing for sure; being with the Jacksons is the best thing that has ever happened to me, and I'm exactly where I'm meant to be.

Afterward, Zack and Samuel take me to bed, and it's only when they're drifting off to sleep that I tell them I love them.

EPILOGUE

There was a time when I thought that having the kind of life that I wanted was out of my grasp. I looked at my friend and her perfect harem of men and couldn't imagine that I would ever have her luck. I'd dream of it and wake up hot and sweaty as my fantasies taunted me in my sleep. I'd feel guilty for wanting something so far from the ideals that my mom and pop wanted for me.

I was the one who convinced Laura to follow her heart into the arms of the ten McGregor brothers, and I don't regret it for a second. When she pushed me to take a chance on the Jacksons, I initially thought she was being crazy. What chance could I possibly have to find ten brothers, who knew nothing about harem living, who would want me enough to share me?

But I took a chance regardless.

Maybe it was losing mom that gave me the kick to try and take life by the throat and wring out all the joy I can. I'm not sure, but I'm glad that I made that decision.

I'm glad that I traveled on a bus to a stranger's home

with the hope that I could find my dreams there. I took a chance on a lifestyle that I had never thought would be something I'd enjoy and found that I loved it.

After the day when Samuel and Tommy returned from the hospital, we made a promise to each other that we would make it work between us, no matter what life threw our way.

And it threw plenty.

There was a newspaper article filled with speculation and showcasing the ICU photo as evidence. Broadsville was awash with gossip, but we agreed on a no comment strategy which worked to snuff out continued speculation. Not that I didn't cop a whole ton of shit at college, mostly from Connor.

The TV crew who were filming the McGregor's reality show got wind of our relationship and wanted to do a special feature on the Jackson Harem. Needless to say, my boys were not keen. Where the McGregors were used to the limelight because of their father's high profile business initiatives, the Jacksons were used to being relatively anonymous.

I didn't want to do anything that made them feel uncomfortable, so I agreed to feature in one more episode of the Laura Plus Ten so I could tell our story; it was my way of making sure that speculation was put to bed.

Eventually, the slow cogs of justice turned and the men who'd been trying to damage the Jackson Ranch and who had attached Tommy, Zack and Samuel were tried and convicted. It was a big relief, and things were quiet after that.

I had to return to college to finish my courses. Even as much as I wanted to spend every waking hour with my men, I wanted to make good on my promise to my pop. I might not want to be a high powered business woman anymore, but I knew my skills would eventually be useful in helping the Jacksons make more from their ranch.

Keeping up with ten men over FaceTime wasn't easy, but we made it work with weekend trips in both directions. I remember the faces of the neighbors the first day they visited me at home. Let's just say that eyes almost popped out of heads as they each picked me up, swung me around, and planted kisses on my lips. I was dazed by the time I could usher them in the front door.

What can I tell you about our lives together?

That they make my dreams come true daily. That I thank the universe that Jackie was watching a reality TV show and had the gumption to pick up the phone to change the lives of her sons forever.

I think it helps that they're brothers. Siblings have an understanding of each other that friends rarely achieve. They forgive where others would hold a grudge. They love with a passion reserved only for family.

I love them so deeply that most days, I feel I might burst with the swell of my heart.

Today is a big day. I'm moving out of my pops house to be with my Jackson boys. As I place my final bag by the front door, I'm swallowing down tears. This house has been my home since I was a baby. Most of my memories are centered in this place. My memories of mom will forever be rooted here.

That's the hardest part for me. Being here makes me feel close to her. When I leave, I'm worried the physical distance will stretch my heart.

"You're all packed?" Dad asks, coming from the kitchen.

I nod. "I think so. There is just one more box to bring down."

"I'll do that," he says.

I stand awkwardly, not really knowing what to say. I know this isn't what dad wanted for me. I know he's had a hard time with the congregation at church who have judged me a sinner. At least he knows that I'm going to be cared for. He's seen the way the Jacksons love me. He's seen the way they protect me. He should have no doubts about my long term wellbeing.

Regardless, I understand that my leaving is tough on him. With mom gone, I was his company. Now he's going to be alone.

"You know, there's something I've been wanting to talk to you about," he says. There's a nervousness about him that I don't remember ever seeing before and my heart clenches. Is he going to ask me not to go? I don't want to have to choose between my favorite men. That would break my heart, for sure.

"What is it?" I ask.

"Well, you know I've been speaking to Jackie on the phone, since...you know." He shuffles uncomfortably, not wanting to bring up the attacks on Zack, Samuel, and Tommy or their long recovery. All that is in the past.

"Yes," I say gently.

"Well, we've formed quite a friendship," pop says. I stare at him, trying to work out what he's trying to tell me and why he looks like I just discovered his collection of

343

Penthouse in the loft.

"Have you?" I say.

Pop nods. "It's just since your mom passed I've been so lonely."

I step forward, putting my arm around his shoulder and hugging him. He seems smaller, somehow. Like a person who's been diminished by the stresses of life.

"Well that's good," I say. "Jackie's a lovely person."

"Yes," he says. "She is. We have a lot in common."

"You do?" I'm surprised to hear him say that. All I know of Jackie is that she loves looking after her boys.

"Yes. Cooking. Gardening. Westerns. Music."

"Well, that's great, dad. It'll be good for you to have a friend. But she's a little far away to pop round for coffee, isn't she?"

He nods, but there's something about his expression. He looks as though he's holding back. "What is it, pop?"

"I don't just want to be friends with Jackie."

Wow. I was not expecting that, and my mouth hangs open lets him know that without a doubt. "What?"

He shrugs. "Neither of us is getting any younger. We like each other's company and want to spend more time together, so I'm going to travel up to the ranch with you."

"You're moving in?" I gasp.

Dad holds his hand up. "No. It's not as drastic as all that. I'm coming up for a vacation to see how it goes. If we

344

get on in person as we have on the phone, then maybe things might move in that direction."

"Do the boys know?"

Dad nods. Jackie told them last night.

"And they're on board?"

Dad shrugs. "They know their mom deserves a life of her own and I think it helps that you're moving up there today and they're going to have their hands full...but I'm sure they have the same reservations as you do."

"You better not get married," I say. "Having ten boyfriends is one thing. If you make them my stepbrothers, that is going to add a whole extra heap of weird on top."

"Like Laura, you mean," he says with a smirk. I forgot that's exactly the situation my best friend found herself in. It hasn't made any difference to her in the long run, I suppose.

"That's different. Nora and Roderick were together first. They wanted this for their children. If it weren't for me, then you never would have met Jackie."

"I'm grateful," pop says. "You don't have to worry about us. Neither of us wants the hassle of getting married again. If anything we'll live in sin."

I make a vomit noise in my throat. I know I'm a grown adult, but the very idea of my dad having sex makes me want to chuck up the burger I had for lunch. "Just keep the ins and outs of your relationship to yourself, dad," I say.

A horn sounds outside, and I run to the door, throwing

it open to see my men arriving to take me to start our new life together. The barn conversion is finished so when I move in, it'll be to our own purpose built place rather than to their family home.

I know we're going to end up eating at Jackie's most nights, but I'm looking forward to that part. Cooking has never been my strength. Their mom can take care of their stomachs, and I can take care of their hearts and bodies.

Damn, the thought of their bodies has me hot between my legs immediately.

They pile out of the car and start towards the door, eyes shining with anticipation.

Zack is first. Well, actually, Frankie bounds towards the house in front of his master and is the first to plant a very wet kiss on my cheek. I pet him roughly in the way he loves and the happy sounds he makes fill me with joy.

Zack waits patiently, his eyes glowing with happiness at the sight of his best friend and his girl reuniting. I stand slowly, leaning into his body for a hug that fills my soul. "I missed you," he says softly, smoothing back the hair from my forehead with his warm hand and planting a kiss there. I snake my arms around his middle and breathe in his warm, woodsy scent. He smells like home.

"Don't hog the woman," a voice says from behind him. It's Tommy, and he's practically bouncing with anticipation.

"The woman has a name," I say as I'm released from Zack's arms and am free to greet the rest of his brothers. "Hey," I plant a kiss on his lips and slide my hand into his shaggy hair. Both the T twins need a haircut, but I love it when they get all floppy on top like this. "Hey yourself, gorgeous," he says, gripping me under my ass and lifting me off the ground. "You ready to come and make us happy?"

"I thought I was moving in so that you can make me happy," I laugh.

"Right," Trent says, throwing up his hands. "The deal is off."

Everyone laughs, and I slide out of Tommy's arms to hug his twin. "Baby," Trent murmurs in my ear, hugging me so tight I feel like my sides are going to split. "Too tight, too tight," I gasp, laughing with joy at his exuberance.

"You guys need to learn how to share better," a voice pipes up from behind. It's William.

"Says the man who told no one that he'd already claimed her," Wade says.

"No one claimed me," I say. "I claimed you guys."

There are nods of agreement because it's true and I'm never going to let them forget it.

I hug each of my boys in turn, loving the way that William, Walker, and Wade wrap my up between them like the filling in a triple-decker sandwich. Xsander and Xane pick me up and spin me around, their strong arms making me feel as light as a feather. York is next with his passionate kiss and eyes that seem to want to check me over in case I've been hurt since he last saw me. Ever the caring one. Last but by no means least is Samuel. He hangs back until his brothers have all finished jostling for my attention. He's still reserved. Still wary.

But now I understand why.

It might take me years to prove that I'm on his side and that I'll never hurt him like his birth-momma, but I'll keep trying because he's worth it.

"You okay, trouble?" I say, cupping my hand over his cheek.

He nods but doesn't smile.

"Have you come to take me home?"

Samuel nods again, but this time he wraps his arms around me tightly and buries his face into my neck.

There he is. The man I uncovered on that difficult night all those months ago.

His brothers are silent as they watch their toughest, most reserved sibling seeking comfort in my arms. My throat burns with emotion too.

Dad clears his throat behind us. "I really hope you're going to get quicker at hellos and goodbyes or you'll never get anything done."

Everyone snorts with laughter because he's right. It's taken me ten minutes just to feel like I've given them the right kind of greeting after all his time.

"Who's going to move my daughter's things, then?" Pop asks.

Ten men step forward, scrabbling for boxes, wanting to be useful and manly in the best possible way.

The drive to the Jackson ranch – my new home – feels longer than it ever has before. I guess because I'm anxious to get there and start my new life. I'm eager to see the barn, knowing how hard the boys have worked on it since

I was last there.

I wonder if they took on board the mood-boards I made for each room or if I'm going to turn up to find a bachelor pad complete with pool table and jukebox.

When we arrive, Tommy covers my eyes as we approach the front door. "No peeking," he says.

I couldn't, even if I wanted to because his hands are so huge.

Someone unlocks the door, and we all pile through into the space which was dilapidated and damp-smelling the last time I was here.

It certainly doesn't smell damp anymore.

"Are you ready?" Zack asks.

"I'm more than ready," I shout. "Lemme see."

Tommy lifts his hands from my eyes, and I blink, stunned momentarily by the brightness of my surroundings.

"Wow." My mouth is hanging open, and I don't even care. This place is amazing. They've taken a building that I wouldn't have felt comfortable housing animals in and made it into something from a home make-over show. The kitchen, dining room, and lounge are all open plan. Stone worktops compliment wooden cabinetry. A huge table that could fit at least twenty is surrounded by gorgeous blue velvet chairs. The table top is actually a slice of tree, with raw bark edges and a lacquered top. It's AMAZING! I take five steps in, gazing up to the vaulted ceiling, peppered with skylights. It's bright and airy and everything I could have hoped for. The whole back wall has been removed and replaced with bi-folding doors that open to our own fenced yard. And the den is monstrous in size, with a massive horseshoe-shaped sofa that could seat twenty too.

"You like it?" Zack asks. I know a lot of the carpentry would have been his undertaking. In fact, the table has his name all over it.

"I love it!" I gasp, gazing around at their expectant faces.

They've made us a real home; somewhere we can be happy together.

I can see our future more clearly now, and it's a good one, filled with joy and laughter and love.

It'll be noisy and boisterous and fun and happy.

Yes, there'll be challenges, but I know I have ten of the most amazing men to stand by my side through anything that life throws at me.

"You haven't seen the best part," Wade grins. He grabs my hand and leads me to a door. He turns the handle and opens an enclosed part of the barn. There are multiple doors in the hallway, and I open one, finding a gorgeous shower room. The next door houses a carbon copy.

"How many of these are there?" I ask.

"Ten," Wade grins.

"And what about me? I have to share with one of you guys?"

He shakes his head. At the end of the corridor, there's another door. Inside...well, I can't even take in what's inside.

It's a bathroom fit for a Hollywood A-lister. Marble tiles cover the floor and walls. A beautiful vanity unit houses the softest white towels I think I've ever seen. But it's the bath that I'm gazing at. Sunken into the ground, it has jets.

I have my own spa bath!

"It's..." I grab him and pull him to me, then move from brother to brother, hugging and kissing them.

"Wait," Samuel gasps, as I pepper him with kisses. He takes hold of my shoulders. "You haven't seen the best bit," he says.

"There's more!" I'm aghast. I don't know how much more I can take.

"Yes, there's more. Unless you're planning to sleep in the bath."

The bedroom.

I can't believe I forgot about the bedroom.

There's a wide door at the end of the hallway with double doors. The Jacksons are following me and allow me to open it first.

They really did save the best until last.

Most of the room is made up of a vast bed. I've seen Laura's at the McGregor mansion, but to be honest, this puts theirs to shame. It's amazing. I've never seen anything that could accommodate eleven sleeping people. It's double ended with six pillows on one side and six on the other.

"We've made it so you can sleep either way," York says.

He puts his arm around my shoulders as I stare around at all the little touches. Gorgeous dove-gray wooden bedframe with crisp white linen, soft rugs, and stylish nightstands. In the corner, there are two more doors. "The closets," York says. "And there are five more bedrooms."

"Five," I gasp.

"Yeah...for the kids," Xsander says. "One day...you know...when you're ready."

"Wow. How many kids are you hoping for?" I say, feeling worried. I've always thought that two might be nice. Two pretty little girls who'll love baking and crafts and riding horses and being bad-asses.

"Ten," they all say in unison.

Holy shit. That's a whole lot of children they're hoping to emerge from my vagina.

"One each," Walker adds sounding hopeful. Their expressions are the cutest things I've ever seen.

"How about six?" I say. "One for each set of twins, one for the triplets and one each for the others. I think that's enough for me to cope with."

There are grins all around. "Told you we needed to start high," William says.

"There was no way she would have gone that high if we didn't," Walker laughs.

They got me good. "You know I'm standing here and can withdraw my offer at any time." I put my hands on my hips like I mean business. I'm only standing for two seconds before Xsander lifts me up and tosses me on the bed like I weigh nothing. I land in the most ungraceful way, like a sack of potatoes, but no one seems to care about that. They're all stripping off their clothes while they look at me like a piece of steak. Oh my god.

My pussy is hot, wet, and aching in seconds.

Did I mention how lucky I am to be the center of the Jackson Harem?

I'm so damn lucky. So, so damn lucky.

Ten gorgeous men strip down to pure nakedness, ten cocks stand proud and ready to please me. Twenty hands flex ready to touch me.

I back up, needing a little space to enjoy the feast of manliness before my eyes.

I can't even count the ab-ripples that are before my very eyes.

Tommy is the first on the bed, stalking me like a big cat. He takes hold of my ankle and tugs me towards him. "Where do you think you're going, little lady," he says. His twin is close behind, with matching eyes filled with mischief and matching mouths set into wicked grins.

"I'm wanting to claim my reward for all of this hard work," Trent says.

"And we need to test out this mattress properly," Tommy says.

Their brothers aren't far behind, taking places around me. Hands caress me, removing my clothing so fast I don't even notice until the cool air hits my warm pussy as my legs are spread wide.

"See that," Tommy says, his finger glancing my clit.

"She's wet for us, boys. Wet and ready."

He leans in to swipe a long lick, his tongue flicking against where I'm swollen and achy, and I moan loudly, unable to hold in my response to so much pleasure.

Trent kisses my lips as his brother licks me, both tongues synchronized to please me. Someone's hand finds my breast, and someone's mouth finds my nipple. My hands are secured around two matching hot cocks, and I don't know who is who, but I don't care. I am the point around which all these men now revolve, and it feels so right.

"I am ready," I say, because I know that's what they all need to hear.

I close my eyes to focus on the sensation of Tommy's tongue on my clit, but then there's movement on my left as a hand caresses my breast, then another hand does the same on the right. More hands find my thighs and my ass, lips find mine and kiss me with passion and urgency. For a while, I don't know who is who but it doesn't matter because I trust each of these men with my body and my heart. I know they will handle me gently up until the point that I'm begging for something more.

Hands softly squeeze my breasts and find my nipples. Lips kiss my calves and behind my knees and my thighs. I'm so hot between my legs, so desperate and needy that I can't keep my hips still.

"She's ready," Tommy says.

"Are you ready," Samuel whispers against my ear, and I whimper. His voice is gruffer than I've ever heard it, and my heart skips a beat. Does this mean that it's Samuel who's going to go first? I hope so because as much as I love him watching, seeing that he's confident enough to take his place between my legs first will feel like a big achievement.

So many hands spread my legs that I can't even count. Tommy backs up, leaving my soft, wet pussy open for all to see.

"Damn." There's a chorus of appreciation I look down and see Samuel taking his place between my legs. Zack passes out the condoms which are rolled on with an eagerness that has me panting. This will be our first time all together, and although I'm ready in mind, I have no idea how my body will cope with the demands of ten huge cocks. My eyes meet Samuel's and I smile. "Come and get it," I say, and he grins an adorable crooked smile.

"You bossing me around, Danna?" His hand takes hold of one of my legs, and he rolls me so that my ass is in the air. His rough hand strokes up my thigh and over the rounded cheek and I brace myself, knowing that I'm in trouble for being sassy, just the way Samuel loves it.

He doesn't spank me hard, but it's enough to make me jump and for my skin to heat. "Samuel," I squeal, and he laughs, rolling me back over.

I gaze around me and find Xsander, Xane, William, Walker, and Wade are the ones who've been caressing me. The rest of the Jackson brothers are near too, cocks in hand, waiting for their turn. The sight of so much man on show makes my pussy clench. I think I could come from just laying here, looking at them and thinking about what they're going to do with me and if I feel like that only from thinking, what is going to happen to me when they are actually doing.

"Fuck her," William orders, his eyes flashing dangerously in the way that they only do when he's talking sex. Samuel doesn't need telling twice. He grins as he settles between my legs.

My hands are pinned to the bed so I am totally in their control, and I love it.

Wade leans in to suck at my left nipple, and Walker squeezes at pinches at my right. Hands stroke my thighs, as Samuel's huge cock notches at my entrance. His arms twitch with the control he requires to work his way into me slowly. Xsander's lips find mine, and he kisses me as though he's imagining pushing his own cock inside me; long, languid strokes of his tongue match Samuel's in my pussy. I have to shift my hips. I can't take the overwhelming feeling of so many hands, so many fingers, so many tongues.

"She's getting close," William says, still watching from the sidelines.

"Her pussy's clutching me so damn tight," Samuel hisses.

"Fuck," Wade grunts as I pull my hand from his grasp and reach for his cock.

Fingers press into my ass, holding me tight as Samuel fucks into me harder. Each thrust rubs my clit and hits me deep inside, and I want to wriggle but I can't.

"That's it," Wade urges. "Don't hold it, Danna. You come on Samuel's cock. You show him how good he's fucking that pussy."

I want to. I want to so badly.

"That's it, you bad girl," William says sternly. "We're all going to fuck that pussy until you're not going to be able to sit down."

It's that thought that has me falling over the edge into oblivion, overwhelmed by a level of ecstasy that feels bright and dangerous. "That's it, girl" Walker whispers, his hand caressing my stomach and hips gently. His brothers follow suit, as Samuel continues to fuck me, prolonging the waves of pleasure until I'm seeing bursts of white light behind my eyelids, and when he comes, it's as though all the pressure of the last few months leaves his body.

I relish the pulsing of his release inside me and the way his strong body goes lax. He hangs his head, chest rising and falling as though he's just completed a marathon. Samuel doesn't get to rest for long, though because William is wanting his turn.

I know how he will feel; long, thick, and hard. His cock nudges at my opening, taking the slickness his brother built up and using it to lubricate his way into me.

"Fuck," someone mutters as William pushes all the way inside. My back arches, and lips find my breasts again. Wade shifts away, and I think someone is going to take his place, but that isn't what happens. He strips the condom off his cock and kneels next to my head.

"Suck it, Danna," he says. "I want to see those pretty lips wrapped around my cock." I open my mouth and lick at the salty sweetness of his pre-cum. He's so big, and the angle isn't the easiest, but he seems to know how to position himself so that he can thrust without hitting the back of my throat.

"That's it," Walker says as he watches his triplet brothers using my body to take their pleasure. Even though I can't really see where he is, I use my hand to feel around, taking hold of his cock and stroking it.

"See how well she can handle them," Xsander says

proudly. I know it's him because his voice is tinged with a cheeky smile.

William is fucking me with slow, deep strokes that feel so damned good. Wade is getting close; I can taste his excitement getting stronger and his cock getting harder. His hand goes into my hair, not to guide me but more as a possessive gesture. His eyes find mine as he comes in my mouth, and it's the sexiest thing to see him releasing. Like Samuel, he has to use a hand to stabilize himself while he recovers.

William's fingers dig into my ass, evidence that he's getting closer. His pace speeds too, his abs working as he progresses towards his orgasm. I want to feel him come so badly. A guttural moan builds in his throat, and I know he's almost there.

"You're gonna make him come," Walker says as he watches his brother release.

"I want to make you come too," I say.

"I'm close," he tells me, "don't stop."

"Let me suck you," I say, and Walker's eyelids go heavy. He moves to kneel by my head, guiding his cock into my mouth as his brother did. It doesn't take long until he comes hard, filling my mouth with his salt-sweet release.

"Who's next?" Xsander asks as William and Wade move away.

"Me and you, bro," Xane say.

"Get her on her knees then," Xsander suggests. "I want to see her pretty ass."

"Is that okay with you, Danna?" Xane asks, ever the

considerate and thoughtful twin. Even though I'm still feeling weak from my orgasm, I manage to roll to my side and onto my hands and knees. Xane kneels in front of me his big cock standing proud. Xsander doesn't rush to penetrate me. Instead, he uses his big strong hands to stroke over my ass, tapping in gently. "Your ass is perfect," he says. "Big and round and juicy."

"Just the way Xsander likes it," Xane says with a grin.

"And what about you? Is that how you like it?" I ask.

Xane nods. "We're identical in most things."

When Xsander pushes inside me, I groan, but then Xane's cock is in my mouth, and I can't talk while I'm working. Damn it feels good to know that I'm giving them both so much pleasure. I can taste Xane's arousal and feel Xsander losing control behind me.

Tommy and Trent take places either side of me, caressing my breasts with this rough hands, tweaking my nipple in time to their brother's thrusts.

"Unnnmmm," is the only sound I can make as Xsander's finger finds my clit and all the arousal these men have been building inside me unleashes.

"She's coming," Xsander groans, then his cock is swelling and so is Xane's, and I can't seem to hold myself up anymore.

When I crumble onto the bed, curled up while I come down from my orgasm, it's Tommy whose lips find mine and Trent whose mouth seeks out my pussy.

"I can't," I say, but he doesn't listen. His tongue explores my folds, never quite touching my clit that is tender and swollen, and it feels good. Then, when he's eaten his full, he fucks me gently, his twin following on.

I'm boneless and broken, but my boys are attentive and gentle, slowly bring me back around until I'm craving more. It's just York and Zack left, and to my surprise, it's Zack who suggests double penetration. I guess he must have liked it with Samuel.

This time, I lay on top of Zack, my back to his front, his long, thick cock seated inside my pussy. York's wets his fingers, and he explores my labia, pulling the skin around my clit in a way that has me shivering with anticipation. He braces himself of top of me, his arm shaking as he focuses on working his cock into my pussy too. That burn is there, but it's not as bad as the first time. I think it helps to have fucked a lot before, building up to this moment. York pushes harder, and the stretch is immediate. I arch backward as Zack's hands mind my breasts. Other hands stroke my arms and my legs as more Jackson brothers take places close enough to watch. York leans down to kiss me, and I find myself relaxing and relaxing until he's fully seated inside me.

The pleasure is immediate. "Go slow," Zack says, and York listens well. The way he fucks me is erotic and sensual, resting upon his knees so he can watch the sight of his cock and Zack's opening me wide. The pressure directly on the little bundle of nerves inside me makes me grunt.

"Look at our that," Samuel says. "Danna's a fucking angel."

"She was made for this," William says.

"She was made for us," Wade says.

My legs are shuddering, my clit grinding against York. I know I'm going to come soon because it's rising fast and I don't know what to do. There will be no holding back when this happens. It's too vast and overwhelming.

"She's close," Zack says, starting to move beneath me. The push and pull take me closer.

"So am I," York hisses.

"Oh god," I gasp. "Don't…"

I don't get to say stop because it's too late. I'm coming and coming and coming, an avalanche of pleasure so big that my head swims out of consciousness.

"Fuck," York gasps. It's got tighter in my pussy as it clamps down with my orgasm and Zack swells too. York is the last to release, pushing inside me so deep that it stings.

We stay like that, joined like one six-legged creature turned to stone.

I struggle to catch my breath, and we're all so sweat slicked that my skin turns cold.

"Damn," someone mutters from my right. I think it's William.

"The girl needs a rest," Xane says.

"I think we all do," Tommy says. My boys all lay around me. Someone finds a blanket to cover me. Hands stroke my hair and fingers lace with mine. The boys laugh and joke with each other, and my heart feels absolutely at peace. In the moment, not a single person alive could convince me that this isn't exactly where I'm supposed to spend the rest of my life.

There isn't one perfect way to live in this world, and following the well-trodden path does not guarantee the greatest happiness.

As I lay between these ten men, I know that loving them will bring me so much more love and contentment than I was ever expecting in my life.

I'm with my boys, and I trust them absolutely. I know they will do anything to please me and protect me, body, mind, and heart, and I marvel at the rightness of this.

Life doesn't always go as we plan. There can be more cloudy days than sunny. More trouble than contentment. More hardship than ease. We don't always travel the roads that will lead us to the happiest place. We don't always dare to seek what will fulfill us.

I'm so glad that I strove to find my ideal life. I'm so glad that I have a best friend who was there to give me a nudge towards my joy when I was weakened from grief.

Most of all, I'm glad that I can bring happiness to this family who has been through so much to come together. Keeping the Jackson brothers in a strong unit to work this family ranch is so important to me.

I've found my heart here in this wild place.

I found my harem.

Ten men.

One love.

Forever.

ABOUT THE AUTHOR

Stephanie Brother writes scintillating stories with bad boys and stepbrothers as their main romantic focus. She's always been curious about complicated relationships, and this is her way of exploring the situations that bring couples together and threaten to keep them apart. As she writes her way to her dream job, Ms. Brother hopes that her readers will enjoy the full emotional and romantic experience as much as she's enjoyed writing them.

CPSIA information can be obtained
at www.ICGtesting.com
Printed in the USA
LVHW090508081219
639802LV00001B/17/P

9 781710 514254